Connec

Martyn Clayton

[signature]

7/04/08

Connection

This edition published 2008 Garbled Noise

ISBN 978-0-9556946-0-8

Copyright Martyn Clayton 2008

Martyn Clayton has asserted his rights under the Copyright, Designs and Patents Act 1988 to be identified as the author of this work

This book is sold subject to the condition that it shall not by way of trade or otherwise be lent, resold, hired out or otherwise circulated without the publisher's prior consent in any form of binding or cover other than that which it is published and without a similar condition, including this condition, being imposed on the subsequent purchaser.

Front cover design copyright Janet Owen 2008

BY THE SAME AUTHOR

Fiction

Take Me Out

Non-Fiction

Roma : A People On The Edge

Ta very much

Firstly huge thanks have to go to my cover artist and spiritual twin Jan Owen. Without her instinctive friendship at a very hard time this book would never have come about. A friend in the fullest, truest sense of the word is very hard to find. I feel blessed to have one. I meant to thank my sister-in-common-law Ellen Simpson in the last book for saying the right things at just the right time and setting me wondering what just might be possible. I received good advice and feedback from countless people, all of which I have tried to take on board in this book. Doubtless at times I have failed but the intention was there. I was helped through a difficult year by countless people who showed the depth of their humanity through their words and instinctive understanding. At the root of everything is my relationship with Rachel. My best-friend, my soul-mate, my confidante and the person who makes me smile more than anyone else. To see my love reflected in her face is the greatest privilege. This book believes in true love, everyday beauty and a crisp sandwich being the best medicine.

For Julie. My Sister.

'I meant to write about death, only life came breaking in as usual'
Virginia Woolf

It had just started raining in middle England…

Just how easy would it be?
Star sat on the edge of the bath. It was cold. There was no heating in the bathroom and she couldn't afford to warm the flat properly anyway. In her right hand she gripped a solution to how she had been feeling. A beautiful pristine razor blade. Left behind after Kyle moved out in a hurry. He never used the things. Someone had bought him a flash old school looking shaving kit one Christmas, he'd purchased himself a set of blades for the razor then never touched them. Stuck to his crappy disposables that always left a stubbled edge on his face. Most of the time Star hated it, she told him so, but he wouldn't do anything to remove it. It irritated her like hell when he went down on her and stopped her fully relaxing into the moment, which led him to accuse her of being frigid which was just a fucking joke wasn't it? Seeing as it came from Mr 'can't keep it up after just two pints of lager' himself. He was alright when he got warmed up but he was hardly dynamite in bed and maybe she wouldn't have noticed his stubble if he hadn't been like a limp fucking jellyfish down there. Now she missed the feel of his face as they kissed. But she mustn't think like that. This wasn't about him. Who was he anyway? What had he ever done for her? What had he left her with?

The razor caught the light and glinted. It looked cold but crisp and perfect. Small but deadly. That was it. Her passport out of this place. The only thing standing between her and complete and total nirvana was her will. All those years of yoga, trying to meditate her way there, or find nuggets of inescapable truth in overpriced self-help books full of platitudes and meaningless drivel. The age of Aquarius was a sick hippy joke. There was no paradigm shift. There was no hope in crystals, or spiritual healing, or seeking messages from beyond the grave. The only meaning, the only real peace was the grave. The sleep of all sleeps and she was never happier than when she was enjoying an extended dreamless stay in the unconscious, so just how bad could an endless perpetual rest really be? There was nothing frightening about it. The prospect seemed inviting. That must mean she'd crossed the Rubicon. Real suicide contenders welcomed oblivion, it wasn't just an attempt at a 'you'll miss me when I'm gone' style cry for help

That's what they'd said about her mum hadn't they? That it was a cry for help that had gone wrong. That she hadn't really meant to take those 68 aspirins washed down with a bottle of neat vermouth. That it was just her way of trying to tell people that she couldn't cope. That life had become too hard for her. The hot pant wearing nightclub princess with the masses of ringlets and legs as long as South America. The faded party girl who no-one could love anymore because she was fat (she wasn't) and had a baby. The girl who was too precious for life, the friend of the stars, the one who glittered in the limelight, famous for nothing except sleeping with a few yahoo footballers who drank away their potential, grew their hair, wore their shirts out of their shorts and felt themselves edgy. If she wasn't riding cocks she was posing for never quite cutting it designers, or taking her clothes off in Leicester Square to promote the album launch for one of her rock star also-ran friends.

It would have been nice to have had a mother rather than a few photos and cuttings of a stunningly beautiful young woman who Star didn't really recognise as real. In her childhood fantasies she imagined an alternative mother. A homely, floral patterned frock and apron wearing type who cut pastry into shapes with her, and dressed her up in party clothes. One who attended parents evenings and was happy for Star's friends to stay for sleepovers, and would amuse them all with her tales about her early boyfriends and the things they got up to, before she met 'your dear father.' They probably lived in the country. The cottage with roses round the door. Her father would be tall, good looking but not overly so, maybe a little overweight, but always dapper in his work suit. He'd do something in the city and largely be away during the week leaving more time for mother and daughter bonding. They'd be so close, like best friends almost.

Come on Star. What are you thinking about those things now for ? There was no ideal mother. Just a series of resentful foster parents and eventual adoption by a pair of dour Jehovah's Witnesses too barren and joyless to ever contemplate sex, never mind any actual product of their union. Even if they didn't really like her name or approve of her family background : 'So she's the daughter of a junkie socialite suicide who came from nothing to feature on the gossip pages of the tabloids principally by looking attractive and opening her legs to wayward sportsmen and possibly diseased sex-addicted rock stars. Oh and we're not sure who the father is.' Star was to be their little project. Their chance to show that even the product of hedonistic amoral scum could be made pure when washed in the blood of the lamb.

Her real name was the first to go. From being burdened with a ludicrously flower-child moniker, she was then given something ridiculously antiquated. Joyce. It wasn't until she was 18 and finally escaped the clutches of her adoptive parents, her birth certificate in hand that she re-discovered her real name. Star Turner. Mother Sarah Turner, Father Not Known. So she went with Star. It would have been easy at this point to slip quietly into the background, become a Karen, a Debbie or a Helen or something. But she didn't want to. Taking her birth name was a way of stating exactly who she was and where she came from, even if she felt little for the vacant looking woman smiling on the fading newspaper cuttings. She looked like countless leggy 70s lovelies. The sort who danced on Top Of The Pops behind Ed Stewart, or who ran around public parks in sleazy lingerie being chased by dirty old men on the Benny Hill Show. Dated clichés the lot of them. As too was the name Star. It was either a modern new age affectation or an authentic piece of old school hippy nonsense. When she told people her name she saw them start to classify her as the kind of woman who worried about auras or thought there might be some truth in tarot cards. In reality Star lived by Nietzsche and latterly Richard Dawkins. Not all Star children were sent to earth gullible.

It would be too easy she thought to blame her upbringing on the situation she now found herself in. To blame it all on the confusion of her early years, the manner of her mother's death or the repressive unpleasantness of her adopted family. That was far too simplistic. Sure Star had her fair share of problems. She'd been a serious boozer back in the day, more so than her friends and an occasional line of the white stuff never did anyone any harm did it ? Except her mother. Which was why she ultimately straightened up her act and taught herself to fly right. Eight years clean of booze, drugs, and casual sex. Star was not her mother and was never going to be.

No, this was all Kyle's fault. It was his hand holding the razorblade not hers, even though she knew he was shacked up twenty miles down the road in his new girlfriend's flat. They were probably fucking like dogs right now. The image of their grubby endeavours entered her head and made her stomach turn. Kyle was never that pretty a picture naked. The face was passable, but the body with its beer induced pot belly was hardly top draw. That didn't matter though when you loved someone. Six years down the pan just like that and what for ? The chance for an unsatisfactory jump with a twenty-two year old shit for brains receptionist at the firm where he worked. Just how fucking cliché can one thirty something middle-manager be eh ? Too unoriginal to make it interesting, to decide he wanted to be called Shirley and wear bold print smock dresses, or shave his head, don saffron robes, then fuck off to India to become the Dalai Lama's favourite second Tuesday of the month comfort boy.

She took a deep breath, wiped a tear from her eye and then realised her nose was running. She fumbled in her pocket for a tissue. What did it matter ? A bit of snot down her face was nothing when compared to the blood bath she was soon to be swimming in. But she couldn't let it just run. She reached for the toilet roll and pulled off a strip, gave her nose a sharp blow, wiped it, then folded the tissue and placed it in her pocket. There. All better. Right, back to the matter in hand.

Wasn't suicide meant to be dramatic and heart wrenching ? This seemed a bit mundane. The phone was ringing in the front room. Fuck. She paused for a second. Who could that be ? No one of importance. Maybe it was Kyle ? Maybe he'd changed his mind and was on his way back. That was it. No, don't be fucking stupid Star, that's how you've been thinking for the past six weeks and he hasn't called, he hasn't sent a text, there's been no emotional letters explaining everything. Just the usual circulars and junk mail. At first she'd get up early with a degree of expectation, watching out the window as the post man made his way up the street, then swung open the big metal gate into the lobby of their block. There she'd hear him filling up the individual mail boxes and then as his figure re-emerged and moved off she'd rush down to check what was in flat 4's. Mostly nothing.

But why would Kyle write a letter ? It wasn't what he did. The odd text speak style email to his mates or his family was about the closest he ever came to written correspondence. It was funny. Now he'd gone all those daily irritants she'd pushed under the carpet came crisply into view. The way he ended his sentences with the line 'so says I ', the way he wore his replica football shirt on Saturdays, the disgraceful nature of his farts, the way he took his tired socks off last when they were getting into bed. So much about him was deeply repellent. But still she loved him. The little dimples on his cheeks when he smiled, his awful jokes, the way he held her when she said she was cold, the total utter tasty brilliance of his spaghetti bolognese. Since he'd gone she'd been living on cold baked bean sandwiches. Made with white bread. Kyle only ever bought wholemeal. For a man who smoked twenty Benson & Hedges a day and drank forty units of alcohol a week he was surprisingly health conscious.

Again she stared at the blade. She could hardly feel it between her fingers. Something so sleight could be so destructive. Just like a bulimic death wish model.

The York Press March 22nd 2001

The police are to today begin investigating the death of a York man found dead in the front-room of his Gillygate flat on Sunday morning. 29 year old Matthew Trethewy, a visual artist originally from the Newcastle area was said to have had a history of mental health problems. Friends describe Mr Trethewy as 'laid-back, loving and brimming with talent.' Investigators say that no suicide note has been found, but they are not currently looking to interview anybody else in relation to this matter.

October 2007, Old York City, Englandshire, Yoo-Kay, roundabout afternoonsies

'Aww Mills !' Lauren was talking with her mouth full.
'What babes ?' Millie didn't look up from the unfortunate photo of a totally trolleyed Amy Winehouse she'd been studying in Lauren's Heat Magazine.
'I've frickin gone and done it !'
'Done what ?' Now Millie turned her head to her flat-mate whose face appeared to be in a higher state of rapture.
'Made the perfect crisp sandwich. It's amazing…aahhhh…it's like sex.'
'You're weird.'
'Yeah I know that, but have a bite of this.' Lauren jumped up and scurried across to where her friend was sitting.
'Errrr get it away you freak ! I don't want your filthy sandwich.' Millie had turned her head to the side and was protecting her mouth with her hand.
'Ahhh come on kitten, it's dead nice…you'll like it.' Undeterred her friend continued to shove the crisp filled roll in the direction of Millie's mouth.
'Oh alright then. Just a small bit.' Millie took a tentative bite. Lauren watched her chewing expectantly. Millie's face slowly assumed a portrait of complete horror before an exaggerated swallowing action suggested she'd finished.
'That was foul. What are you talking about ?'
Lauren looked hurt. 'Aah didn't you like it.'
'No, it was vile. What did you put in it ?'
Lauren went and sat back down on the sofa and took another bite. 'Well,' she continued talking regardless. 'I went and bought a granary roll from Thomas the Baker this morning. For health.'
'Nice'
'Thanks, and then I bought a packet of Seabrook's Cheese and Onion and brought them home. I grated some cheddar cheese, which took ages and gave me a dodgy wrist, anyway….'
'Finish it before you carry on.'
'Oooh OK'. She hurriedly put the last piece of the roll in her mouth and started chewing. 'I spread the roll with brown sauce, chopped up a pickled gherkin, stuck it in, along with the crisps and hey presto…'
'You've made a disgusting sandwich with neglible nutritional value.'
'Nooo…I've gone and made the perfect crisp butty. God, I'm amazing.'
'You're not. You're eating yourself into an early grave.'
'Millie…look at me ! There's not a millimetre of extra fat on these bones.' She pinched her stomach. 'I'm like a rake. You've said so yourself.'

'That's because you never eat proper meals. You live on crisp sandwiches, chunky Kit-Kats and beans on toast.'

'No I do not ! I cooked spaghetti bolognese the other week. You said you liked it.'

'I did like it, and it wasn't the other week was it ? It was like, three weeks ago, and before and after that momentous date in our culinary calendar I've not seen you eat another proper meal. It can't be doing you any good. What with that and the smoking.'

'Aw god,' she put her hands over her ears, 'don't get started on that again.'

'You are like a one woman crematorium. You're always puffing away.'

'It's relaxing. I'll pack up one day.'

'When exactly ?'

'Don't nag. You're getting terrible at it. I thought you might let up a bit now you've got yourself a boyfriend who isn't mental …or gay… or a nazi.'

'Oooh…jealousy is a terrible thing.'

Lauren gave her an exasperated look. 'Millie, I know you like to think I spend my life resenting your fabulous relationship successes but as far as I'm concerned, Damian appearing on the scene has been a total blessing. It means you stay over at his place for nights of seedy passion and I get this salubrious address all to myself. I eat crisps, smoke fags, drink tea and watch TV without someone nattering their commentary in my ear. It's heaven.'

'Aaahh…my DeeDee. He's luvverrlllee.'

'Now don't start going gooey. You'll make me hurl.'

'That'll be the sandwich.'

'Or the presence of a love struck best mate who's driving me up the wall with her health fascism.'

'I am not a health fascist ! I just happen to realise that the five basic food groups are not tobacco, alcohol, crisps, chocolate and…' Millie hesitated. This was a fatal error when attempting to intervene in the life of Lauren Seymour. Anything other than total certainty and 100% clarity would be shrugged off as easily as a cagoule off the back of a smooth coated spaniel.

'See that's only four.' Lauren smirked.

'Shut up weirdy. I'm reading my mag. ' Millie flicked the page over and started studying the horoscopes. 'Ooh get this Ms Taurus.'

'Oh not that rubbish Mills.'

'It's not rubbish. You might change your mind when you hear what it has to say.'

'I think that's unlikely to be honest, but go on then if you must.'

'Well, it says that the coming week 'is one of real celestial significance to those born under the bull."

'Woooh', Lauren stuck her hands upside down under her chin and wiggled her fingers like tentacles whilst making her eyes wide.

'Lauren ! If you're not going to listen properly I'm not going to continue.'
'Oh go on then stroppy pants, I'm only teasing.'
'Well because of the 'alignment of several key planets in your chart, this week could see some dramatic events that have the potential to change your life dramatically for either the better or the worse'.'
'Well lets hope it's the former then.' Lauren picked her cigarettes up off the coffee table and stood up.
'Wait there's a bit more.'
Lauren sighed. 'Go on .'
'It says that, 'only you have the ability to determine which it is to be."
'Is that it ?'
Millie nodded.
'Well please excuse me if I don't immediately wet my pants with excitement won't you ? Kit-Kat and fag are now calling so must dash. Laters loser.'

   Lauren left the room and headed for the back landing, by the door where metal steps led up to the flat from a tiny snickleway below. Out here, you could see into the backyards of retail premises and into the grubby looking accommodation above them. Living so centrally was cool as far as Lauren could see. Fossgate was a street within the old stone walls, just off the city's central shopping area. Their flat was above a kitsch shop that sold household things you never really needed but made for a marginally brighter life. A stream of young women and their complaining boyfriends made the shop's bell ring, followed by a handful of gay men and groovy looking older people who didn't look as if they lived on a cul-de-sac. But probably did, just in really kitsched up houses with pink walls and a surfeit of retro-tat. Lauren liked it. Millie was forever dropping in the shop to see what she could find. Consequently, their flat was filling up with camp fridge magnets, cup cake trinket boxes and pink fluffy things the identity of which Lauren remained sketchy about. Hello Kitty was beginning to feel like a third flatmate. One who got out of paying rent by looking cute and waving.
   She took a drag on her Lucky Strike. She'd ditched the roll-ups. They were making her wheezy. So it was back to ciggies. This she felt was probably slightly healthier. Blowing a smoke plume into the air she looked at the grey sky. The summer had been a disappointment. Endless rain, broken by breezy days where a weak watery sunshine gave no hint of the identity of the season. It had seeped slowly into a dull grey autumn devoid of colour where even a walk under the turning leaves of the riverbank failed to fill her with much in the way of joy. Usually it was one of life's simple pleasures. The whole year had lacked much flavour.
   Everything was different. No more living in the little house in the terraced maze of the Groves with her overweight jovial gay nemesis, Millie back in

town and falling in love yet again, no more repetitive copywriting job at Accent Advertising. And the whole thing with Robert. That was particularly weird. No one ever mentioned it now. Occasionally Beth, who popped round to see her now and then brought his name up. Francis alluded to 'strange men' in the general, but she knew this was his way of talking in the particular. Millie, who only ever knew the guy as a student, remained oblivious. She was always so wrapped up in her own world that the ins and outs of Lauren's never seemed to cross her mind. Or so Lauren had thought. Now after 15 years of friendship in which Lauren had avoided sharing an address with her best friend, proximity was revealing a side to Millicent Croft that Lauren Seymour had never previously seen. She was attentive. Motherly even. Forever asking what she was up to, what she'd been eating, how she was feeling. It wasn't unpleasant. Unsettling maybe. Francis used to enquire about her general well-being and at times set about skewering withheld information from her with a directness that it was hard to wriggle away from. But Millie was defined in Lauren's mind by her charming self-obsession. The woman who went halves on the rent for the flat was very different. Maybe it was the presence of new love, Damian, the self-deprecating gentle young son of Tony her former housemate's equally charming civil partner. Maybe it was the lesson of the cancelled engagement or perhaps, and most troublingly, Lauren just didn't know her as well as she thought.

This idea bugged her. She'd always prided herself on being a decent judge of character. She could root people out fairly easily. Give her half an hour with someone and she'd be able to make some tentative judgements about what made them tick. After her confusion regarding Robert her confidence in her own abilities was no longer what it once was. But Millie ? Surely she knew her better than she knew anyone ?

Jude put his phone back down on the counter. He wasn't having the best of days.
'Where are you ?'
There was no answer from his best mate and he needed to sound off. He'd texted her twice, then phoned her mobile, then attempted to get through on the land line but nothing. Maybe he should be worried. Two large men in FCUK and Ralph Lauren t-shirts grabbed two four packs of Carling from the fridge and slammed them down hard on the counter, making Jude look up with a start. They stared at him quizzically. One jabbed the other and smirked.
'Excuse me mate.'
Jude tried to appear impassive. 'Yes ?'
'Are you a boy or a girl ?' His friend immediately burst out into drunken

laugher. Jude just glared. Then sighed and scanned their lager.
'Six pounds fifty please. Did you want a bag ?'
The other man recovered and spoke. 'Eh, you didn't answer me mate's question ? Are you a boy or a girl ? The thing is from where we're standing it's a bit hard to tell sweetheart and I don't want to be disappointed if I take you home tonight.'
Jude finally snapped. 'Go fuck your ugly mother up the arse till she bleeds.'
Nice work.
'You cheeky fucking bastard.' The man reached across the counter and grabbed Jude by his brown and cream company tabard, then turned his head to face his equally ugly friend.
'Shall I twat the ponce or will you ?'
At that point from the back of shop emerged Barbara the acting store manager. She was only in charge whilst Glynis was away in Bournemouth with Harry and the grandkids. Jude hated Barbara. She'd never liked him. Not her pot of Earl Grey at all. Or pot of watery supermarket discount bag tea. Barbara was definitely a joyless penny-pinching kind of girl. Jude imagined her loveless life with her predictable husband in a spotless house full of chintzy knick-knacks but little warmth. Daily Mail to her core.
'Is there a problem gents ?'
The man let go of Jude, who brushed himself off, pursed his lips and started examining his fingernails.
'That there is love. Your fucking shop boy or girl or whatever it is just told me to shag me own mother. Up the shitter as well.'
'Travers. Is this true ?'
'It's not that simple.'
'It never is, is it Travers ? Look I'm sorry gents, tell you what you take those cans on the house and I'll sort out this one for you. We don't stand for abuse from either customers or staff. It's in the company manual.'
'They were the ones who started it.' Jude jabbed his finger towards his tormentors.
'Please calm down. We'll talk about this shortly.'
"No I won't fucking calm down, I was minding me own business when they started on me.'
'And what did they say ?'
'Yeah, tell the lady what we said love. Be a doll.' The larger of the two men spoke, folding his arms across his chest and smiling.
'They asked if I was a boy or a girl ?'
Barbara laughed. 'Ha, oh gents, I'm so sorry about this. I've often wondered myself sometimes. Quite a little character is our Jude.'
'Do you mind ?' It was happening again. The norms ganging up on him. They always did. Just because he was slightly different. The narrow-minded

conspiratorial bastards. He hated them with a passion.
'I really am sorry gents. Leave this one to me.'
The men took their cans off the counter and turned to leave the shop. One of them blew a kiss at Jude as he went, prompting him to respond with a two-fingered salute. Barbara was almost incandescent. Her face was red and a little vein on the side of her neck was quietly throbbing. There was brief lull, a moment's charged silence before Barbara opened her mouth giving Jude a full display of her yellowing teeth. Her breath too. It wasn't good. It stank of the decades and too much gammon.
'What the hell do you think you were playing at !'
'They started it.'
'I've been in retail for nearly thirty years and I've lost count of the number of times someone's pulled my leg or had a bit of a tease. It goes with the territory.'
'This was different.'
'How was it different hmmm ? It's not as if you don't bring it on yourself looking like you do.'
'What do you mean ?'
'You've not got an inch of muscle on you, your hairstyle wouldn't look out of place on a girl, you've got more bracelets than Gerald Ratner and I'm sure you're wearing make-up.'
'Only a bit of eyeliner. It's no big deal.'
'See what I mean. You wouldn't catch my Gavin wearing eyeliner.'
'No because he'd look like the world's worst fat hairy tranny if he did.'
'I beg your pardon ?' Barbara's mouth fell open in an expression of mannered disbelief. Her hands resting on her hips.
'Because he'd look shit in it that's why. He's got them snidey little piggy eyes hasn't he ?' Jude made little circles of his fingers and thumbs and held them up to his big eyes like glasses.
'Are you saying my son is ugly ?'
'Well, yes. Duh ! Everyone else does. Fatty Venereal they call him.'
'Our surname is Venables !'
'Yeah whatever.' Under his breath Jude muttered, 'Babs fanny itch'. Not for the first time. Luckily his acting manager was too angry about the slight on her precious offspring to hear.
'Just because my son feels no need to preen around looking like a male prostitute and talking like a school girl it doesn't mean he doesn't care about his appearance. He makes a lot of himself.'
'Yeah because no one else is likely to are they ? Not when you're his size. Is it all down to pie eating or has he got something glandular going on ? That's always the excuse lazy fat slobs give isn't it ?'
'Now that really is it. I don't think we'll be needing your services any longer

Travers. I always had my doubts about you anyway. You looked like trouble from the off. Quite the little oddity. No, I said to myself I said, 'Barbara, that one's got baggage. I can't imagine he's one for hard work not like...'
'Yeah your fucking fat son, I know.' Jude made a pointed yawn. 'Well tell you what trout face, as I know for a fact that as only the acting manager of Toddy's Neighbourhood Store you don't have the power to hire and fire, I'll save you any embarrassment and quit. Fuck knows why I stuck it as long as I did anyway.'
'Good. Good. You go. Take yourself out of my sight. There are lots of people out there, mothers who want a bit of pin money, students and the like who'd give their eye teeth for a job like this, I've not been in retail for nearly thirty years without...'
'Turning into a smelly old harridan who should probably be put down. Ta-ra.' Jude walked out of the store waggling his fingers and pronouncing his wiggle for her benefit. He looked extra confident but inside he was shaking. Star had better be in.

Ding-dong.

'Fuck it.' The doorbell broke her concentration. The blade was hovering a couple of centimetres above her upturned left wrist. Just ignore the bell. This couldn't wait. She mustn't lose her nerve. Remember the pain of the last few weeks and stay strong. Kyle would be punished.

Ding-dong. Ding-dong.

Two sharp impatient chimes.
'Go away.' She had to act, she dropped the blade so it was making the lightest of contact with her skin and held it there.

Ding-ding-ding-ding-dong-ding-ding-dong.

Someone was holding their finger on the buzzer. It had to be Jude. He was her escape route. She imagined how he would feel if he found her. Imagine doing that to him. His life would be destroyed. She didn't have to do it. She mustn't do it. God bless you Jude. Bang on the button as always. She lifted the razorblade from her arm and shoved it in the bathroom cabinet, quickly wiped her eyes on a piece of toilet tissue and ran to the voice entry unit by the front door. She pressed the red button, took a deep breath and then spoke into it.

'Yes.'
'You would not believe what's just happened ! I can hear my heart beating in my chest Star I'm that shook up.'
'Jude ?'
'Of course it's Jude. Let me in.'
'Ok, Ok.'

   Jude sat on the sofa in the front room drinking a cup of tea and was gesticulating wildly with a Hob-Nob.
'I couldn't believe what I was hearing. Making ME out to be the villain when THEY fucking started it.'
'Calm down sweetie. It doesn't matter.'
'Doesn't matter ? Doesn't matter ? Hah ! I'd expected some sympathy from you.'
'Oh Jude, you know I'm sympathetic. I'm always sympathetic. It's just you were saying the other day that you were going to quit because you hated it.'
'I did, I just wanted to do it in my own time.'
'I always thought you were one for the big dramatic gesture.'
'I am, but now I've given that ugly old cow reason to gloat.'
'From what you've told me I think she's more likely to be seething. Did you really call her son fat ?'
'I did.'
'And you actually suggested a customer violently bummed their own mother ?'
Jude grinned devilishly. 'Yeah I did.'
'God I love you. Come here.' Star reached across and gave her best mate a huge hug.
'Aww bless you. That's much better.' Jude loosened his grip and straightened up. 'Now, tell me why you've been crying ?'
'I haven't been crying.'
'So why are your eyes red raw then.'
'Oh.'
'You can't hide stuff from me you know. I know what you're thinking. We're psychopathic.' He tapped her forehead and smiled.
'It's just…'
'Kyle ?' She nodded. 'He's gone Star and you should be grateful he has as the man was a wanker. I always thought so.'
'Just because he didn't like you.'
'No, and the feeling was mutual. He was just jealous of me. Didn't like another bloke being close to his bird. Especially one as pretty and refined as me.'

'I hated when he called me his bird.'
'So did I. Tosser.'
'And the way he used to pick his nose and then examine what he'd found whilst we were watching the Antiques Roadshow.'
'He did that ?' Jude had a look of appalled disbelief on his face.
'Fraid so.'
'Urrghh. Gross. Was this specifically brought on by the sight of greedy grannies touting their hand me down tall boys and dodgy porcelain to men in bow ties in provincial leisure centres , or was it more general ?'
'Definitely general.' Star paused and thought. 'And there was how he used to keep all his Mojo magazines in month order on his bookcase. I used to mix them up when I was dusting.'
'I'd have found the fact he read Mojo irritating in itself. I'd probably of used them to wipe my backside with. All those arse-licking articles about Eric Clapton and how Radiohead are more important than gravity. I hate music bores. They give me a migraine. You never see Girls Aloud on the front cover of Mojo. Why I ask myself ? Why ?'
'Ha !' Star spluttered her tea all over the laminate.
'Now look what you've done. Messy girl.' Jude smiled at her.
She returned it. He'd done it again hadn't he ? Turned potential tragedy into laughter in just the space of a few hours.

Jude had been busy in the kitchen knocking them up some food. There wasn't an awful lot in the cupboards but he managed to find all the component parts of his special cheese on toast. It was just what the doctor ordered. The richness of the cheese and mustard mix would take away from the staleness of the bread.
'When did you last go food shopping properly ?' He asked as he carried the plates into the front room.
'Must have been ? Let me see. About seven weeks ago before…'
'Don't tell me, before Kyle left', Jude rolled his eyes. 'Star, you can't go on like this ! Life moves on you know. You've got to get yourself together and get back out there. There's plenty more fish in the sea and all that.'
'Don't say that Jude.'
'What's that ?'
'The fish in the sea line. Everyone keeps talking about bloody fish. I don't want fish, I want Kyle.'
'Now you listen to me.' He put his hand on her shoulders and took hold of her chin, gesturing with his fingers like a stage hypnotist for her to keep her eyes fixed on his. 'Repeat after me. I do NOT want Kyle.'
'I do not want Kyle.' It didn't sound very convincing. Star sighed. 'If only it were that easy.'

Having finished their food, Jude washed up their plates and began rifling through the DVD rack next to the TV. The small portable that had once sat in the bedroom had been promoted following the removal of Kyle's flat-screen. It was odd because she could never remember it being specifically his until he decided to leave. Then like so much of the more expensive kit they'd shared it all got strangely co-opted by the groin-led man-boy quitter.

'I'm presuming the entire first series of Battlestar Galactica belonged to the dickhead.'

'Yup. Left quite a bit of stuff. Cheap stuff.'

'Well give it all to me then and I'll stick it all on Ebay. I'm going to need the readies seeing as I'm unemployed. Carly will do her nut when she finds out. I'm three weeks behind on the rent as it is.'

'Jude what have you been playing at ?'

'Don't know really. I had me hair done at Toni & Guys which set me back a bit, then there were the cocktails at Jekyll's.'

'Toni & Guys ? Bloody hell no wonder you're skint. And when did you go to Jekyll's ? Why wasn't I invited ?'

'You were invited. You just didn't want to come.'

'Was I ?' Star looked confused.

'Yes, you were too busy staring at your navel to come out for a drink with me and Jess.'

'Aw Jess. How is she ?'

'Not too bad, got into a fight with some woman who was eyeing up Emma.'

'Emma ? Is that her girlfriend ? I thought she went out with someone called Holly.'

'She did but she chucked her when she met Emma. That girl is nothing but a womanising heart breaker if you ask me.'

'She is sweet. Like a cute little pocket dynamo.'

'Don't let her hear you say that. She hates being called sweet. Once kicked a bloke in the bollocks for calling her it whilst we were cueing for a pizza. He had to go to A&E in a hurry but was too embarrassed to press charges, thank fuck. I did NOT want to spend a night in the cells with an angry lesbian. I'm still suffering Prisoner Cell Block H flashbacks now.'

'Right. Thanks for the warning.'

'You'll be alright. She thinks you're hot.'

'Does she ?' Star smiled. 'Aww nice one.'

Jude resumed flicking through the DVDs 'Terminator 3 - utter shite, Lethal Weapon - yawn, the entire CSI series 5 - tedious crap. Is there nothing here decent. Where's your stuff ?'

'Mine are in the draw. Couldn't find room for them on the rack he said apparently.'

'The cheeky bastard.' Jude pulled the draw out and lifted out a selection of

what looked to his eyes to be much more promising films.
'Oooh Moulin Rouge, Dirty Dancing naturally, Pretty In Pink, god I soo badly wanted to be Molly Ringwald first time I saw that. Hey, now you're talking.' Jude pulled a DVD out of the draw.
'What ?'
'Thelma & Louise. The perfect fuck-you movie. That's what you need. Two fingers in the air. Make yourself look fabulous. Less of this moping.'
'Aww I love that film. You bought me that for my 24th birthday remember.'
'Ooh so I did.'
Star leaned back on the sofa, let out a huge sigh and ran her fingers through her hair. 'Wouldn't it be lovely just to take off like that. Go on a road trip. Leave your troubles behind.'
Jude put the DVD down on top of the telly and turned as an invisible light bulb seemingly flicked into life above his head.
'What's stopping us ?'
'Eh ?'
He scurried across and sat down on the sofa next to Star.
'Why don't we do it ? Just take off. Go on a road trip.'
'Jude, we can't just go…'
'Tell me why not ? You're freelance you can do what you want and as from today I'm dole scum *yet* again. There's nothing to keep us here. We could go anywhere.'
'No, I couldn't. I've got this place to look after and…'
'Stop the excuses. Your work can wait, and this place isn't going to go to pot in a month. Anyway, you worry way too much. You've got all responsible too early.'
'Jude, I'm thirty next birthday, so are you. We're not kids anymore.'
'That's all the more reason to do something exciting. We don't need to get bogged down. Think about it..'
'It is tempting.'
'See ! I told you. Let's go tomorrow.'
'I've not said yes yet.'
'But you're going to, your just doing your usual let's pretend to put up a bit of resistance thing because actually I'm dead sensible and grown up.'
'I'm more sensible than you.'
'No you're not ! You're just more hung-up. You think stuff whereas I do it.'
'So I'm sensible.'
'That's not sensible that's cowardly.'
'You cheeky sod.' Star attempted to tickle Jude but he grabbed her hands before they could make contact. He was well practiced in defending against her 'chuckle-hands'.
'So ? Are we doing this or not ?'

'Ok, Ok. We'll go. We'll definitely go.'
'Yay ! You're a star.'
'That kind of goes without saying Jude.'

Star drove Jude round to the flat he shared with Carly his landlady. He was hoping she was going to be out.
'No lights on. Looks promising.' Star looked up to the first floor bay window in the Victorian converted town house.
'You don't know Carly, she's practically the undead, she prefers to operate in the dark.' Jude shuddered.
'You make her sound like a monster J, she's only a teacher.'
'Only a teacher ? Teacher's have made my life a misery let me tell you.'
'I know. Along with your parents, your siblings, every employer you've ever had, everyone you've ever been out with, most of your friends and everyone you've ever lived with.'
'Aww, but you're nice to me poppet.' He touched her nose and felt all brave.
'Best go get my stuff. Wait there.'
'Won't you need a hand ?'
'Nooo…you stay out of it. You don't send a girl to do a woman's job.'

    Star looked out at the streetlight illuminated avenue. It was a street of Victorian town houses, with mature trees that overhung the pavement, giving the place a leafy, sleepy feel. Most of the houses had been turned into flats and bedsits, and had an elegant dishevelment that Star always enjoyed. So different to the faceless new build block she shared with Kyle. Sorry, had shared with Kyle. She sighed and then saw a light go on in the front room of Jude's flat. Carly must be out. Thank goodness. She seemed alright, a bit stuffy and buttoned up perhaps but fundamentally a good sort. Star wasn't sure what she'd make of Jude though, didn't really seem like her cup of tea. Flat-sharing made some unlikely bedfellows. Eventually, Jude scurried out of the front door and down the path, almost tripping up over himself to get back in the car.
'Was she out then ?'
Jude caught his breath, then spoke. 'Noooo…she wasn't.' He shook his head gravely. 'But I didn't see her.'
'Why not ?'
'The place was in darkness apart from her room.'
'And ?'
'There were sex noises coming from behind the closed door.' Jude's face ran pale.
Star gulped. 'Carly ? Sex ? I didn't know she had a boyfriend.'
'Me neither, and to be honest I don't think she has.'

'She's not…'
'Nooo, she's always going on about how she fancies that bloke from Blue Peter.'
'Gethin thingy ?'
' Yes him, the dancing man.'
'Right. So, what was happening ?'
'I think I could hear a bit of a low electrical buzz and I don't think she was drying her hair from the noises she was making.'
'All of a sudden Jude I have a very unpleasant image in my head.'
'Me too ! It's just the thought of her. All twenty four stone, lying there on her bed, probably starkers, moaning around as she…'
'Yes, that's quite enough thank you. I think we've got the picture now.'
'Not expecting me back just yet clearly.'
'Well the main thing is you've got some stuff.'
Jude tapped his huge rucksack. 'Loads in here, just shoved everything in I could lay my hands on. Aww poor Carly. I think she's just lonely and dead horny. Fat people having feelings too you know.'
'No more of that.'
'And I mean she's not likely to see much action is she, not looking like she does. Just where does a plumper go to find sexual solace ? '
'Don't be cruel Jude.'
'It's not cruel it's just an observation isn't it ? I think I might make a pitch to BBC 3 to put together a documentary about the sex lives of the morbidly obese.'
'It's a disability Jude, not something to laugh about.'
'Fuck is it ! Someone born with only one arm has a disability, Carly just eats a lot of chips. It's lack of self-control that's the problem. I grew up poor but I'm not a porker. I did wonder if it was something glandular until I saw the amount of shit food she puts away. There's not an evening goes by she's not gorging herself on a tub of Ben & Jerry's. People who do have an under active thyroid I've sympathy for. Greedy cows just bring it on themselves.'
'That's enough J. Let's get going.'
'Did I ever tell you that she came onto me ?'
'Noooo. You're joking !' Star's eyes lit up and she immediately forgot about her earlier distaste for the subject of Carly's sex life. 'When was this ? Why didn't you tell me ?'
'I wanted to but you were too miserable and not wanting to see me. There's loads of stuff I could have told you about if you hadn't been so self-pitying.'
'Aww sorry treacle. Give me a kiss and then tell me all about it.'
Jude leaned across and kissed her cheek. 'I came home one night to find her lounging on the sofa in her dressing gown.'
'And ?'

'She'd been drinking and she asked me if I'd like to join her, so, innocently I said yes, poured myself a glass of her wine and started watching QI with her.'
'Then what.'
'Then she wrapped her arm around me and started telling me how attractive she found me. I was flattered and just presumed she was being friendly so I thanked her and then lied when I said that she was alright as well.'
'Oh god no.'
'Then all of a sudden she lunged at me, pushed me onto my back and tried to shove her tongue down my throat.'
'You didn't relent ?'
'Bloody hell no ! What do you take me for ? I wiggled out from underneath her and then went and locked myself in the bathroom until I heard her go to bed.'
'Haha ! That sounds priceless. Carly and Jude, sitting in a tree, K-I-S-S-I-N-G !'
'Shut up and drive you ! I'm suffering post-traumatic stress.'

Jude slept on the sofa at the flat, waking up at 7.30 as he heard someone moving about in the front room of the flat above them. He turned over, put his head under a cushion, but someone somewhere was listening to Chris Moyles, and irritating snippets of the idiot's voice kept infiltrating his brain. 'Will you please shut the fuck up.' He threw the cushion across the room, sighed and sat up. It was no good. He was going to have to get up before eight. This might possibly mean he turned into a pumpkin but needs must. If he did perhaps Star could make him into a spicy autumnal soup. Or she could if she knew how to work the cooker. That girl was hopeless with anything connected to the kitchen. For all of Kyle's general uselessness he did at least ensure Star wasn't living on crisps and chocolate. This road trip would give Jude chance to look after her for a bit. He smiled and walked across to the kettle, filled it, flicked it on, and threw a couple of teabags in the pot.
'I'll be mother shall I ?' He said to himself, and then started whistling.

Star was munching on a bacon sandwich. Jude had found some bacon hidden away in the bottom of the freezer, defrosted it in the microwave and then stuck it under the grill. He toasted the remaining pieces of stale Mother's Pride and managed to knock up two passable butties, which were made more palatable by the copious addition of plenty of brown sauce.
'It was a bacon butty that did for my vegetarianism you know.' Star spoke with her mouthful.
'It's always the way isn't it ?'
'I think so. Kyle made a lovely bacon sandwich. He'd put rocket and tomato

into a toasted panini, smear it with mayonnaise and…'
'That's enough. Kyle's not here remember. My handiwork will have to do. '
'Sorry, sorry. I forgot.'
'Soon young lady, you and I are going to be out of here anyway.'
'Erm..Jude. Do you know where we're going exactly ?'
Jude caught a bit of stray bacon on his lip with the tip of his finger and edged it towards his mouth. 'Mmm..wait a minute…erm…no, not really. Where do you fancy ?'
'Don't know to be honest ? Anywhere's better than here.'

Which wasn't perhaps that much of an exaggeration. Newtham was a nowhere town, east of the Midlands, North of the South, but neither one thing nor the other. It had never been fully industrial, neither could it claim to be a well-preserved market town. The high street had given way to mobile phone and charity shops, the pubs were full of old men, or white shirt wearing townies who smashed glasses over each others heads of a Friday evening before going home for unsatisfactory sex with their dumb compliant girlfriends.

There was only one decent place in town where non-conforming free-thinking determined not to get too old and too conventional too soon types could hang out. That was Jekyll's, a funny little bar in the corner of a 60s development that housed a discount supermarket and some vague unspecified offices. It had a little room upstairs which it let out to different groups. Everything from the Newtham Writers to the Socialist Workers Party would meet there.

Jude and Star could sit for hours in their little corner, shooting the breeze finding refuge amongst the ageing grebos, loved up gay couples, underage emo kids and the handful of artists and creative types brave enough to stand out in a conventional place like this. A gathering of outsiders. In it they found a degree of comfort and togetherness, whilst at the same time it emphasised their difference from the rest of the residents. This was no place to stand out, and what's more Newtham was just one of thousands of similar places right across the country. It was a nothing place, full of largely nothing people, shuffling their way through nothing lives until the reaper called time, and they then went purposefully into the nothing.

It didn't suit Star, but at least she could blend in. Throw on some anonymous clothes, get her head down, hide her weirdness from the world. Jude's difference was always on display. It wasn't just in the way he dressed, which was not that dramatically remarkable in the grand scheme of things. But in the shape of his face, the big heartbreaking eyes, his full-lips, the way he carried himself with his narrow shoulders back, his nose in the air, an understated elegant glide to his walk, rather than the usual Neanderthal broad-shouldered slouch of his male contemporaries. It would of made more sense if he was gay perhaps. Peoples lazy stereotypes would have been satisfied. It was regularly presumed he was. From his mum, his school contemporaries, the people he had worked with, random strangers in the street. But he only ever slept with girls. When he could be bothered. If anything he seemed almost asexual, yet remained deeply sexy. He was always so intriguing. Star had long since concluded that her best friend from childhood was just different and that difference was ineffable and difficult to define. He just didn't seem much of anything, but whatever he was it was deeply attractive. To Star at any rate. As a friend. You couldn't imagine a relationship with someone like that. Too confusing.

Jude stood up, picked up his plate and took Star's from her out reached hand

'I hate Newtham. I always have.' Jude had clattered the plates into the sink in the kitchen into which they'd both moved. Star was leaning against the units, eating stale digestives from the biscuit barrel. They'd had this conversation countless times before.

'So why did you never leave. You've got A-levels, you could of gone to university ?'

'Don't know. Comfortable I guess.'

'You're dead out of place here though aren't you. You were the only rake-thin pretty boy wearing eyeliner in town until someone invented emo.'

'I fucking hate emo. It's ruined everything. Stealing my USP like that.'

'I know, I'd be wandering around town seeing all these fifteen year olds dressed like you. I thought you'd set up some weird cult initially.'

'Now there's a good idea.'

'That is just too awful a prospect to contemplate.'

'No it's not, it makes sense. I am pretty darn hot and I do talk a lot of sense. I shit on David Koresh let's face it.'

'But where are we going to grace with your hot-ness then sweetie ? We need to make a decision.'

'We should toss a coin. Heads we take the A1 north, tails we head south. What do you reckon ?'

'Well it's a start I guess, but I don't want this road trip to be about us hanging out in Doncaster or Peterborough for a few weeks. We need a bit of excitement, interesting places. The seaside maybe ?'

'Ok, Ok, whatever. I've got a pound coin.' Jude reached in his pocket and retrieved his coin. 'Do you want to do it.'

Star bit her lip and shook her head. 'Nooo…too nervous. You do it.'

'Ok, right, here goes.' Jude threw the coin in the air, they watched it rise and the stood out of the way as it headed towards the kitchen lino, where it landed, bounced a little, spun on its axis and then toppled still. Star leaned down.

'Heads. We go north.'
'Cool. I'll get my coat.'

I get my kicks…

It was raining as Star's little eight year old Renault Clio pulled out of town and onto the A1 northbound. She still had no idea where she was meant to be driving them.
'So we've established that we're going north, but whereabouts did you have in mind ?' She asked her passenger who was looking at himself in the wing mirror and playing with his hair.
'Nowhere really. Don't know. Sheffield first or something ? That's always nice I hear.'
'You're not serious. A road trip to Sheffield ?'
'Just a thought.'
'How about Leeds. More happening.'
'We could do that yes.'
'You don't seem very enthusiastic Jude. Come on, where did you have in mind ?'
'Erm…what about York ? We went there on a school trip once remember ? I got put in a group with the girls to go and draw pictures of the period costumes at the Castle Museum, whilst the boys went and pulled bits off the Mallard at the railway museum. Didn't we go to that Viking place as well ?'
'Aww yeah, we did didn't we. That was a lovely school trip wasn't it ? We hung out together all day and talked about everything except what we should have been talking about.'
'We must have been such a weird couple of kids. Me the nervous little girly boy, you the girl who looked as if she'd been a child actor in Witness who none of the other kids would talk to. Very Amish I found you.'
'Haha ! You didn't know what Amish was back then you liar. Bloody hell though I always felt out of sorts. My folks were just so different.'
'They were that bless 'em. Make me look normal. Actually, how are they these days, you still speaking ?'
'I speak to mum, she's alright. Dad's an elder now or something. They still don't call me Star. I love them in a funny way, they're good people. They just believe an awful lot of mumbo-jumbo.'
'I've always believed myself to be the reincarnation of Dorothy Parker but it's never held me back.'
'You're not a gay bloke Jude no matter how much you protest to the contrary. That camp stuff never suits you. You and I both know you're just a

weird variation on a dyke. By all accounts you should have been really.'
'True. But I'd be quite femme. I don't know enough about car maintenance or team sports to be butch. Jess is a whiz with a spanner you know.'
'Haha, you crack me up dude. York, let's do York. Old buildings, nice pubs, we can knock around there for a bit until we get bored.'
'Sounds good to me but where are we going to stay ?'
'I've not really considered that. We could do a B&B ?'
'I'm broke Star, I've no cash for a B&B, you'd have to pay the lot and you aint loaded honey.'
'Sleep in the car ?'
'You can think again if you think I'm going to sleep in your rubbish strewn car with you snoring and farting your way through the night.'
'Just a suggestion. Wait a minute….?' Star had just remembered something. 'I think I've a cousin lives in York.'
'Oooh popping in on the family. How lovely. As long as it's free and they feed us I don't mind where we stay.'
' Mum's sister's daughter. Bit older than me. Only ever met her at family parties and stuff. Always seemed a bit sullen and quiet.'
'Sounds a laugh a minute. She's not another religious nut job is she ? I'm not sure I could stay with someone who never changed out of corduroy and faded Runrig t-shirts.'
'If my dad had worn a Runrig t-shirt I would of considered it a step into dangerously new liberal territory.'
'Cousin. What about her then ? If you don't know her how do we go about kipping at her place ?'
'Wait a minute, let's pull over.'

   Star pulled the car into a small service station that had seen better days. There was a dodgy looking, slightly dilapidated transport café next door, in a couple of cut and shut portakabins, that cluttered up the lay-by.
'Cup of tea on me. I think I'll phone my mum and see what I can come up with.'

   'Oh hello Joyce, lovely to hear from you ? How are you ? I understand you're not living with Kyle anymore.'
   Star winced, firstly at the use of the name her adopted parents gave her, second at her mother's immediate prying into the former boyfriend issue. Her parents had never approved of her shacking up with a man without her getting a ring on her finger first. It was a constant, never allowed to just lie quietly, issue that always popped back up. The traffic rumbled past the window, lorries created draft that rocked the cabins slightly. Star put a finger in her free ear as she struggled to make out what her mum was saying.
'Yeah, erm, that's difficult mum. Look, I'm phoning about that cousin of

mine.'

'Which one ? Oh you mean Lionel ? He is a lovely boy. Do you know he has his own used car garage now ? Lives up on the new estate where the Willows Care Home used to be, not far from Auntie Flora and Uncle Humphrey. Your great aunt and uncle. Nan's sister. You know who I mean ?'

'Yes, mum I do..I was..'

'He always held a candle for you did Lionel. Well he's still single, still looking.'

From what Star had heard of perfect cousin Lionel he was indeed still looking, but wasn't really in the vagina business. What's more he'd been quite successful in finding what he was after. On an almost weekly basis as well. He spent most weekends in Nottingham and rarely needed to pay to find a bed for the night.

'No mum, not Lionel.'

'Oh, I see… I had thought seeing as you weren't…'

'Mum, I know cousin love is quite normal in your church and all that, but I'm not sure it's right and anyway I don't think Lionel would have me.'

'I'm sure he…'

'No, it's the one from Nottingham.' Star intervened to prevent that line of conversation going any further. 'Tall girl, Laura or something.'

'Oh you mean Hilary's girl. Lauren. I see. What do you want to know about her, I don't really know her myself. Although I did hear rumours that she might be a bit that way.'

Star was confused. 'What way ?'

'You know. The kind of woman who wears men's clothing and plays football.'

'Mum, I'm not really sure I'm getting you here.'

'I mean' her voice dropped to a hushed whisper. 'I think she's a lesbian.'

'Pardon mum, I didn't hear ?' Star was smiling, she had heard she just wanted to hear her adopted mum repeat it.

'A lesbian !'

'Ah right. Well, whatever. Do you have her number ? Does she live in York ?'

' She was there a while back, no idea if she still is. Not spoken to Hilary for a few years. It's difficult.'

'Well could you give me Auntie Hilary's number so I can find out ?'

'If you like. Why do you want it ? You're not thinking about becoming a lesbian as well are you ? Since you can't find a man to marry ? One of the pastors at church gave a lecture about deviance and he said inability to find a suitable life partner was one of the major causes. Told us all to be careful. Is that what all this is about ?'

'No mum, I don't want to become a lesbian and I'm not really sure it's that simple.'

Overhearing this it took all of Jude's self-control not to splurt his mouth full of stewed tea across the chipped formica table.

'That's good. I wouldn't want to explain that one to your father Joyce. He's not really one for all these new things.'

'Right, no.' Best try and get off the subject of sapphism as well. This wasn't the time or the place quite frankly, and Star's phone battery was starting to flag.

'Alright here's your Auntie Hilary's number. Don't remember me to her. We haven't spoken since the incident with the cream cleaner.'

Star jotted down the number, made her excuses and got off the phone. Telephoning the number she was greeted by a breezy woman who sounded suspiciously like her own mother.

'Oh Joyce, yes. Of course. Young Joyce. How are you dear ?'

'I'm very well Auntie Hilary.'

'Oh you can drop the auntie thing now love, we're all adults aren't we.'

'Yes, thank you.'

'To what do I owe this then ?'

'It's about Lauren.'

The woman on the other end of the phone hesitated a little before answering. 'Oh yes.'

'Does she still live in York ?'

'Yes she's still up there. We've talked to her about moving back to Nottingham but she's not interested. Had chance to go to London you know, but turned it down. I wasn't disappointed because you hear a lot of things about London don't you, but I was surprised. I'm not sure what's keeping her in York. It's certainly not a boyfriend.'

'Ah right.' Maybe this was the coded message for 'my daughter the lesbian' but Star couldn't be certain.

'Would you let me have her number. It's just I'm on my way up in that direction, thought I might say hello.'

'Oh right. I can do that for you. I'll let you have her mobile, she only ever answers that one in my experience and then only if she feels like it.'

'Right. I can text then, introduce myself.'

'Yes dear, I think that might be a good idea. She's not really the over-friendly type my daughter.'

Star was beginning to wonder if this really was such a good idea.

'Oh no problem.' Auntie Hilary read out a number which Star jotted down.

'Thanks for that.'

'That's alright love. If you do see her, could you just remind her she's got parents ? I think she sometimes forgets.'

'What about character development?'
Francis had dropped into the flat for a coffee and a natter. He was taking the week off to decorate the Groves house but so far had spent the first three days making social calls, watching afternoon screenings at the City Screen and chatting on the telephone.
'Are we talking about my story here?' Lauren asked. Francis had been scanning through a print-off of the first section of her putative novel.
'Of course.' He looked up at her over the rim of his reading glasses. 'What did you think I mean?'
'Oh it's nothing.'
Francis put down the manuscript and took off his glasses. 'Come on. What's bugging you?'
Lauren sighed.
'I don't know.'
'There's something up. You're not regretting not taking the London job are you?'
'No, it's not that.' She was certain of that. Being surrounded by her few friends meant emotional safety. That was undoubtedly a good thing.
'So what is it then?' Francis got up from the chair and joined her on the sofa. 'Shove up fatso.'
'Cheeky sod' She smiled and digged him in the ribs. Francis in turn attempted to tickle her, but Lauren grabbed his hands and stopped him making contact. He pulled them out of her grasp instinctively wrapping his arms around her and hugging her close.
'Ah my poor old Lauren. I do miss having you around.'
Lauren pulled away and looked at him. 'Do you? Everything's alright with the Silver Fox then?'
'Oh yes, thing's are going swimmingly there.' He gave her a wink. 'It doesn't stop me missing you though. We spent a lot of time with each other. You were like part of the furniture.'
'I'm just like an occasional table me.'
'I had you down more as a hat stand.'
'Ah cheers. Yeah a hat stand. I can see that.' She took a sip from her coffee mug.
'So what's bugging you then? You can tell your Uncle Francis. You always used to.'
'I don't know. It's just I wonder sometimes if I'm a bit stuck. Life's sort of stuttering a bit.'
'Stuck how?'
'Well in my skin kind of. I don't seem to be growing as a person that much.

I've always been this chain-smoking singleton who minds her own business. Am I going to be like that for the rest of my days ? Millie seems loads different somehow. She's still the same Millie, but she's more grown up. I don't think you can say the same about me. If I were a character in a book I think there's a danger the readers might get bored with me. I think I need an adventure.'
'Oooh bloody hell. Right' Francis raised his eyebrows, paused for a second, his out of focus eyes steered in the direction of the ceiling. Gathering his thoughts he spoke. 'Well, firstly Millie had more growing up to do. There was too much of the little girl about her. She never thought things through and rarely thought of anyone else. She's a lovely person, but she's always been immature. It's part of her charm. You on the other hand.'
'Think too much.'
'Yes, but that's part of *your* charm. You're very different people.'
'We are, but we get on.'
'You get on because you're so different. No you've nothing to worry about.'
'But one day one of those useless blokes she's always hooking up with is going to turn out half-decent and she's going to be gone.'
'Yes, it's what people do Lauren. Most people want that from life. All the years I spent on my own I used to wish there was someone special who'd always be there for me.'
Lauren momentarily looked hurt. 'But I was always there for you ?'
'You were. You still are and I'm here for you, but it's different somehow. It's more primal, it's a need we have.'
'I'm not sure I do.'
'Really ? I'm not so sure.'
'Meaning ?'
'I think you do but you're very self-protective, you don't want anyone getting too close in case they hurt you so you tell yourself that you're above all that. The trouble is Lauren, unless we're very lucky we all have to go through the hurt until we find Mr or Ms Right.'
'Nope. I'm not having that.' She shook her head and stood up. The atmosphere in the room had suddenly got cooler. It was purely of her doing. Francis knew this mood. He'd touched a nerve, he needed to step back a little, give her chance to cogitate. All he had to do was plant the seed.

Walking across to the window Lauren looked down on Fossgate. A teenage couple were unselfconsciously necking at the end of an alley between two shops. Lauren looked back at Francis.
'Shit happens Francis. I'm not going to try and be someone I'm not in the vague hope that it will bring someone to my door. I'm just not like that.'
Francis smiled. 'You're certainly different Lauren and I love you for it. But I personally think you deserve some love.'

'Deserve it ? How come ?'
'You don't get it do you ?'
'Erm.' She looked confused. ' No I don't.'
'In that case then I'm not going to tell you.' Francis glanced at his watch .
'You haven't got any cake in have you ?'
   Suddenly her phone launched into Sheila Take A Bow by The Smiths. An incoming text. It wasn't from a number she recognised. Opening it she started to read :
'Hey Lauren, I'm Star, but you probably know me as Joyce. I'm your cousin. I'm on my way up to York with a friend and wondered if we could pop in ?'

'Frickin weird.' She was just about to hit delete but hesitated.
'What is ?'
'Text message out the blue, someone called Star or Joyce or something says I'm their cousin. Doesn't make any sense. Wants to see me.'
'Oooh how intriguing. Let me see.' Francis took her phone and read it.
'Aww that's nice.'
'What is ?'
'Your cousin. She wants to come see you. Do you remember her ?'
'There was a girl called Joyce. I met her one Boxing Day at my nan's house when I was a teenager. She'd be about four years younger than me. Weird actually. Her folks were dead religious. Seemed really old fashioned.'
'What's all the Star thing about then ?'
'Don't know. Probably means she's rebelled and become one of them new age crusty drop out kids who do hair braiding and stuff at festivals. I could see Mills doing that if life had turned out differently. Frickin cotton wool brain at times that one.'
'Less of that Lauren.' Francis tried to make a stern face but failed. 'You know I won't hear any bitching about your best friend.'
'Francis, I don't frickin bitch. I don't know how to.'
'Hah ! Anyway, what are you going to do about this cousin of yours. You can't turn her down can you.'
'Just delete it probably, pretend I never received it.'
Francis looked horrified.
'No you will not.' He took the phone and moved faster than his cumbersome body would ever normally allow to the privacy of the bathroom, where he quickly bolted the door. Lauren was left stranded in the front room open mouthed. When Francis finally emerged he was grinning like a Cheshire cat.
'I think you should expect a couple of visitors you great lanky anti-social sod you.'
Lauren shook her head. 'Just great, just frickin great.'

Star's phoned beeped an incoming message.

'Hello Joyce, so lovely to hear from you. I would be absolutely delighted to see you. It will be wonderful to share a sedate meander down memory lane together. Sorry to be a complete pain, but could you talk to my dear old friend Francis to find out where to come to ? I'm very busy at the moment with my needlework project and cannot be disturbed. Fear not though dear heart, the kettle will be whistling and the cake will be sliced for you upon your arrival. I shall have to change my pinny now won't I ?'

There was a telephone number for Francis attached.
'Right, blimey. Not what I expected.' Star raised her eyebrows at the message.
'Ah, has she said no ?'
'No, it's OK. Just I was expecting a full-on grumpy dyke and instead I think we might be staying with Mrs Beeton.' She showed the message to her best friend. Jude chuckled.
'Haha. She sounds a bit mental. Guess it goes with the territory with your family.'

Almost the boy next door…

Mum always said he was such a good boy.
'You're a good boy our Lee. I'll give you that.'
Incompetent. Over-sensitive. Clever if not the brightest button in the box. The kind of lad you wouldn't be overly-proud of as a parent , but they wouldn't let you down by beating seven shades of shite out of someone every Friday night or raising a fist to a girlfriend. Not our Lee. You could be sure of that. Lee was of his time. When his dad was worrying about his son's perceived lack of backbone, it was mum who would always leap to his rescue, 'it's the generation. They're not like we were.'
 Skip back a generation again and things were different still.
'Of course when I first got married,' Nan would say, 'you expected the occasional slap. We all did. It was par for the course. In a way it showed your fella cared about you.'
That kind of attitude had definitely gone down the historical toilet. A man couldn't raise an open hand to his wife, sorry, partner without them calling foul. Political correctness gone mad granddad predictably called it. 'In my day, when there were proper jobs to go to, the Labour party concerned itself with real things, like wages, and conditions. None of this fannying around with the nanny state. Telling a man how he can and can't act in his own home. Thatcher were a bastard but she never interfered in what people did

with their own lives. This lot are like Thatcher crossed with a bloody social worker.'

You had to just nod your head when granddad was going off on one. Keeley would say to him, 'you're a miserable old bugger gramps but I do love you,' but Lee couldn't say either. He knew if he called him miserable he'd cuff him one, no matter how old he was and the second bit about loving him, well that wasn't true was it ? He wasn't really a man for whom the word love could easily be applied. Respect at a push, but only on one of his better days. Most of the time he generated a mild rumbling and definitely unspeakable contempt. Unspeakable if you wanted to remain breathing that is.

Dad was more sussed.

'Yer granddad were always a hard mean bastard and I hated him fer it,' he'd confess. 'Sound principles and all the rest of it, but when it came to the personal stuff he didn't have a bloody clue. ' Lee's dad was himself of a different generation. Came of age in the sixties. He might have been sweating cobs in the steel works by day, but by night he was a Mod. Sharp Italian tailoring purchased on the tick, previously written off Italian scooter rescued from the scrap heap with a bit of TLC and the help of a mechanic mate. Just a shame there were no Italian women knocking around Rotherham to complete the perfect picture. As it was, he ended up with Lee and Keeley's mam. Not that she were anything to complain about. Quite a looker was Jenny Fawthrop. And her dad ran an ironmongers. One step up from the factory monkeys. No, dad knew what was what.

'There are three things for you to remember son.' He'd told him the night before his 18th birthday as they'd sat at the end of the bar at the local working-men's club, the first full initiation into the rights of the adult proletarian man at precisely the time when the proletariat were ceasing to have any real historical function.

'Always pay your way. Don't be beholden to anyone. You'll only live to regret it. Secondly,' he continued wiping his mouth on his sleeve and reaching for the open crisp packet sitting on the bar. 'Never cross a picket line. There's only one thing worse than a scab in my book.' He gestured with a handful of Seabrooks Prawn Cocktail a flavour innovation he'd previously described as stinking of a 'prozzies unwashed minge.' Despite these clear misgivings he crunched them to a soggy nothing, then began on the third and final no-no.

'Never, ever, under any circumstances, no matter what the provocation should you hit a woman. Not even a slap lad.' With that he'd downed his pint, washing away the false fishy remnants, looked at his watch and called time on the evening. 'Son, you're a man now. Don't expect any big emotional gesture or manly hug or owt. This isn't Hollywood. This is Yorkshire. We do

things differently here, but you should be grateful we do them at all.'
Which sort of made sense if you thought about it. In a dad kind of way.

Lee knew it all to be true of course. It was a simple, yet pertinent threefold credo for the post-war working man. It had served dad well, who was to say it wouldn't him. The third rule of life though ? Was that really still relevant ? Did that really need repeating ? In the world that dad had grown up in men routinely hit their spouses. Not a hospitalisation job, but enough to enforce a perceived proper order. It was a dying attitude then, and it was an abomination now. Go to a few unreconstructed parts of the country and you might still find a few recalcitrant male throwbacks willing to countenance a little back-of-my-hand discipline on his family, but they were definitely in the repugnant minority. It was completely beyond the pale.

Surely it just wasn't an issue for men of Lee's generation ? He would go one step further of course. What was between the legs didn't matter at all. You just shouldn't hit. It was a sign of defeat. Even if that meant riding a few blows along the way. Nations that bombed their less-armed antagonists back to the stone-age were senseless moral cowards. The same applied to people. And so as the generations moved on, man became more civilised, more ready to turn to diplomatic solutions to the daily frustrations of life.

Lee hardly ever seemed to lose his temper, rarely cursed or spoke ill of someone. He was too good to be true at times was Lee. Maybe he was too soft for his own good. He'd much more likely let a woman walk all over him than strike out in the heat of the moment. That was what people said of him, that was how he saw himself. Lee Canning was definitely one of the good guys. His heart had been broken along the way but he kept his faith in human goodness, tried his best to keep a smile on his face. The kind of man who always looked for the mutually beneficial and peaceable solution.

So why the fuck was his open hand now in a slow-motion retreat from the red stinging face of his shell-shocked fiancee ?

'Oh my god Lee !' Cassie was open-mouthed and completely incredulous. 'I cannot believe you just did that.'
Lee couldn't find the words. 'I'm…'
'You're what Lee ? What are you ? A wife beater. A fucking wife beater ? Is that it ?' She sneered, in her fury ignoring the fact she wasn't actually his wife just yet. The principle wasn't ring dependent.
'No, no, no,' he couldn't look her in the eye. His stomach was in revulsion. Then he found the words he'd been searching for. 'I'm sorry.'
'Sorry ? Sorry ? That's meant to make it all better is it ? I'm meant to forgive you am I and we're meant to move on ?'
Ahh if only life were that simple.

It wasn't meant to be a night when he hit his girlfriend. Far from it in fact. They'd not seen each other for a week. She'd been away at some conference or other in Milton Keynes discussing how recent changes in child protection policy were going to impinge upon their daily practice. To Lee's ears the endless meetings, discussion groups and lectures from 'key practitioners in the field' sounded deadly dull. As she shared the details of her week, he found himself zoning out, thinking instead about her pussy and how he'd like to be burying himself deep inside her.

'It was dead interesting actually,' Cassie had told him over an Indian take-out at the flat they shared in a new development just beyond the York city walls. It was her place. He didn't earn enough at the record shop to afford anywhere of his own, but in return he kept the place clean, cooked their meals, soothed her furrowed social work brow. 'Some of the case studies though would make your hair stand on end. I thought I'd seen it all but shucks.'

She'd poured herself another glass of wine. They were on the second bottle. The sex tonight was going to be fantastic. Lee was certain of it. A week without a shag and a goodly amount of alcohol would surely see to that. She was telling him all about the week, the people who'd been there, what she'd been learning and all he could think about were her middling to decent sized breasts, the way her legs parted, and just how soft her inner thigh felt as he brushed up inside it on the way to the promised land. A land which felt a long way from suburban York. It was a design classic was the female genitalia. Something that looked so unpromising could deliver so much in the way of everyday practical transcendence.

They were listening to The Shins. Both of them had fallen in love with the band purely on the strength of that bit in Garden State where Natalie Portman tells Zach Braff that they'll change his life, and passes across some oversized headphones for him to listen. They'd not long been together when the film first came out. She'd rested her head on his shoulder as they watched it at the City Screen Cinema and he'd felt as if the world was going to be alright. That Kirsty was long gone and that love wasn't a once in a lifetime event. That it was perfectly possible to have been totally in love with someone, for that to die and for it to then reprise in the shape of someone new. That someone was the feisty little brunette who he met one night in Lendal Cellars. He was in there with the guys from work, leaning against the bar, attempting to remember a line from The Mighty Boosh when she brushed past him knocking his drink slightly as she did so. He was about to let rip with a 'you clumsy bastard' when he saw her. She was perfect. Diminutive, with big brown eyes and a strong, fixed curious expression. He wanted to be strong and together but he melted.

'Sorry about your drink mate. Can I buy you another ?' A girl had just called him mate. One he didn't know.

'Er, no you're..' She was looking at him quizzically, holding his gaze for slightly too long under the circumstances.

'Yes ?'

'OK…I'm OK.'

'Well I'm pleased to meet you Mr OK.' She'd grinned at him and held out a hand. ' I'm Cassie.'

He quickly placed his beer back down on the bar, wiped his wet hand on the back of his jeans and shook it.

'Lee, I'm Lee.'

'Well, tell you what Lee.' The drink was giving her extra confidence. She liked his cute teddy-bear looks, his collar length dishevelled hair, the slight pot-belly underneath his slacker t-shirt. He had the air of an American college musician, his Yorkshire accent sitting incongruously with the paler skinned take on laid-back West Coast charm. 'Why don't you let me buy you another drink, then you can tell your friends that you've met this nice young woman who wants to ask you where you bought your trainers.'

He was wearing his scuffed old school Adidas Gazelles. Italian in design but perfectly English in their downbeat provincial execution. 'Oh these old things.'

'Don't get me wrong Lee. I like them, but not overly. You and a thousand other blokes knocking round York are wearing them .They're just a perfect excuse for you to give to your mates so you can come and sit with me.'

'Sit with you ?'

'Yes, sit with me. Do I have to spell it out ? I quite fancy you. I've not had a shag for over six months and I'm sure you would more than happily provide a bit of easy relief at the very least. If you're good at it, we could make it a regular arrangement.' Lee's mouth dropped, a quick head rush rapidly headed south causing his cock to stir slightly. Cassie looked at him then raised an eyebrow. 'Now, what was it you were drinking ?'

Or should that have been thinking ? To Lee's eyes the woman standing before him seemed effortlessly assured. Black jeans, a pink and black fitted stripey t-shirt, a shemagh tied around her neck and a scuffed up pair of old trainers. She seemed to have complete confidence. There was nothing particularly demure about her, and her looks if not totally top draw, were beyond what he'd normally set his sights on. What's more she was talking to him. A gimp in a difficult to remove stain ridden t-shirt, wrapped over a belly that was far too fond of Scotch eggs for its own good.

He wasn't a bad looking fella in his day was our Lee, but that day was becoming more of an historical moment with each passing year. Now here he stood in his mid- thirties, a perennial bloke-ish underachiever, sans relationship, sans settled life, still looking for that certain something that was going to see him right. The moment when all that family faith in his potential ('the first Canning to get to University', 'ooh our Lee the graduate', 'he'll be rolling in it before long will our Lee') still hadn't arrived and that earlier lazy belief that it would one day simply descend from a clear blue sky, bestowing on him the funky pad, the perky doting girlfriend (with almost daily acrobatic, experimental but very well scrubbed sex) , the edgy employment in some tossy PR agency which found new ways to linguistically bamboozle stuffed-shirt clients into parting with ridiculous amounts of wonga. But it hadn't happened yet. And let's face it, it wasn't going to ever happen was it ? This was what the thirty something Lee Canning was all about. A job in a record shop, a room in a shared house with similarly success challenged housemates and the occasional student passing through, presumably on the way to the perfect lifestyle he'd seemingly been denied. Of all the pet niggles of his daily existence, they had been the worse. Their fresh faced good looks, their knowledge of what was happening musically, their ceaseless fucking optimism, their round of parties, nights-out, hanging about with their mates discussing their fantastic future lives, their trouble free cross-gender friendships which never became anything more, just developed, got stronger, more supportive, their continual reminder of his lost youth, his already vanished opportunities. What hurt most of all was the perception they had of him. Lee was the cuddly, older, underachiever. The harmless impotent old chancer. When the academic going was tough, his student housemates would console their friends with ,' yeah but look at my housemate Lee, he's got a degree and he's not really done anything. You don't need letters after your name to be successful.' Which was true of course, and as each new group of graduates spewed out onto the city streets every year, wafting around town in their gowns, briefly allowing themselves to believe they'd somehow gained entry to the intellectual elite, he knew his chances of ever being anything other than a fat slacker drudge were diminishing faster than a pricked dot.com bubble. Or a bubble dotted prick. Whatever one of those was.

  Now this woman wanted him to fuck her. Just like that. He didn't have to lech over her all evening. He hadn't had to buy her a drink, ask her what her star sign was explaining how he'd always had an affinity with Pisceans, or compliment her on what she was wearing, or try and get her mobile number, or wonder what the fuck she really thought of him for days on end before something someone told someone else in 'complete confidence' got back to him and made him wonder even more. She just asked for it. Just like that. She'd been drinking sure, but this wasn't like a proposition from an overweight Bacardi Breezer binged single-mum five minutes before kick-out time at the Saturday night, low-rent sleaze central of Ziggy's. You only went for that when you were truly muntered, or truly desperate or a combination of the two. Things like this just didn't happen to Lee Canning. They might conceivably have been a possibility once but not now. But as Cassie Wilde rode his cock to the inevitable premature release of his first pussy induced orgasm for several months he began to wonder what else might just still be possible.

'You had a fucking vasectomy and never thought to tell me ?'

That was how it had begun. The piece of previously neglected to share information that for some reason or other had just been blurted out. Maybe it was the wine. Maybe it was the insistence from his partner, who 'had been doing a lot of thinking whilst she'd been away' and 'was wondering if now might be the time to think about starting a family' that 'they really needed to talk about this kind of stuff' because they 'weren't getting any younger.'

Lee wasn't anti-kids per se. He wasn't a chuntering child-hater moaning at women breast feeding their pink smelly babies in restaurants. As with most things in life he was largely indifferent towards the whole kids question. They were cute as far as it went. Maybe in his perfect life scenario, sketched out in his head sometime around 1992 and repeatedly modified ever since there might have been room for a couple of cute but well-behaved offspring to seal the family line. He'd joke at dinner parties about the RP accents little Cosmo and little Pixie had picked up at their progressive fee-paying school, and did you know the children of Radiohead's bass player are in the same class ? How far the Canning's had come in just two generations. If only grandpapa (the miserable old bastard), had been alive to see it.

But the miserable old bastard wheezed on, and his future great-grandkids had been strangled at the spermatozoa stage. Radiohead's offspring continued their alfalfa rich nurturance a millions miles away from Lee's daily reality.

'A fucking vasectomy ! I cannot believe you !' Cassie was apoplectic. She'd only eaten half of her meal but picked it off the table, and scraped it into the integral swing bin with a loud clatter.
'Why the fuck did you have a vasectomy ?'
'Kirsty.'
'What ? What's she got to do with anything. She traded you in for a better model Lee, you ought to be thankful I was on my sexual uppers when I bumped into you, otherwise I might have held out for something better myself.'
'I know I'm not perfect Cas.'
'Ha ! The day you get to passable will be an achievement.'
'What's that supposed to mean ? It's not my fault Kirsty didn't want kids.'
'If she was so fucking certain why didn't she get sterilised then ?'

'I don't know…it's more intrusive isn't it.'
'Oh how fucking valiant of you Lee. Rushing to the little lady's aid, and doing the decent thing. Had it not crossed your mind that your relationship to her might not see fucking Christmas, never mind happily ever after ?'
'I don't know really. I just thought…'
'You never thought to tell me first off ? Before all this. Before you move your scraggy stuff into my flat, before you nip into Argos to buy me a thirty quid engagement ring and then fucking sulk like a slapped three year old because I don't want to wear it, even though I still said I'd marry you.'
'It never crossed my mind.'

She moved across to him. Put her nose right next to his and jabbed him hard in the stomach.
'You mate are an absolute fucking disgrace. You're no fucking use to anyone. And do you know what else ?'
'No, I…'
'You're fucking useless in bed as well as everywhere else. You've only given me one real orgasm in all the time we've been together. I've had to lock myself in the bathroom and finish myself off whilst you lie back on the bed snoozing with a contented look on your fat ugly face.'
Lee could feel his rage beginning to rumble. It rarely made a showing, but this was different. This was humiliation.
'You telling me you've been faking it then ?' That was more pointed than before. Not quite masterful though. More pathetically aggrieved.
'Does this ring a bell sunshine.'
Cassie closed her eyes and began a soft girlie groan, gently brushed a stray strand of hair from her face, suggestively bit her lip, began to increase her breathing, making her moans louder, and more provocative. Lee couldn't take this. This was worse than Kirsty telling him she'd been secretly shagging a trainee mechanic. At least she hadn't re-enacted, her doubtless earth-shattering grease monkey induced multiple orgasms as she'd done so. This was out of order. This was just…

Then it happened. The right hand. It had clenched into a fist, then released and moved swiftly, as if by itself, to her expressive groaning face.

'Oooh yeah…Lee…that's right…ooooh aaahh aaaahh'

Slap.

The performance immediately stopped. She opened her eyes and looked at him astounded, touching her cheek which was slowly beginning to turn red. Lee knew he'd just crossed the line but which one. How was this going to play. A momentary lapse into unlikely optimism flitted across his mind.

Maybe this was what she needed. Maybe he had needed to be more assertive. Maybe he had to draw a line somewhere, to re-assert, that no actually, I'm the guy here and this kind of thing isn't…

'Oh my god Lee. What have you just done ?'

Maybe not.

At least the sun was shining. It might be a mid October day but it was a warm one. That was something to be grateful for. Under different circumstances Lee could perhaps have felt like a new man rather than enjoying that gut stirring feeling of not really knowing who or what he was anymore. Six months in a psychiatric hospital can do that to a guy. Particularly those two months on a locked ward. At least in the other four he was able to enjoy the gardens, go on mentally ill jollies with the other inmates up to Sutton Bank for a stroll and some flap jack. At least then he could play cards with the other head cases, keep taking his medicine and get brownie points in the form of smiles and ' you're doing really wells' from the staff. It wasn't a bad existence as it went. You got fed, you knew what your role was in life. Being a nutter had a noble lineage. It was an honest vocation. Look at your Picassos your Sylvia Plaths your Spike Milligans and your Stephen Frys. Top talented people all of them. All confirmed nut-jobs. He wasn't just a domestic abuser, he was a loon which kind of excused it, even if the lunacy took a while to manifest itself. It must always have been there.

But we need to go back a bit. When your girlfriend has decided that actually you're, 'too much of a risk' and that she 'just couldn't trust you anymore', in case this was 'just the beginning of something', and as a consequence throws you out, it is of course your mates you turn to. You need a mate who truly gets you. Who'll take you under his copious sheltering wing. Help you get back on your feet again. A man like Noah. He was ark-like in his ability to help you keep your feet dry in the middle of a flood.

'You did what ?' Noah looked incredulous and put his pint down on the table. Reliable Noah. Rock-like Noah, unflustered family man Noah. Good old Noah.
'It was just a slap.' Lee shrugged.
'Did I hear you right pal ? Did you say *just* a slap ?' Said Guardian reading local government officer Noah.
'I didn't really do owt, I don't know what came over me.'
'Just a bloody slap ! You slapped your girlfriend.' Disbelieving Noah

continued.
'She was provoking me for crying out loud.'
'Ah right' said product of a violent alcoholic father Noah. ' She were asking fer it were she ?'
'No that's not what I meant.'
'What did you mean then pal ? Tell me that ?' Said remembering the repeated body blows to the crouched sobbing figure of his mother Noah.
'I just mean.' But the words were gone.
'You fucking appal me Lee. I can't believe what I'm hearing. I thought you were my mate. I thought I knew you.' Said painfully recalling the midnight flit to a women's refuge Noah. The you can't fucking trust anyone Noah, the surely not your best mate, Noah.
Then even though he wasn't actually there, Lee's dad decided to chip in :

Never, under any circumstances, whatever the provocation should you hit a woman lad, not even a slap.

And Cassie. Her voice seemed incessant. Shrill, cold and piercing. Totally loveless where once it had been warm :

Oh my god Lee. Wife beater Lee. I cannot believe you could do that Lee.

Dad, Noah and Cassie. All agreed on the non-negotiables. Little bullets of intentional friendly fire from former allies. The walls of his ramshackle mental shelter coming under repeated attack.
'But I love her.'
'You want to be grateful that I don't take after my bastard dad Lee. I should be teaching you a fucking lesson mate.'
  With that Noah downed the remains of his pint, gave one last hate-filled look at his former best mate and stormed out the pub. Such looks are always much more effective and meaningful when they come from the head of someone who once only looked at you with poorly disguised but never mentioned affection. His head full of the past he hit the delete button on his phone, removing Lee's number from his SIM card forever, wishing that he could do something similar with the paternal name on his birth certificate and the ugly violent heritage of his sex.

   There could be no more hesitation. Lee had to cash in those 'if you're ever in trouble' last resort parental chips.
'The Algarve ?' He'd been expecting Tickhill. For the retirement bungalow.
'Yes, your dad says our money will go a lot further out there and you know how I'm one for the sun.' Mum laughed unselfconsciously. Her enthusiasm

was palpable. 'Ooh you should see some of the places he's found for us to look at. Some of them, you're never going to believe this, actually have their own swimming pools.'
'Blimey. Mum..'
'And the other thing is of course, your dad was wondering about maybe doing B&B on a small scale, just to top up the pension.'
'Sounds..'
'People keep saying to us 'will you miss England', and we say 'I shouldn't think so. Not now.''
'Can I just…'
'Of course you'll be able to come out for your holidays. You and Cassie. That'll be nice won't it ?'
'Yes, I..'
'I'm sorry love, I've nattered on. What was it you wanted again ?'
'Oh, nothing.' He couldn't do it. 'I just wanted to see how you were.'
'Oh, you did. Well that's nice love, you're always such a good boy.'

People might let you down but booze is always there. A trusty old standby. The wayward old friend whispering in your ear, saying ' you and me, we're both fucked, let's get off our faces, let's do the decent thing. We're shit, let's be shit together, let's laugh about it. You know you want to.'
It worked for a while. The few cans of lager of every evening made the damp surrounds of his Burton Stone Lane bedsit seem that much more bearable. Despite the damp, despite the constant comings and goings, the raised voices in Slavic, the banging on his door in the early hours. The sound of ceaseless, vigorous, aggressive underclass sex. It sounded far more liberated than anything he'd ever enjoyed. Then the next morning he'd see the drug wasted faces of the practitioners as they left the building for a day of skulking and drinking and wonder where exactly he'd come to. This was what he was about now.

No, mustn't think like that. He still had employment. He was just gathering himself then he'd move on. Find someone new, stop thinking about Cassie, stop rehearsing in his head what might have been. He'd take the drinking in hand, he'd clean himself up, he'd find himself some full-time employment and get a proper place.

Then came the crash.

'Oh, hi Cassie.' He'd been sitting on the grass in the Museum gardens circling job adverts in The Press when someone had tapped him on the shoulder. 'Not at work today ?'
'No, I'm not at work anymore. I gave it up.'
She looked different somehow. More grown-up. She'd stopped to talk to

him. That had to be a good sign.
'Why? You loved that job.'
'I know,' she sighed 'but your priorities change.' She glanced around distractedly. 'Listen Lee, I saw you there and just wanted to know how you were doing. Have you had any help yet?'
'Help? I'm sorry?'
'With your anger. Have you done anything to address it?'
'No, I…'
'Lee, it's not going to go away you know. I saw Noah last week.'
'Oh.'
'He said he wasn't talking to you and last thing he knew you were wandering around town looking like a tramp. He said he thought you might have a drink problem.'
Lee made a false nervous laugh. 'Oh, I'm alright. I'm still working and everything. Just looking for something full-time actually.' He lifted the paper towards her. She looked at him slightly disbelieving. 'Anyway, why did you give up work? What's that all about?'
'That's what I wanted to tell you Lee. I've met someone. I live with him. He's a web designer.'
'And?' Must not look bothered. Must not look as if guts had been pulled out with bare hands. Must not look as if world has been torn apart by a nasty vindictive bitch.
'We're having a baby. I'm pregnant.'
'Eh?'
'I'm having a baby. Max and I.'
'Max?'
'Yes, he's my partner.'
'But you can't!'
'Sorry Lee, I know this must be hard for you.'
'Fuck off!'
'Now don't get aggressive again Lee.'
'You're going to have a baby with some cunt called Max!' He was standing up now, the pages of his newspaper being lifted and carried off by the wind. Passers-by were beginning to look on.
'Why didn't you have a baby with me?'
'You can't have them can you Lee. You've had a vasectomy.'
'I could have had the fucking thing reversed. It's do-able, we have the technology.'
'You're being totally ridiculous now. I've not seen you in months and had hoped we could be adult and friendly. I hoped you were sorting yourself out but clearly…'
'Stop talking to me like you're my fucking social worker.'

'Right, I'm going. It's clear you're not adult enough to be able to be friends.'
'Friends ? Friends ? After you ruin my fucking life.'
'Spare me the melodrama purlease. Let's just remember who it was who hit who here.'
'For Christ's sake Cassie it was only a fucking slap. One solitary fucking slap.'
'I cannot believe you are still talking like this ? That you still haven't accepted your transgression. That you've clearly got a problem.' She looked him up and down. 'One of many it would appear.'
'I don't need this kind of shit. I was getting myself together until you came along. Why did you have to rub it in ?'
'If you can't even accept an overture of friendship from someone who has your best interests at heart Lee then I'm afraid you deserve all you get. I've no sympathy for you.'

With that she gave him one last long withering look and headed off towards town, doubtless to see Max and tomato feed her foetus. Lee stood there frozen to the spot watching her disappear before finally shouting. 'You're meant to care. You're meant to be a fucking social worker.'

There was nothing else for it. He distractedly blustered his way into the nearest off-licence, his behaviour alarming the staff, but not enough to prevent them serving him with two of their cheapest bottles of vodka. The encounter had left them feeling strangely out of sorts and wondering what they'd been party to. Finding himself a spot on a bench down by the river, Lee began drinking. This time with a clear intent towards self-destruction. There was no pretence of pleasure at play. A local character, a short older guy with long hair, often found drinking in The Maltings, who Lee vaguely knew as Capers nodded him a look of recognition, but Lee was too preoccupied with his own misery to properly notice. His dwindling hold on the acceptable parameters of social normality were making him more noticeable yet more purposefully anonymous. Soon he would slip away entirely into that messy alternate reality occupied by the dregs.

People who passed him by were staring at him, teenagers jeered him, mothers steered their toddlers out of his way. As the first bottle emptied he became more and more oblivious to his surroundings. The second bottle securing the promised black nirvana. Consciousnessless as clear as anything experienced by a life-denying religious ascetic. The easy route to the complete cessation of self. It was accompanied by anonymity, or at least a perception of anonymity. Angry and invisible he had no idea that he was swaying dangerously along the edge of the bank howling incoherent garbage at the empty sky. Or that the two dark figures who came blurrily into his vision were policemen. He had no idea that he was in fact threatening to kill one of them, then himself. He had no idea where he was being taken to, arms and legs flailing, screaming random blue murder at his professionally automaton captors.

Then he woke. His head feeling like it was being rammed into a brick wall repeatedly by an assailant. Only the soothing voice of the middle-aged woman before him made much sense.
'Mr Canning' it said, so hushed you could almost classify it as whisper. 'Mr Canning, I'm Beryl Young, I'm a psychiatric nurse. You're in Bootham Park Hospital.' He had been sectioned by society for his own good. A safety net of sorts had caught him.

So it began. For a week he played the angry alcoholic card. Being difficult, banging his fists against the wall, screaming meaninglessly, or demanding his freedom. The freedom to destroy himself how he saw fit. In his incoherence he made perfect sense. Then as the booze seeped slowly from his purgatory system, he discovered some of the best sleep of his life. There then followed weeks of therapy, painting sunflowers in art groups, assertiveness training, cookery, activity to divert his thoughts to more productive ends. Soon he realised that you could win brownie points by being the model patient. He did as he was told. Was always polite. He was a good boy. Just like his mum had told him to be. This was the Lee of old. The get your head down, try to be nice, don't aim too high, never expect too much and in turn you'll be left alone to get on with what passed for your life.

Cassie had always been out of his league. He needed a younger girlfriend. Someone not as bright. Stupid even. A shopgirl or something, one who had never lived anywhere but York and who would be naturally impressed by him just by virtue of his extra age and sophistication. That was a word that didn't sit easily on the head of Lee Canning but these things were always relative.

As he sat on a bench in the Museum Gardens passing time before he headed back to his bedsit just off Walmgate he wondered where life might be heading next. Being mental did at least come with benefits. There was no need to work if he didn't want to. He was ill after all and no one could take that away from him. Maybe he could allow himself a small degree of optimism. Perhaps he wasn't so bad. Perhaps he wasn't a failure. Maybe he was just what he was and what he was remained nothing special. But that was better than nothing.

He sat feeding the squirrels, talking to them individually. He had come to know and name a number of them. There was cheeky little Nutkins, shy Bushy, aggressive young Grumpus and delectable Deirdre. He had no real idea if Deirdre was really a girl. He just thought he'd better have one to address the gender imbalance. Then someone tapped him on the shoulder. It was a young woman, medium build, short hair, long fringe. Alongside her stood what he thought to be a guy. He was tall-ish, rake thin and distracted looking. He had soft features and a similar hair-cut to the girl. He looked smart and together. Therefore Lee hated him immediately.

'We're looking for Fossgate. A shop actually, it's called Stroke The Pussy or something. I don't think it's as rude as it sounds.' The young woman chuckled.

That was that kitschy shop that girls liked. Always seemed a little on the gay side to Lee. Cassie had popped in now and again to laugh at things she found amusing but which he didn't understand. It sold fridge magnets and greeting cards, lamps and trinket boxes. Pink stuff. Things Lee couldn't see the point of. What did they want that place for ? It was hardly a tourist attraction. The strange girly-man was staring at him, smirking slightly he was sure of it.

'Er yeah. It's in town. Kind of over there.' He pointed vaguely in direction of town.

'Could you be more specific ? We're not from here you see. ' The woman asked.

'Or better still you could show us.' The girly-man spoke. His voice was a bit soft and slightly effeminate. Not like Dale Winton, but not like Noah's either. He missed Noah. The girly-man's voice would really get on your nerves if you had to listen to it for too long though. It was definitely too pleased with itself. Like one of those smug fashionable older girls who used to take the piss out of him when he was a teenager but in the body of a skinny man. He unsettled him. Lee wouldn't speak to him. The fucking weirdo.

'Yeah, could you show us where it was, if you're not too busy. ?'

The girl was cute though. She had a sunny smile. It made him feel warm when he looked at her. He wanted to help her out. Yes that would be something to do. It was near where he lived anyway. He'd head home and show them the shop on the way. The girly-man would have to come too though. He couldn't be her boyfriend could he ? That wouldn't be right. He must be a gay best friend or something. Lots of girls had them. Madonna's was Rupert Everett. He didn't like Rupert Everett. Posh and queer. He was glad no girlfriend of his had ever had a GBF. That was what they called them wasn't it ? GBFs ? He'd read something about it in Cassie's Marie Claire, the whole article irritating him more and more as it progressed. These gay blokes getting special access to the emotional lives of straight men's girlfriends ? Girls talking stuff through with their girl mates was bad enough but with a bloke ? He wasn't sure how he'd have felt about that. Everything is too complicated these days. Then the girly-man spoke.

'Yeah, and I'm not being rude or anything but you do look as if you could do with the exercise.'

The woman jabbed him sharply in the stomach with her elbow 'Jude ! Behave.' She turned and gave him a dirty look, the girly-man grinned and looked away. 'I'm sorry about my friend, he can be a bit of a tease. Just ignore him.'

47

Lee looked down at his shoes. He was fat. He hated being overweight. He definitely knew he hated the girly-man now. Talking to him like that. It wasn't on. He was a good bloke. A decent fella. One of the lads if they hadn't all done a runner as soon as he went mental. He didn't do anyone any harm. Just where was the issue exactly ?
'Would you mind showing us ?' The girl touched his arm.
Lee looked at her hand on his arm, and then up at her open face and smiled. 'Sure.'

From the back of beyond…

Lauren was doubled up in laughter on the sofa as Millie put a hand on her hip and tried to appear stern. It wasn't very convincing.
'Lauren ! It's not funny.'
Lauren wiped a tear from her eye, sniffed back some snot, wheezed and then spoke. 'Dimitri Montage ? Are you really telling me the guy is called Dimitri frickin Montage ? Jesus Christ on a pedalo Mills, where the fuck do they find them ?'
'Dimitri is one of this country's finest psychic mediums Lauren.' She sounded like a disapproving primary school teacher. 'He's very well respected. Have you not seen him on Spirit Ways ?'
'Spirit Ways ? Is that the thing where that dodgy bird who used to be on Blue Peter visits allegedly haunted houses with a load of other gimmers, they make stuff up and a psychic goes a bit mental.'
'Pretty much yes.' Millie nodded and looked slightly awkward. 'They've recorded some very credible phenomena I'll have you know.'
'Millie, when exactly did you have your reason bypass operation ? Of course they haven't. They're a frickin TV crew with access to thousands of pounds worth of equipment designed to bamboozle the gullible. It's all bollocks. I'm surprised an educated woman like you believes a word of it.'
'Oh you shouldn't be so sceptical !' Millie waved a frustrated arm at Lauren's words. 'Anyway, I've got two complimentary tickets and I hoped you'd come with me.'
'You want me to go to a night with a medium ?' Millie nodded. 'Alright then. Should be a laugh. See the fraudster in action. How did he get his name anyway ?'
'Well,' Millie sat down, her face immediately losing some it's earlier frustration. 'According to the blurb I read this morning, he's the son of a descendant of the displaced Russian aristocracy, and his mother was a dancer at the Folies Bergiere.'

'So why is the French bit of his name his surname then ? That doesn't make sense ?'
'Now there's a reason for that.' Millie was getting animated. ' When he was first visited by Basking Otter.'
'Basking Otter ? What, a particularly chilled out river side creature beloved of children's fiction ?'
'Nooo silly.' Millie slapped Lauren's leg. Lauren in turn raised a bemused eyebrow. This was solid gold Mille-world. Completely random, slightly bonkers, but always endearing and shared with total gushing sincerity.
'Basking Otter is his spirit guide. He was a native American berdache.'
'Now you're losing me.'
'They were like inbetweenies, not quite properly men or women. Bit like you.'
'Yes, OK, right. We've established I don't really measure up in the female stakes, but I'm in no way spiritual. I daydream about fire-bombing Jonathan Cainer's house for fuck's sake.' Lauren shook her head as she started to get progressively more confused. She'd read something once regarding berdache people in a book about the opening of the American west. The female born ones would hunt with the men and were often fearsome warriors. She'd have been well up for it but was wondering precisely what they had to do with the price of fish. Or the naming of fraudsters who think they see dead people.
'Anyway, they were regarded as being spiritual, go-betweens between different worlds sort of.'
'Like a shaman ?' This was actually quite interesting. Just the context was all wrong. A mental note was made to Google the word berdache next time she was online.
'Yes, like a shaman. Basking Otter is Dimitri's spirit guide who came to him when he had a near death experience after almost choking to death on a hazelnut whirl.'
   Lauren burst out laughing again.
'Lauren ! It's not funny, he nearly died.'
'I'm sorry Mills' Lauren shook her head. 'It's this story. You don't actually believe all this do you ?'
'It was on the blurb at the Opera House. I've been having some amazing conversations with people who have been buying tickets for tonight. They way he's touched them.'
'Is he a sex pest as well then ?'
'Right, that's it. If you're not going to take this seriously I don't see anymore point in telling you anything.' Millie started to stand up.
'Sit down, sit down. Carry on. I'm listening.' Millie stuck her bottom lip out and turned her nose away slightly. 'I am interested Mills.'
'Oh, Ok then.' Millie's enthusiasm immediately returned. 'Anyway, Basking

Otter told him that he wasn't going to die, but had to go back into the world to spread the word about the afterlife and bring comfort to the grieving. He told him that before he took on his mission he had to change his name as a symbol of his new beginning. He was told to take his father's first name and his mother's surname, the latter in particular recognised the fact that the psychic gift generally comes down the female line. Women are more naturally attuned with these things you know.'
'A moment ago you were telling me that Red Indian inbetweenies are spiritual, now it's just common or garden women is it ?'
'It's complicated I think.'
'You're telling me. These things usually are. It helps the gullible airheads who believe this kind of rubbish think there must be something to it. If it's too straightforward they get a bit short-changed. Most new age stuff is pseudo-intellectual ripping up of eastern mysticism mixed with a bit of native American, chuck in something vaguely scientific to give a veneer of credibility and as if by magic.' Millie pursed her lips and gave Lauren a disapproving look. Lauren wasn't bothered. She had zero patience for quackery. 'What was his name then, before he changed it ?'
'Oh, erm..Ivan Felch I believe. He used to manage a Rumbelows in Nantwich before he received his calling.'
'Oh fucking hell no !' Lauren couldn't help herself, she doubled up in laughter as the entry phone buzzed that someone was giving them a calling.

  Lee glanced back at the two of them standing by the heavy black wooden door to an alleyway next to Stroke The Pussy. The girl was laughing, and the girly-man seemed to be tickling her. He just couldn't be her boyfriend but he was very familiar. As they had walked through town, Lee finding it impossible to make conversation in his current mindset, the girl had kept calling the girly-man things like 'sweetie' and 'honey' . It was hard to tell. They did walk arm in arm at one point. They kept making little comments which as far as Lee could tell were not about him, but they still made him feel uncomfortable. In-jokes. They were the worst kind as they highlighted the fact that you were excluded. As they eventually reached the shop, Lee had stood awkwardly for a second looking at the girl who had thanked him for his help. He paused for a second too long and became aware of the girl and the girly-man starting to look a little amused. Who did they think they were ? After he'd helped them like that ? It was the girly-man of course who instigated all this. He was definitely a bad sort, of that Lee had no doubt. Probably just confused. Not like Lee. Who smiled and sauntered down Walmgate without looking back allowing himself to think what it would feel like to be moving inside the girl as she lay beneath him. It was thoughts like that which kept you warm at night.

Standing at the open front door to the flat stood a woman who Lauren vaguely recognised as bearing some resemblance to her younger cousin Joyce. She seemed to have undergone a successful fashion transplant since 1990. Didn't look anything like the mousey Sunday school teacher she'd been expecting. Alongside her stood a berdache. Or at least a boy so beautifully beguiling Lauren was finding it hard to keep herself from salivating. This didn't happen very often. In fact she was struggling to remember when it last had ?

'Lauren ! Hi ! Lovely to see you.' Star made to give her older cousin a hug but Lauren pointedly shoved out a hand to shake. Star looked down at it , embarrassed at being rebuffed.

'Er yeah, cheers. Nice one.' She couldn't stop glancing at her cousin's companion.

'Oh this is Jude. My best friend.'

Best friend. Right. Not an item then. Probably gay though. An authentic GBF. Just like Francis. No scrub that. Franny could never be considered a GBF. Fashion-wise he was a disaster zone. Lauren moved her hand towards Jude who took hold of it in both hands and warmly shook it. He had that big-eyed soulful thing going on. They looked straight at Lauren who made a metaphorical gritting of the teeth in an attempt not to swoon. Was he really here ? He looked far too pretty to be real. She'd noticed this. Extremely attractive people often had an aura about them. An almost celestial glow accompanying their every move.

'Thank you SO much Lauren for letting us stay. I can't wait to try your cake.' The pretty-boy gushed.

'Stay ? Erm..did you want to stay then ?' Lauren looked back towards her cousin.

'Oh god, didn't we mention that ?' Of course she hadn't mentioned it. The aim was to get a foot in the door then casually drop it into conversation. Just as long as Lauren hadn't turned out to be too much of a headcase. So far, so good on that score, even if she did seem a bit surly. At least it was an apparently sane kind of surliness.

Jude opened his mouth wide in mock horror and looked at his friend. 'Star ! You said it was OK ? You were meant to ask first.'

'Sorry Lauren, I've not been totally honest with you. The thing is we're on a bit of a road trip, both needed a break kind of and we fancied hanging around in York for a few days, and were sort or wondering if...'

Millie bounded down the hallway her face alive with the excitement of it all. 'Of course you can stay ! As long as you don't mind kipping in the front room. I've got an inflatable airbed one of you can borrow and there's always the sofa.'

'Really, we don't mean to…' Star looked towards Millie anxiously. This one seemed an awful lot more welcoming. Pretty too. Very pretty. Too pretty in fact. Star felt frumpy by comparison.
'We'd love you too.' Millie looked up at a furtive faced Lauren who was still glancing discretely at Jude. Where the hell had he just come from ? 'Lauren.' Lauren was in a pretty-boy induced haze. 'Lauren.' Millie jabbed her. 'We don't mind do we ?'

Jude noticed Lauren was looking at him and gave a small devilish smile back. He was used to being admired/looked at/pointed out in crowds. He had a massive armoury of suitable responses. Ranging from shy coy for the compliments to 'fuck you, you ugly bastard' to the derogatory. Everyone seemed to have an opinion on him. There didn't seem to be much room for blind neutrality where Jude was concerned.

Lauren finally turned to her flatmate with a cheeky grin plastered across her face. Bingo. Or some other such tired exclamation of delight normally inserted at this point to signify mutual attraction. 'Nooo..we don't mind.' It wasn't Christmas, but sometimes you felt as if you'd just unwrapped the best present ever.
'Did you change your pinny for us then ? You don't seem to be wearing one ? I hope this doesn't mean the cake is off as well.' Asked Jude. Lauren looked back at him a little confused. Please don't be mental or difficult will you ? Pretty blokes often are. Goes with the territory. Being a bit girlie or sensitive as a boy often resulted in your head being forcibly introduced to flushing school toilets and the like. This then led to unresolved, deep rooted personal issues in adulthood that generally made them appear a bit flaky. Which of course told the world that their tormentors were right all along, and that kind, gentle, un-blokey, empathetic men were somehow just weird aberrations who were best not encouraged. Which was just bollocks.

Lauren thought the world needed more sensitive blokes. Men who had more in common with Millie than they did Danny Dyer. This would immediately render a greater proportion of the male population more fanciable in her eyes. As things currently stood, she was going through another of her 'all men are one-dimensional cock-led idiots with no dress sense,' kind of periods. They were becoming more regular of late. 'Someone please pleasantly surprise me,' she'd written in her journal after briefly musing on the issue. Maybe Jude just might. She'd just have to see. Pretty features do not automatically equate with a similarly attractive personality.
'I'm sorry. Which pinny would that be ?'
'You mentioned in your text that you'd have to change your pinny if we came to visit.' Star answered.
'Did I ? Can I see.'
Star handed Lauren her phone. 'There you go, look.'

'Frickin Francis the cheeky get.'
'Oh Francis. He was that the guy I spoke to. He seemed dead lovely. Gave us directions and everything. Told us where to park and not to risk trying to find anywhere near here.'
'Oh right. I see. Organising your life for you. That sounds like my Francis.'
'How long have you too been going out ?'
'Sorry ?'
'You and Francis. How long have you been an item. He said he was your fiancee ?' Now it was Millie's turn to burst into uncontrollable laughter. Star looked at her. 'Have I said something wrong ?'
'I'll kill him. I will absolutely kill him.'
'He's not then ?'
'No he's definitely not. He's my former housemate and he's currently shacked up with another man in the warm afterglow of civil partnership conjugal bliss. He's also impossibly interfering and doesn't know when he's gone to far.' Lauren shook her head and then smiled. 'Bless him. But I can assure you that I don't do pinnies and there is no cake waiting for you. I've got a six pack of Hula-Hoops and several packets of Hob-Nobs in my cupboard though if you're interested.'

Jude rubbed his hands together. 'Now you're talking.'

The four of them were settled in the front room eating Hula-Hoops which Lauren had poured into a bowl, and dunking Hob-Nobs into their tea. It was Millie who was doing the most to engage their guests in conversation. It had a kind of pleasant scripted flow to it. She was good at this kind of thing. It was part of the Millie/Lauren ying-yang double-act that had served them so well over the years. It was the kind of small talk Lauren found impossible. Not because she didn't know what to say, she was far too socially astute not to, but just because she couldn't be bothered and wasn't really interested anyway. Why would anyone want to know if the traffic was busy, or where someone was going on their holidays when you could be considering if it were possible to teach a ferret to juggle grapes, or what Jeremy Paxman might look like with a full-on Billy-Ray Cyrus style mullet ?
'So when was the last time you saw Lauren ?' Millie asked Star. Head tilted to one side, eyes widened in expression of interest. Definitely Desmond Morris primate behaviour Lauren was thinking.
'Gosh, it must have been about seventeen or so years ago. Is that right Lauren ?'
Lauren was still casting glances in the direction of Jude who was sitting perfectly cross-legged on the floor whilst studying Lauren's Heat Magazine. He appeared equally disinterested in pleasantries and had instead made himself immediately at home.

'Sorry ?'
Millie had noticed Lauren's lack of concentration and cast her a scowl. 'Star wanted to know if it's been 17 years since you last saw her.'
Lauren shrugged. 'Er yeah, must have been.'
'Oooh look at this.' Jude slid Heat magazine across the laminate in Lauren's direction. 'See that plaid shirt Alexa Chung is wearing in that photo ?'
'Yeah.'
'I reckon that would look just right on you. You've similar frames.'
Lauren picked the magazine up and studied it. 'Hmmm, think you're right. Only twenty notes as well. Nice one. Cheers.'
'Excuse me !' Millie looked annoyed. 'Are you listening to me Lauren ?'
'I was just talking to our guest Mills, don't be so rude.' She made a little pleased with herself purse of the lips and smiled at Jude who was grinning back at her. Unexpected allies. They always gave you a little buzz of satisfaction didn't they ?

New beginnings…

Lee was browsing through the picture folders on his old computer. Here he is with Cassie on the day they went to Whitby, there's Cassie in that dress she used to wear, the only one she used to wear. There's Cassie with the sunlight reflecting off her hair as they sat on the top deck of a tour boat on the Ouse one perfect sunny Sunday last year. There they were at an earlier Christmas, she was kissing his cheek as he took the photo at arms length, the angle of the shot giving him the mother of all double-chins. They'd laughed about it, she'd teased him into losing a bit of weight but hadn't minded because he loved her and you did things like that when you were in love didn't you ? They looked so happy and together. Like a normal, well-adjusted couple. The kind of couple who chose paint shades together in Homebase but who didn't seem to find each other annoying. The kind who tripped down supermarket aisles in their matching trainers on a Sunday morning filling their baskets (only ever baskets) with speciality houmous and boxes of expensive muesli. For a moment he felt a mild degree of regret and jealousy. That was the life he should be leading ? Why wasn't he leading it ? What had happened ?

He thought of Cassie. Her belly contentedly growing with someone else's child. Squatting in the womb that by rights belonged to his own offspring. The perfect little children he'd once imagined. Now some alien foetus was being nurtured in there. The thought made him feel sick. He shouldn't mope like this. He should try harder to win her back. He glanced at himself in the full-length mirror next to the bed in the bedsit. He looked a state. There was no way that Cassie would want him back. Then he imagined Max. That clueless cunt of a baby father. The bastard probably had it all. Job, looks, the right emotions in the right places. Words to say at difficult times.

That was what women craved most of all wasn't it ? Men who could express themselves and talk their language. For a second the image of the girly-man of earlier popped into his head. Gross. He could fuck-off. That was what you became if you let yourself lose your masculinity. He might not have Cassie, he might be a bit overweight and currently out of work, but at least he wasn't like that. The girly-man was like that odd lad at school. The one who had a slight lisp, and couldn't play football. Just stood there like a weedy plank. No wonder he got his head shoved down the toilet. What did he expect ? Not that you could condone bullying or anything but some kids just bring it on themselves don't they ? That was always what the games teacher Mr Gravely you used to say to him . 'Stop acting like such a girl and people will stop treating you like one.' Didn't make any difference.

What was his name ? Simon Redburn that was it, but everyone called him Simone. Definitely a faggot. Ian Cockrill once caught him looking at Paul Brayley's arse. The dirty little fucker. Not that he had anything against gays. As long as they left him alone. Redburn had been a great deflector of abuse. You always knew you'd be spared any teasing or fists whilst he was around. No matter how odd or strange you felt, you knew that Redburn would appear far stranger. Thank fuck for the effeminate boy. He's a shoe-in for the position of class victim. The rest, the borderline weeds and social oddities can then breathe a sigh of relief. The first time Lee had seen Redburn mince his way to write on the blackboard and heard him lisp his way through the first few pages of a Saki short story, he felt an almost overwhelming and primal sense of relief. A connection to the group. They'd found their outlet. Their punch-bag. It was just bonding wasn't it ? Someone had to be singled out for that purpose. It was nature, and in the survival of the fittest world of a boys school you got nowhere by being a girl.

Lee lay back on the bed and allowed his hand to wander to his crotch. He might not be able to father children but at least the equipment appeared to still be in working order. He thought of the girl from earlier. Her cute smile, the pert ass he'd spied as she'd been talking to him in the Museum gardens, her long legs. He imagined them wrapped around him as he ploughed deep inside her. Man, that was a good thought. His chain of thought took him further and further into what he'd like to do to her, and what in turn she'd do to him before he was finding release in a hot sticky spoonful, that suddenly left him with a vague sense of ennui.

This was him now was it ? A handful of cum, on a bed whose sheets hadn't been changed for weeks, in a grim bedsit fantasising about women he'd just run into in town. He definitely needed an interest. Something to take his mind off all this. Wiping himself he stood up, his trousers and pants still around his knees, his sickly white belly casting a gross silhouette on the wall, as the flickering light of his computer monitor pulled his attention. His photo browsing had been left on an arty shot he'd messed around with on Photoshop. It was of the west wing of the Minster. Sepia tinted, the sky looking oppressive, white fluffy clouds turned almost gothic brooded a kind of everyday malevolence. It wasn't bad. He wandered across to the computer and looked at it closer. Not bad, not bad at all. Maybe he wasn't too bad at this photography lark. That had been one of the best bits of his psychiatric stay. The photography group. Rae, the cute young occupational therapist used to take them around town snapping things. He'd enjoyed it. Maybe that's what he needed to do now. Less of this moping about. He picked up his camera. It wasn't bad. It would do the job and if he got good and maybe sold a few of his photos he could invest in a better one. This could be a whole new career. Of course. Photography. It was so fucking obvious.

The vision of himself as a busy paparazzi dashing about snapping minor celebrities entered his mind. It's Liz McLarnon look. Smile for the camera love. Did Jessie Wallace look in a mirror before she left the house ? Probably not judging by that dress.

Nah, way too sleazy. He wasn't interested enough in slebs anyway, whatever the cash incentives for the right shot.

Try this for a future vision instead : Here he is looking all thoughtful and ponderous as he takes a picture of a beautiful landscape. Lost in the scenery. Somewhere stunning and atmospheric. Ah yes, that was much more his cup of tea. Wait a minute, what about nudes ? Not tacky glamour shots. No porn or nothing. Arty, black and white photos of beautiful women. Fucking hell, now that was a good thought.

Wherever it led, the viewfinder of his digital camera had to find him some better circumstances than the ones he was currently looking at. He pointed the camera to the street below. A teenage girl was walking past his window. He looked through the viewfinder. Focusing in he could see her mouth. It was full and expressive. Quite perfect really. This zoom was powerful. She had lovely looking skin as well, as much as he could tell under the streetlight. Perhaps it was the light itself being kind. Before she had chance to move out of his vision he pressed the button and the camera clicked satisfyingly. Looking back at his photo on the screen on the display at the back of his camera he felt the first feeling of contentment he'd experienced all day. There she was. In his camera. His possession. She would remain there until the day arrived when he tired of her and hit delete, reducing the zeroes and ones that gave her form to nothing. This was power. The chance to record and maintain the world as you wished. Yes, Lee Canning would be a photographer. He'd start tomorrow.

Most Haunted…

'Get a move on Lauren. We've not got much time.'
Lauren was lying on her bed in the dark, getting a bit of much needed respite from the company. This was a well practiced coping mechanism to the demands of other people. If she had to suffer the presence of others, she could cleverly engineer herself a few precious moments of solitude. These were sometimes the difference between managing to live with humanity, and secretly wanting to rip its continually chattering head off. No, that was unfair. Star and Jude were pleasant company. It was making a change to have some new faces around. One in particular. It didn't do much to alleviate Lauren's ever present urge to escape but it gave her some pause for hesitation.

There was another knock on the door. Whereas Lauren was in the same long-sleeved t-shirt and jeans she'd been wearing all day, Millie had changed for the evening. Better put a fresh one on or Millie would be wondering what she'd been doing in her room for so long. Quickly she laid a hand on the new green striped long-sleeve skinny-fit t-shirt she'd found in the blokes section at H&M, sprayed deodorant under her arms, pulled on the shirt and made for the door. No wait a minute. Better do something with the face. She had a make-up bag, mainly full of stuff she hadn't touched for years and which was slowly congealing, drying up and perishing. She had bought most of it during one of her earlier 'must try to be more feminine' moments. Although she'd never been entirely sure what it was she was purchasing. Millie would be the obvious person to ask, but that would precipitate a full-on girlie make-up session the thought of which gave her a slight migraine. Best not bother. She'd got this far without worrying, why change now.

Feminine moments. They never lasted more than a day or two and whenever she cack-handedly tried to apply anything other than eyeliner she always ended up looking like a half-hearted drag queen. Carefully outlining, her big brown eyes with her Boots No7 kohl pencil, she smudged it with the brush end, ruffled her hair and then looked at herself in the mirror.
'Hmmm…the oldest frickin emo in town.' No, actually, she didn't look too bad. Millie wouldn't approve. She never did. Always used to complain that people would think that Lauren was her dykey lover when they were out together, to which Lauren would reply.
'Frickin hell Mills ! I wouldn't go out with you. Way too high maintenance.'
Which would always send Millie into one of her momentary, and highly

unconvincing sulks.
  When Lauren finally emerged from her room, Millie looked her up and down, crossed her arms and made a well rehearsed disapproving sigh.
'Didn't make an effort then.'
'Lay off will you.' Lauren responded with an equally familiar bristling. 'I've got changed and we're only going round the road to see some dodgy bloke pretend to speak to dead people. It's not like I'm meeting the queen or owt.'
'You wouldn't dress up if you were.' Millie glanced at her watch.
'Nah, fuck it. She can take me as she finds me. Sour faced old crone.'
'Lauren ! Enough. We need to get off.'

  They said their goodbyes to their guests who were sitting in the front room channel-hopping and seemed just as relieved to be getting a little respite from their hosts as Lauren was to get out. As they heard the door slam, Star turned to her best friend. He was watching a feature on The Now Show about indoor winter sports in specially made warehouses that resembled aircraft hangars, and which were filled with very realistic looking fake snow.
'They must be mental. Doing that. What's wrong with people ?'
'How do you mean ?'
'Having interests.'
'You've got interests.'
'Like what ?'
'Watching telly. You do a lot of that. Moaning. You moan all the time about how misunderstood you are.'
'True. Do you think I should put it on my CV ?'
'I think it's an essential skill for most workplaces.'
'Never hung round long enough to find out.' He hit a button and chanced upon Emmerdale. The Dingles were discussing a scam gone wrong. Did people like this really exist somewhere in the Skipton area ? Jude scratched his forehead, trying to grasp at the threads of a plot of which he had no prior knowledge. It all looked a bit dowdy. Northern in a way that no north he'd ever experienced actually resembled. Not like Hollyoaks. For a while in his early twenties he'd wanted to move to Chester purely on the strength of the attractiveness of the cast. All the best looking people were clearly born there. It would be lovely to know such well-scrubbed folk. Only later did he realise they were all in fact dodgy bit-part actors and aspiring models, all too willing to get their silicone baps out for the hated lads mags. He shuddered as he thought about the kind of three-fingered meatheads who lapped up that kind of publication. They gave his 50% of the population a terrible name. Mind you, the women who posed in them didn't do much for the other half. He'd once bought the line that said women showing themselves in magazines, lap-dancing or stripping in dodgy clubs were empowered, doing it to express

their sexuality and sense of control. Now he saw it as being just a clever piece of casuistry to hide the fact that they were merely playing along with the objectified fantasy image of their sex held by much of the male population. The kind of male majority who had made his life a misery because he didn't buy into it, refused to play along. Come a real live battle of the sexes he'd undoubtedly elect to be a traitor.
'Didn't Lauren say she watches this ?'
'She did. Asked us to tell her what happened.' Star had picked up the local paper.
'I think she was joking.'
'Right.' Jude had moved his eyes away from the TV and was staring blankly into space. Star noticed and watched him in silence for a second. Smiled and then spoke giving him a poke in the ribs as she did so.
'Jude.'
'Ow. Gerrof.' He flinched, his attention swinging sharply back into the room.
'What do you make of her then ?'
'Who do you mean ?'
'Lauren. My cousin.'
'Oh..' He touched the back of his hair absentmindedly. 'She's..er..she's nice. Not what I'd expected.'
'She fancies you.'
'Fuck off.'
'No she does, she fancies you. I saw the way she's been looking at you all afternoon.'
'Well, that is understandable Star.' He tried a little jokey bluster as means of deflection.
'You fancy her don't you.' It was a statement. Not a question.
'Erm…' Jude's face was starting to seep crimson.
'You do.'
'She's alright.'
'Haha ! I knew it ! She is so your type. She's a ringer for Kate Moennig and she always gets you very agitated. You've always been into tomboys. You had a massive crush on Sam Mahoney in the last year of juniors. You wrote her name all over your roughbook.' She grabbed his left cheek and gave it a little squeeze. 'Aww bless. He's not changed a bit.'
'Soooo…she never fancied me anyway. Love's young dream. I think it was the way she beat up Kevin Harwood when she saw him nicking my sherbert dib-dab that did it you know. She was very handy with her fists if I remember.'
'Too right she was. Nice girl if you stayed on the right side of her. She lives in London now, in a squat with her boyfriend. They're in an alternative circus. Apparently she fires things from interesting places. Saw a photo of

her on Myspace. She's got a shaved head and loads of piercings. You should see if you can find her.'
'I might. Sounds a bit mental.'
'Right up your street then flower. All the women you fancy generally are. Lauren seems a bit too sane.'

Jude chuckled and hit the remote control again, this time landing on Channel 4 News. Star leaned back in her seat smiling.

Lauren was in a familiar and totally portable posture. Leaning against the bar in the Opera House necking back a bottle of Becks, looking a picture of disinterested cool in her stripy top, distressed leather bomber and trusty old Converse. She was ignoring everyone else, whilst around her hordes of menopausal women were busying themselves with discussions about the amazing powers of the Montage. He was featured on a glossy wall poster with a list of dates down the side. Last night he'd been in Buxton, tomorrow it was Carlisle. Live the dream thought Lauren as she drained the last of the bottle, wiped her fringe from out of her eyes and put her empty green one down on the counter.

Montage looked as if he'd come straight from central casting. If you were going to do a comedy send-up of a celebrity psychic you'd probably make yourself look just like him. Middle-aged, orange tan, slicked back thinning hair, shiny ear stud and matching bracelet, his cheek resting on his clenched fist, his eyes slightly closed and downcast, an expression of concerned knowing on his face. Frickin sleazebag thought Lauren. It was so utterly predictable. What was she doing here?

Millie had nipped to the toilet. She was full of nerves for some reason and kept being called away by her bladder, giving Lauren agonising details of the hassle her leggings and skirt outfit combo were giving her every time nature called. The leggings were tighter around the thighs than they should be. She'd been seriously hitting Lauren's Hob-Nobs of late. Lauren would go to her cupboard for a mid-afternoon biscuit or two only to find a little note from Millie promising to replace them. This could only mean one thing. Something was bothering her. She always comfort ate, whereas Lauren starved herself when stuff was playing on her mind as a means of reasserting a bit of self-control. Lauren was clueless though as to what was bugging her best friend. Could be anything. Remembrance of a major wardrobe malfunction perhaps? Or concern over whether or not she could ever get away with those high-waisted jeans that were making a comeback? Definitely not thought Lauren. Millie had short-arse legs and a backside that had a tendency to spread like an ink-splodge on blotting paper following a few days of bad eating. She'd definitely look all wrong. Lauren made a mental note to tell her before she spent her money.

Lauren didn't mind Millie's absence as it gave her chance to grab another drink before she got back, then she'd make out she'd just been sipping on the first one before her increasingly abstemious friend had chance to disapprove. Friday nights out with Millie were now more often than not accompanied by loud prudish disapprovals of younger women falling in the gutter off their faces. Lauren wasn't really sure what to make of this disturbingly adult development.

'Just think of the damage it's doing to their reproductive systems Lauren.' She'd said as she stepped over a pink boob tube and plastic cowboy hat wearing size 20 who was singing Mika songs slumped on the pavement outside Yates's Wine Lodge as the drizzle intensified one Saturday in September.
'Men have been at it for centuries Mills, it's no big deal. They're happy. We've all got an equal right to make an absolute tit of ourselves. They'll all probably grow out of it.' They stepped over a tragically York paving stone splayed kofte kebab. 'And what's with all this reproductive thing anyway ? We're not just walking wombs you know. Some of us have interests. Like skateboarding or macramé.'
'I'm not sure how you can be so blasé. It's the future of the nation we're talking about here.'

Lauren looked at her best friend with an eyebrow raised. The future of the nation ? That was bordering on the fascistic wasn't it ? It conjured up images of proud-jawed ruddy faced hausfraus looking into the middle-distance as their uniformed men folk set about recapturing the Sudetenland. The Nazis were obsessed with cranky health and efficiency ideas. A bit like Millie then. Was she about to start giving herself home colonic irrigations whilst loudly humming Tomorrow Belongs To Me? Lose that image straight away.
'Bringing life into the world is very important.'
'It is, but don't blokes play a part in it as well then ? Heavy drinking fucks up their sperm count you know. It's not all down to boozing birds.'
'You'll feel differently when you're a mother.'
'Ha !' Lauren spluttered. 'Surely you've been friends with me long enough to know that's never going to happen. Anyway, I'm thinking of getting the old tubes tied, failing that I might just drink myself sterile. Might be less intrusive.'
'Lauren !'
'What ?' It was far too easy to wind up Millicent Croft. That name really suited her when she was being like this. A stuck-up prudish bluestocking. Definite school ma'am.

Lauren couldn't see what all the fuss was about. Much of the moral panic regarding heavy drinking young women came down to the old school disapproval of the female of the species larking about, or of partying as hard if not harder than the blokes always had. The same rules applied to both. Do it to too much of a degree over too long a period of time and you'd have problems. But that was your choice. Most heavy drinking women like their male contemporaries got bored, or found love, or discovered something else on which to spend their money. It was a rite of passage and in a small way a pissed up bordering on the obese underdressed young woman rolling in her own kebab on the kerbside was a small step to liberation. A very small step admittedly. But then Lauren longed for the day when what you had between your legs was as much of an irrelevance to everyone else as it always had been for her. But the muggles still persisted in their sex games and considered Lauren the oddity. Ah fuck the lot of them. Who wants to be normal anyway ?

Lauren removed a fiver from her pocket, held it between her thumb and forefinger and gave it a quick wave. The movement caught a bar man's eye, causing him to put down the glass he was drying on a tea towel that looked as if it had seen better days.
'What can I get you mate ?' He moved across with familiar blokey bluster then paused unsure for a second and looked again. 'Sorry…love.' Lauren just smiled and gave her order.

When she finally flustered her way back into the bar Millie tried hard to look as if she hadn't just spent the last five minutes wrestling with her leggings and struggling to open the dodgy lock on the cubicle door. She'd been seconds away from shouting for help.

Millie was beautiful thought Lauren, that went without saying, but you'd never call it effortless. The kind of beauty that gave hope to mere mortals. Even as an 18 year old if she'd stepped out of her room with flawless make-up and a demure expression on her face, within a couple of hours she'd look like a bedraggled, flustered mess. She still pulled though. It was the lips and the eyes that did it. Actually, now she looked at her lips they reminded her of Jude's. Pillowy. Wasn't that what they called them ? Kissable. Oh god. Too weird. Concentrate.

'Gosh, Laurers…I'm so excited about this.' She took hold of Lauren's hands. 'Awww so glad you came babes.' She then threw her arms around a startled Lauren whose heart slowly melted.
'Yeah, yeah. Could hardly turn you down could I. Even if I do think it's all bollocks.'
'I've not got any other friends.'
Where had that come from ?
'You have ! You're the sunny popular one remember ? I'm the miserable loner who never goes out.'
'No, but I haven't Lauren. They've all moved on and left me. There's just you.' She sighed. 'And Damian of course.'

'How is loverboy at the minute then ? He's not been to the flat for a while. I want to give him back that Enemy At The Gates DVD he loaned me.'
Lauren had long fancied herself as a Second World War Soviet Sniper. There had been some proper cool feisty women doing that job back in the day. Imagine that, hiding in burnt out buildings taking pot-shots at Nazis. A more perfect use of her time she thought she'd struggle to find.
'Give it to me then, I'll give it to him next time I see him. Whenever that might be.'
'Is there a problem Mills ? I thought he was perfect.'
'He is. He was. He's just…'
'Just what ?'
'A bit distant that's all. Can't see me this week because of work commitments or something.'

So this was what was prompting the biscuit binges. Lauren didn't like the sound of it. It sounded all too neat an example of Millie's usual relationship pattern. Millie meets very fit, charming bloke. Very fit charming bloke falls head over heels in love with pretty, ditzy girl-woman. Very fit charming bloke soon starts taking advantage of pretty ditzy girl-woman's devotion and generous nature. Pretty ditzy girl-woman gets lonely and sad, and very fit charming bloke soon dumps her for someone sunnier who made less demands. It had such a naff rom-com gone wrong predictability about it.

Lauren had seen it countless times before and it always both broke her heart and made her irate. The clueless, insensitive bastards. Treating someone so special so atrociously. If she had been a bloke she'd of held onto Millie for dear life aware of what a good thing she'd just found. Which in many ways was precisely what she did.
'Anyway, enough about me.' Millie seemed to gather herself. 'I can tell you fancy that pretty boy currently watching our telly and eating our biscuits.' She was grinning mischievously.
'No I don't.' Lauren attempted to shrug it off but it lacked the usual force of her denials.
'You do. I saw you looking at him. I know that look. You don't see it very often but when you do see it, you immediately know what it means.'
'Mills, you sound like Kate Humble talking about a badger or something. Are you some kind of animal behaviourist ?'
'No, but I am a qualified Lauren behaviourist and I know when she's got the hots for a hottie. And let's face it, he *is* a hottie.'
'Not your type though.'
'Definitely not my type. Way too scrawny and I could never go out with a man who was prettier than me, but you…'
'Yes ?'
'Well, he's kind of your mirror image isn't he ?'

'What do you mean ?'
'You've both got that skinny ambiguous thing going on. It's very attractive. You'd make a striking couple.'
'Do you think ?'
'Just one thing though.'
'What's that ?'
'I think he might be gay.'
Lauren sighed. 'Me too. Fuck it.'
'Mind you.'
'What ?'
'Everyone presumes you're a dyke.'

In a disinterested voice the public address system began telling the milling believers that they needed to make their way to their seats for an evening of psychic enlightenment. Or deluded nonsense depending on your point of view. Lauren definitely concurred with the latter.

They found their seats in the stalls. Way too close to the action for Lauren's comfort, and the middle of a row. Definite double discomfort. Usually she hogged the end of one near the back whenever she was in a theatre in case she had to make a hasty getaway. It had been known. She never knew how she was going to react to what she was being subjected to.

Culture had a peculiar effect upon her. It was a bit like a kebab. OK in principle if you were in the right mood, but it generally left you regretting it after a while. It was OK on the TV. If you found something of interest on BBC Four you could tune in for as long as it grabbed you. Then when the boredom threshold was inevitably reached, flick one up on the remote-control channel shuffle and enjoy a Beeb three prog about dodgy bloaters. Or just how terrible kids are to have in your house. Those in particular always made her feel smug. Whilst Millie would sit there trying to understand why the little darling was biting the legs of strangers and hanging the cat from the washing line, and to imagine what she would do to make things different, Lauren would sit smiling saying things like; 'thank fuck for contraception' or 'all that pain of childbirth and you end up with that little shit' and her own personal favourite, 'can't they give it up for medical science or something ?'

Just occasionally though culture could be difficult to avoid. It kind of went with the territory of being a poncey arts graduate knocking around a cathedral city. People just expected stuff. One birthday Francis had taken pity on her regular Wilhemina no-mates or anything planned status (a status she was more than happy with) and bought her a ticket to see some dreary world music event at the National Centre For Early Music in the city. She could hardly say no. It was in a beautifully converted church just down the road from where she now lived. The setting was mildly distracting but the music, something latin American and weird, gave her a migraine. At the interval she went outside into the floodlit graveyard for a cigarette then unilaterally skulked off to the pub without word of explanation, leaving poor Francis stranded. There had been a slight freezing of relations between them for a while, but he ultimately forgave her. He always did. Lauren winced a little at the memory and looked at the stage as the house lights dimmed. You could hardly call the impending nonsense culture though could you ? Hardly likely to see the divine Verity Sharp discussing the Montage oeuvre on the Culture Show. Actually, she would definitely go gay for Verity. Millie had been asking her the other day who might make her consider a dabble on the other side. She'd offered Justine Frischmann and Emily Maitliss , but now she thought about it Verity would definitely float her proverbial boat. One way or another. Her pleasantly wandering mind was dragged back into the auditorium as Twilight Zone style plinkety music began playing, dry ice puffed its way across the stage and then a small explosion heralded the arrival of the man himself.

'Here he is,' chuckled Lauren. 'The frickin Montage massive. Brace yourself ladies.'

Millie gave her a sharp dig in the ribcage. Lauren looked around at the wide-eyed audience. Nearly all women of a certain age, many of them open mouthed at the perma-tanned sleazebag before them. He was wearing a white suit for fucks sake. And slip on shoes. Lauren wanted to vomit over the person in front but thought better of it, seeing as the person in front was so large her folds of fat were seeping over the back of her chair into Lauren's territory. If she did they'd only hit the woman-mountain then drip down onto Lauren's Converse. She found this thought alarmingly distracting. The woman next to her was loudly crunching Murray Mints and had a slight odour of moth balls which the mints were only going some way to alleviating. The man next to her, who Lauren took to be her husband kept sniffing and wiping his nose on the sleeve on his cardigan. Gross. It was all gross in its own way.

Then away went Dimitri.

'Friends. I come to you this evening to share with you the good news. The good news of eternal life. But no. I'm not going to ask you to convert your beliefs, or join a church. I'm merely going to bring you messages from the people we know and love who have gone into the spirit world before us.'

His voice was dreary. Kind of non-specific north-west and he had the delivery of a particularly jobs worth middle-manager. It contrasted with his spray-on showbiz posturing. Lauren was wondering what all these people saw in him. Then he began his discussions with the undead. A man two rows back let out a loud yawn, Lauren turned and looked at him smiling.

'Nice one'. The woman immediately behind her tapped her on the shoulder and pointed at the stage. 'Yeah whatever.' She sunk low into her seat. 'Mad old bint.'

Dimitri Montage was oblivious. To lots of things. The main one being how ludicrous he looked. Mind you, from the no-visible-seat left in the house returns on this evening alone, there was clearly a tidy paycheque or two to be had in cynical, immoral, preying on the emotions of the vulnerable fraud wasn't there ? Lauren sighed. What was she doing here ?

'Basking Otter is bringing into my mind now a man. A tall man with grey hair. He says he's got a message for someone called Irene.'

Lauren looked around the auditorium. Up shot a hand. That must be Irene. It wasn't too much of a shot in the dark was it. A whole theatre full of women in the middle to the end of their lives, one of them was bound to be called Irene. And just how many of them had recently lost tall men with grey hair. What a fucking joke. She would leave at the interval. This was just embarrassing. On he went, messages for Doris from Bob, for Catherine from Nigel, for Terry from Alan, none of them saying much specific, none of them really that enlightening.

Next came a message from a little girl whose mother said that she had died of childhood cancer twenty five years earlier. The mother had been unable to move on, her life stuck in a grieving stasis, her mind full of whats, ifs and maybes. The woman was crying, so too was Millie next to her. Lauren moved uncomfortably in her seat. This was bordering on the pornographic. The whole audience were giving the woman meaningful looks. This had gone from being a mildly amusing piece of anthropological distraction, into different emotional territory. It unsettled Lauren. How long was it until the interval ? Montage looked deep in thought.

'Ok Basking, Ok. I've got that.' He kept making these asides. Supposedly talking to his berdache. 'I've a young man wanting to speak now. He's very determined. Tall, thoughtful looking. He looks like a student but he's a not a student if you get my meaning ?' There was a slight chuckle. Ooh those students with their traffic cone stealing, dressing up like naughty nurses and staying out till the early hours ways in between two lectures a week on their BA in Reality Television. Is this what we pay our taxes for ?

Lauren shook her head. It was like being stuck in some kind of weird middle-England supernatural nightmare. These people were so dissatisfied with their mundane lives that they sought solace in a fictional past or intimations about their future. A future which only they could do something to effect. Not some sleazy middle-aged man manipulating their most treasured memories.

Dimitri Montage continued. 'It's as if this man hadn't really grown up and didn't want to. He's got a book in his hand, something by Virginia Woolf I think. He's showing me a drowning woman. Or is it a drowning man. I can't really say.'

Lauren looked up. Woolf was her favourite author.
'He's telling me that he didn't mean to die. That it was all a mistake. A horrible mistake. And that…' Montage closed his eyes and furrowed his brow a little. He looked almost in pain. 'He loved someone here tonight.' He touched his forehead. ' What's that Basking ? Oh, I see…he says his name is Matt.'

Lauren felt her blood run cold. She fixed the stage. This couldn't be true. Someone called Matt ? Carrying a book by Virginia Woolf. At least she hadn't been named, didn't have to engage in this uncomfortable charade.
'He says his message is for someone called…let me..see…Laura.'
Ha ! Got ya. Not frickin Laura is it. Lauren eased back into her seat feeling her cynicism vindicated.
'No, sorry, my mistake. He's shaking his head. It's Lauren. It's a message for Lauren.' Millie her red tearful eyes wide stared at Lauren and mouthed a silent 'Matt.'

Lauren wasn't going to make herself known. It was all just lucky coincidence. These guys were highly skilled fraudsters. They knew what they were doing. This oily buffoon wasn't going to infiltrate his way into her precious memories of her soul-mate. She wouldn't play ball. Suddenly Millie grabbed Lauren's arm and flung it into the air. Dimitri's eye turned immediately onto the two of them.
'Ah Lauren. You're there. He's telling me that yes, it's you he's after.'
Lauren could feel her fury beginning to rise. How dare Millie do that ? She focused her eyes hard on her feet as she felt the eyes of everyone around her focus in.
'You two were an item yes ?'
Lauren didn't answer. Didn't make eye contact. Millie grinned sheepishly.
'Ok, he just wants you to know that he loves you and that he thinks it's time you let yourself move on. He wants you to be happy. Does that make sense love ?'
Don't call me fuckin love thought Lauren as she continued to glare hard at the floor. This was awful. Make it fucking stop. Make it fucking stop right now before her head fucking exploded all over the fucking row in front.
'He's laughing at me now. Oh he's a character this one…he says this wouldn't be your normal cup of tea and you're only here under duress.'
At this point Lauren finally looked up and mouthed at the grinning psychic. He really was exceptionally smug. Just the sight of him made her stomach turn :

'*Just fuck off.*'

It had just come out. An involuntary reaction to what she was being subjected to. She couldn't help it. He repulsed her. His very existence appalled every moral value she had ever held. He was human excrement. None but her immediate neighbours had heard. They shuffled uncomfortably in their seats and pretended nothing had happened. They'd only gone and got a nutter sitting near them hadn't they. Just ignore her. Stroppy little madam. Ruining it for everyone else.

Dimitri saw she had spoken and looked at her with his wide ice-white tooth grin.
'What was that love ? Is there something you wanted to tell Matt ?'
Lauren couldn't stand this any longer. She didn't care who was watching. She shot to her feet and hollered back; jabbing the air as she spat, 'no, I just want to tell you to fuck right off and mind your own fucking business you filthy fucking fraud !'

There was an audible gasp from the audience, Millie's jaw hit the floor as she stared at Lauren who began shoving her way roughly out of the row. Millie shot to her feet, slung her bag quickly over her shoulder and dashed behind her. Dimitri watched them go smiling. He looked unruffled. You had to be fairly thick skinned to enter this kind of work didn't you ?
'Oooh proper little drama queen there haven't we ladies and gentlemen ? Never mind, we can't please everyone can we Basking ? Basking's laughing ladies and gentleman.' Of course he was. Right on cue the audience of acolytes joined in with their own mannered chuckles. Montage looked at the ceiling, down at his feet and then out again towards the audience. 'Is there anyone here tonight called Gladys…'

Lauren darted out of the Opera House and onto the street. Millie tailing behind managed to grab hold of the hood on her bomber and tug her to an abrupt halt. Lauren turned sharply on her heels and glared at her best friend.
'What the fuck do you think you were playing at ? Embarassing us like that ?'
Millie was shaking with rage as Lauren could feel herself growing dizzy. Passers-by were staring at them.
'That fucker !' She jabbed her fingers in the direction of the theatre.
'That's where I fucking work Lauren ! You are such a selfish bitch at times. You never think about anyone but yourself. I've got to go in there tomorrow and explain all that away. Some of my colleagues were watching on, you stupid, insensitive cow. I fucking hate you at times.'

Millie stamped the ground and clenched both her fists. Lauren could barely focus. She was shaking with rage and confusion. The bastard, the fucking oily bastard, picking on her like that.
'Why did he go for me then ? Why the fuck did he single me out ? I didn't even want to fucking be there.'

'He didn't, it was Matt. Your fucking soul-mate, the bloke you always talk about being the one, the fella whose photos you look at every night before you go to bed and wonder what might have been. It was him Lauren, him. He wants you to move on. You can't feel sorry for yourself, or him for that matter for the rest of your fucking days.'

Lauren scowled, a gaze so incendiary it could be classified as a potential weapon. 'No it fucking wasn't Matt and I'll tell you why shall I ? Because Matt wouldn't do that to me. He would know how uncomfortable something like that would make me and he just wouldn't do it. Even if he did want to talk to me.'

'Can't you see how selfish you are Lauren ? Can't you see that it might be Matt who needed to talk to you, had to tell you these things ? You've built him up into some kind of perfect man, the only man who ever really understood you despite the fact you only saw him for a few months before he died. It's not fair on him you making him out to be some kind of plaster saint. He was a flesh and blood bloke Lauren, not the perfect man by numbers that you seem to want to remember him as. He's not your fucking property.'

'He was my boyfriend Mills, I'll remember him how I fucking well like. And as for you…' Lauren gave her friend a pointed shove which caused her to wobble slightly. 'You can fuck off back home. I'm going to the pub.'

Jude and Star were sitting on the sofa at the Fossgate flat zoned out in front of something meaningless on BBC 3. Star was resting her head on her best friend's shoulder, taking in his familiar smells. Deodorant and moisturiser. He smelt far too nice for a boy. She was wondering why exactly they were sitting here in the slightly dishevelled front room of a cousin she barely knew a hundred miles from home. Then she remembered. It was a road trip. So far so uninspiring then. This wasn't America was it ? There was nothing that romantic about hitting the road in Britain. We didn't even call them freeways and you could never imagine someone penning a rock standard about the A1. Maybe a novelty record with barely risible rhyming couplets by someone cosy like Pam Ayres, but never anything credible.

England sucked much of the time. It was a dead-end dreamless place soaked in self-satisfaction and comfortable smugness. You still had a hard time if you were in anyway different, and all most people aspired to were patio heaters and sat-nav for their ugly family cars. A comfortable, unimaginative, sterile, passionless, living death. That was all Newtham offered. That was all most places offered. She sighed. Where were these thoughts coming from ? Maybe she should pop to see her nice Malaysian doctor when she got home. Plead depression, see if she could wangle some happy pills. They'd worked for Jude. He was always like Tigger when he was on Prozac.

Then they heard the front door click open and both immediately sat up. The psychic thingy must be over already. Star had thought that an odd thing to be going to. Surely they didn't believe in all that rubbish did they ? Jude's face had lit up when Millie had mentioned Spirit Ways. It was one of his favourite programmes. Not that he believed a word of it, he just enjoyed the inadvertent comedy of it all. Millie had briefly wondered if she should ask Jude if he wanted Lauren's ticket, but knowing madam she would have undoubtedly been offended and hurt by this. Didn't want to go but equally hated to feel she was being displaced in Millie's affections.

The front room door flew open and there stood Millie. Her hair all over the place, her face wild and red with tears. Jude and Star glanced at each other frozen into surprised silence. Awkward moment alert. Somebody say something.
'Are you alright ?' Jude finally offered.
'No ! I fucking hate her. I fucking hate her !'
'Hate who, come here sit down ?' Star tapped the sofa then jumped to her feet. ' Would you like a cup of tea, just point me in the right direction ?' Millie said nothing. 'OK, I'll find the tea no problems. She put her hands on Millie's shoulders. 'Talk to Jude. He's good at it.' Jude mouthed a silent alarmed 'Star' in her direction as she left the front room and tried to find the kitchen.

Millie sniffing flounced down on the sofa next to Jude who immediately stiffened his posture. Oh god. He didn't need this. All he ever asked for was a quiet life but drama just seemed to follow him round like flies around a cow turd. Millie looked up at him, her bottom lip protruding, tears still flowing.
'Lauren shoved me !' She sounded like an indignant six year old telling tales on her teasing older brother.
'What sweetie ?' He took hold of her and she instinctively threw her arms around him. He in turn pulled her close and tried to comfort her.
'Lauren. She pushed me away. She doesn't like me anymore. It's all gone wrong.' Millie let out an anguished bawl and slipped out of practical communication for a few minutes of near hysterical sobbing. All Jude could think about was the line of advancing snot which was trailing down her face and heading south to his t-shirt. Just in time he found a clean tissue in his pocket and handed it to her. She wiped her face, blew her nose and then sat up.
'She's totally let me down Jude. Totally. I'm not sure I'll ever be able to forgive her for this.'
Just then the door swung open with Star carrying a tray and three mugs of

tea.

'Forgive her what ? What's happened ?'

Jude gave a little shrug and looked towards Millie for guidance. She leaned back on the sofa, sighed and then ran her fingers through her hair. Jude was hoping they were clean. There had been a lot of mucus flying around.

'It's a very long story.'

Millie launched into the evening's proceedings and the complicated and convoluted story that preceded it. Star and Jude just sat there slightly overwhelmed by it all, but Jude in particular was getting more and more drawn in. This was like walking in on Hollyoaks or something. She was pretty enough to star in Hollyoaks. Or would have been eleven years ago. People over twenty five didn't exist in that series. It was Star who finally delivered her verdict.

'Look, I'll be honest with you. I'm not really sure I believe there's anything in this kind of psychic stuff, but I do think Lauren was a bit mean and well…'

'What ?' Millie asked.

'Dramatic ?' Jude offered. Star looked at him and nodded. He knew all about being dramatic and felt he should try to find a means to defend their host a little. 'The thing is though Millie, from what you've been saying this stuff is really like..kind of..erm..complicated. There's a lot going on in her head regarding this guy who died. And you say she doesn't believe in any of that stuff and then suddenly out of the blue she's confronted with this information, with a whole theatre staring at her, it's going to stir up all kinds of emotions. It would be dead pressured. Excuse the pun.' He smiled sheepishly but Millie didn't return it. 'If I were being honest I think I might of reacted in a similar way.'

Millie looked at Star. 'Would he ?'

'I think it's quite likely. He's pulled tricks like that before.'

Millie turned back to Jude and gave him a slightly distrusting look.

'It's not that I want to be a drama queen or upset people, it's just the intensity with which I feel stuff. Sometimes situations just completely overwhelm me and I need to escape. All you can think to do is run away.'

Star remembered her best friend's disappearing act from countless parties, classrooms, workplaces, relationships. He was one of life's wanderers. 'Millie do you reckon Lauren will be alright ? I'm a bit worried after what you said,' she asked.

Millie shrugged. Jude touched her shoulder. 'Yeah, do you think one of us should go find her ? Did you say she said she was going to the pub ? Have you any idea which one ?'

'It'll be The Ackhorne. It's always the Ackhorne. That used to be Matt's pub. It's where she goes when she wants to mooch about without me. Anti-social cow.'

'Tell me where it is then and I'll go see if I can find her.'

Star gave Jude a knowing glance. He didn't seem to need much encouragement did he ?

Connection…

Jude stepped out into the night. This was definitely interesting. Millie's directions had been straightforward enough. Just head up and out over the river until you reach a little cobbled alley down by the side of a disused church on a corner, opposite an 1980s theme bar. The Ackhorne was half way down the alley. He got his head down and pushed on. This wasn't really what he'd had in mind when he suggested he and Star take off for a bit, but at least it was different to his usual uneventful drudge. If he were being honest the opportunity to spend some time alone with Star's cousin wasn't too terrible a prospect. Something about her intrigued him but he couldn't work out what. After a bit more time with her maybe it would come. She was certainly attractive, if not conventionally so, but then he'd always found conventionally pretty women as appealing as they'd found him. Not at all. He liked Lauren's long choppy brown fringe, the big questioning brown eyes and her general sense of together aloof cool. The fact that she appeared to be quite feisty just made her seem even more compelling in his eyes. A difficult person at times he was sure, but one who had lots of layers, plenty to say for herself and didn't feel much need to fit in. Self-sufficient. That was always attractive wasn't it ? He might be wrong of course. He'd only had a short period of time with her, but he liked to think he was a good judge of character. All this surmising might amount to nothing, who could say. Maybe tonight would help him find it.

He found the alley and hurried down it. The cobbles were greasy from the dank mild weather they'd been having and once or twice he threatened to lose his footing. The church yard looked slightly creepy. He imagined a Magwitch type crouching behind one of the head stones. He briefly shuddered, realising he was freaking himself out, and pushed his way into the pub. This always made him slightly nervous. He was different. He looked different. Not everywhere welcomed that difference. He'd lost count of the number of scrapes that difference had landed him in on nights out. This place seemed OK though. It was only moderately busy. Glancing around the pub, a low ceilinged, low lit, cosy hideaway, the kind of place you came to when you didn't want to be bothered. There on a small table by the fire sat Lauren. She gave the impression of reading the newspaper, but Jude didn't think she really was. Just using it instead as a means not to have to engage

with the rest of the room. He'd done it himself. Walking across to where she sat he made a small polite cough. She looked up instantly with a look of surprise on her face.
'Mind if I join you ?' He asked.
'Er..no…if you want to.' Hardly the most effusive welcome ever but then he wasn't expecting it. She folded up her newspaper, rested her head on her hands and looked across at him.
'So. What's she been telling you ?'
'Who ?'
'Millie of course. That is why you're here isn't it ?'
'Well..'
'Yes or no ?'
'Yes.'
'Right. What's she's been telling you ?'
'Just that there'd been a bit of an incident at the opera house and then you had a row.'
'Come to tell me off have you ? You hardly know me mate.'
'Oh no. I'm not taking sides. No, I'm just here to see if you're alright.'
'Well, as you can see I'm quite alright. I've got a pint of Kronenbourg, I've got the paper, I've got my own company…sooo…'
'You're fine.' She nodded. Jude stood up. 'I'll get off then. I'm sorry if I…'
   Lauren seemed to soften. She looked at his big beautiful eyes and embarrassed awkward expression. He really was exceptionally attractive that one. Blokes like that didn't just come looking for you very often. Not her anyway. Most of them probably went looking for each other. What harm would it do him joining her ? 'Oh fucking sit down then. You may as well stay now you've made the effort.' She reached inside the pocket of her jeans and pulled out a five pound note. 'Go buy yourself a drink and get us some crisps.'
Jude took the note and smiled, unpeeling his coat and placing it down on the stool opposite her.
'Not frickin salt and vinegar though. I hate them.'
   Jude nodded and wandered to the bar. Lauren peered around the corner as he went. What a stunning arse as well. Looked perfect in those jeans. Glad he didn't go for skinnys. They had a Max Wall quality on the wrong man. Jude would be able to pull them off though, but still. She associated them with smelly early twenty something boys with big back combed Russell Brand hair but none of his rakish charm. Nope, Jude had got it just right. Nicely fitted t-shirt which showed off his sylph like frame, straight leg jeans, trench coat complete with judicious use of the badge, oh and what was he wearing on his feet ? She glanced down as he carried a pint of lager and two bags of crisps. Black Converse. Just like hers. They were shoe twins. Actually, they were

practically identical. She raised an eyebrow and sipped her lager. Maybe tonight wasn't going to turn out to be quite so disastrous after all.

Millie had taken herself in the bath. Star was relieved. She was finding conversation with her awkward. It was understandable that Jude might want to see if Lauren was OK but that didn't mean she wasn't going to feel like a bit of a spare part. Even Millie seemed to clamp up once Jude had disappeared. He just had one of those faces that made people want to tell him all their secrets. It was always happening. Star was used to it by now, no point getting territorial. Not with someone like Jude who everyone seemed to want a piece of. She knew that when all was said and done, he was her best friend and their friendship superseded all others. They would always be joined. As they had been since Mrs Durrant's reception class all those years ago. Walking hand in hand around the playground. The two little odd kids. Fielding the abuse of the other children and the perpetual misunderstanding of the teachers who kept on at them to make more of an effort to fit in.

Star flicked through the TV channels again and thought about her own bed, her own flat, the work she could be getting on with. At times there was nowhere better to be than by her drawing board. It was in front of a window that overlooked the park across the road. You saw the seasons change in the trees, children playing on the swings, people walking their funny looking little dogs. They should head back tomorrow. This was a bad idea. It had been nice to catch up again with Lauren, and maybe they could keep in touch still, but this whole thing was just rash. They had lives to live. At least she'd barely thought about Kyle. Maybe she was at last beginning to get over him. She hoped so. Then a two-tone signal emanated from her phone.

'*Star, I miss you. I think we need to talk.*'

'Don't think I'm going to tell you all about what's just happened you know. It's none of your business.' Lauren was at least pretending to remain defiant.
'I wouldn't expect you to.'
'Good. Anyway, I imagine Millie has already done that for me.'
'She was very upset.'
'Well, good. It's all her fault this happened. She dragged me there, she shoved my frickin arm in the air when that sleazy gimmer was talking about me. I didn't want any of it to happen.'
'Does stuff like this happen often ?'
'Who are you ? My frickin therapist ?'
'Nooo, nooo…don't think I'm prying, it's just that I'm the same. I react in similar ways, I understand totally why you'd of needed to escape.'
'You do ?'

'I do.'
'Oh right. Er..cool. Nice one.' She clinked his glass and then quickly changed the subject. 'So then, what brings a pretty little thing like you to a mean old town like this ?'
'Haha ! Ohmigod Lauren..you would not believe what happened to me the other day. It's the reason I'm here actually, not in the pub, in York I mean…I was in the shop where I used to work, it's just this shitty convenience store, smells constantly of rank luncheon meat, anyway…'

    Star looked at the text message. Her heart was beating double-time, and as she noticed the hand which was holding the phone had started shaking. She stood up and began pacing the room, thoughts in her head beginning to fly, crashing hard against her cranium and rebounding all over the place, sending her dizzier and dizzier with each impact. Where was Jude ? He'd of known what to do. This was all she'd hoped and prayed for over the past few weeks, now it had actually happened she was paralysed. Kyle. Her boyfriend. Of course she needed to talk to him. But wait a minute, he'd dumped her hadn't he ? He'd been unfaithful. He'd spent the past few weeks living in ditzy la-la-land with a legs spread wide bimbo. He was soiled goods. Did she really want him back ? What had brought this on anyway ? Had he realised that the airhead was not a patch on his sexy together professional of a life-partner, or had his shag just got bored of him ? Hope thought the former, common sense told her the latter.
    She tried to imagine what Jude would be saying right now. He'd be angrily pacing the room firing off expletives about Kyle's general uselessness. They had never got on. Kyle just couldn't understand why Star should insist on having a bloke as a best friend, he also couldn't get his head round Jude's general lack of blokeishness. A man who preferred the company of women but didn't seem obsessed with shagging them. Yet who wasn't gay. Had no interest in football, couldn't drive (and didn't want to), liked watching chick-flicks, doing his hair and talking about feelings into the early hours. It was definitely a bit suss.
    It was all wrong in Kyle's mind, although to Star it just made perfect sense. Jude wasn't a bloke with all the associated baggage that came with it in terms of impenetrable moods, baffling hobbies, emotional paralysis and tedious taste in films. Jude was just Jude. The kid from primary school who homed in on her on the very first day, who wouldn't let her leave the wendy house one afternoon. Both of them had sat in their so stubbornly their respective parents had to be called to coax them both out. When they weren't together they were planning what they would do when they were. They went to school together, played out together, grew up together, told each other all their secrets and shared countless major life events. And now, as she tried to

decide the best course of action in this one, she needed him again. He would be the one to stiffen her resolve, to help her make a decision that was best for her, not just to react to Kyle's latest whim. To not be a passive victim of circumstance. That was Jude's job, but right now he wasn't here.

'Man, you're just like me. It's freaky weird.' Lauren had finished her second pint, and after three quarters of an hour of probing Jude about his life so far she'd reached a few conclusions. 'Do you ever get the feeling you're not really much of anything ? I haven't the faintest clue about what I'm meant to be as a woman, I forget I am a lot of the time, yet I find men, so-called proper men I mean here, hairy ones who like football and shit, completely baffling. I see how they think and how they act, but I can't comprehend why. It's as if I'm in a completely different category of humanity. I remember when that book 'Men are from Mars, Women are from Venus came out I bought it and read it, and neither men nor women made much sense to me according to that. I understood both, and could kind of see what the guy was on about, just couldn't relate personally to either. I just remember thinking to myself, well what frickin planet am I from then ?'

Jude looked pensive and thoughtful. 'You get that too ! I think we're the ones from planet earth. We're the flesh and blood humans in a world of walking clichés.'

'True but then you sort of say to yourself, well all this 'blokes do this', 'women do that' stuff is all bollocks and we're all essentially the same and then you see someone like Millie who just does girlie stuff and really enjoys it. She thinks like women in magazine articles, and says stuff that women are meant to say, she wants things that women are meant to want and is still wrapped up in little girl handsome prince fantasies, but it's not like an affectation or something she's just learnt. It's her identity, and it's as real to her as my not being like that is to me. To deny her that would be cruel, in the same way people who tell me I should be more feminine or have kids are missing the point where I'm concerned. She came out the womb that way, as I came out the womb my way, and you...'

'Always preferred dressing up to playing war.'

'Precisely. I'm guessing most of your friends are probably girls.'

'They are, but that's only really because most of the lads I grew up with were freaked out by me. They thought I was , to use their terminology, ' a fucking shirt-lifter'. Small-town, working class attitudes, honest toil and casual deep-rooted bigotry. You know how it is ?' Lauren nodded. It was an utterly predictable story. One she'd guessed at the first time she set eyes on him. That kind of ostracism was a rite of passage for a bloke like Jude. They all went through something similar, either eventually kowtowing to the norm for an easy life or becoming more outrageous to wind up the antagonists or in a few rare cases, not reacting either way and just getting on with being themselves. Like they should in order to be happy. Like she tried to do. Her youth hadn't exactly been a wonder of acceptance and understanding.

'Girls just seemed to accept me pretty much,' he continued, 'well some of them did. I had loads of girlfriends and my best mate was the girl all the lads ended up fancying. I think it gained me a bit of begrudging respect.'
'Joyce ? Sorry, Star you mean ?'
'Yeah, she kind of blossomed from about 15. Up until then she was dead nerdy and awkward, then she grew into this stunning young woman. They all wanted her.'
'Did you never fancy her then ?'
'Kind of. I saw she was attractive, but it was weird as she was like my mate from tiny so I just couldn't think of her that way. I don't with anyone very often. I think I'm probably a bit asexual, it just doesn't motivate me that much. I like conversation and being with someone who understands me but the whole physical thing just feels a bit of an effort a lot of the time. Unless it's someone really special, but I have to be sure that someone's broadly on the same wavelength before I start taking my clothes off. I just can't get off on the sex alone .Does that make sense ?'
'Ah yeah, totally. And it's refreshing to hear. A bloke who isn't steered through life by the demands of his groin. I think a lot of men's trouser areas operate as an autonomous republic.' Lauren wiped her mouth on the back of her hand. 'Another pint ? I'm enjoying this.'

Jude smiled and nodded his head. This night could go on forever as far as he was concerned.

'Oh god Star. What are you going to do ?'
Millie was sitting next to Star on the sofa. She'd walked into the front room to catch her distractedly pacing up and down. Her curiosity opened her mouth and asked Star what the problem was. As soon as Star outlined the bones of the whole sorry episode Millie was hooked and seemed to forget her own woes entirely. Now she held Star's hands in a mannered fashion and looked directly into her eyes as she spoke. Millie the love ally and relationship counsellor. She so rarely got the chance to do this with Lauren. Her flat-mate solved her problems by isolating herself in her room until everything had blown over. Then she'd emerge to make herself a sandwich and go out for a walk. She could be gone for hours. On her own as well. Usually down by the river in either direction. What was the point of that ? The mardy-cow. Star made for a refreshing girlie change. She seemed quite normal.
'I'm not sure what I'm going to do to be honest. I'm all over the place. I should try to be strong and think to myself, he left me for someone else, treated me like shit and then expects to just waltz back into my life but…'

'You're still in love with him ?'
'I think I am. We were together six years, you don't just suddenly fall out of love with someone after that length of time, just because they decide they can't live with you anymore.'
'In that case Star, I think you know what you have to do.'
Star looked at Millie's special big sympathetic face which she saved for just such occasions and nodded.
'I'll text him. We do need to talk.'

'Oh fuck it.' Lauren put her head down on the table. The alcohol induced feelings were just starting to slip from tipsy into mildly drunk. As she did so she slapped her face with her open palm, making Jude jump, then look awkwardly around the room to see if anyone else was looking. After about twenty seconds of Lauren lying face down on the table making groaning noises, she looked up, pulled her fringe down over her face, hiding her eyes, and shook her head. 'I just made an arse of myself in the Opera House. Why am I such a twat Jude ? You seem like a wise man, tell me that ?'
'You're not a twat.'
'Yeah, yeah.' She waved it away and took a glug of lager. She seemed impatient with herself. 'Doing that to Millie as well. I put that girl through fucking hell at times.'
'I'm the same with Star, but at least you're aware of it.'
'I am, I just don't know how to change.'
'Maybe you can't. Maybe you don't need to.'
Lauren shrugged and started pulling apart a beer mat. 'Fuck knows really. All I want from life is books to read, music to listen to, enough cash to pay my way and plenty of time left on my own. It's simple really, I don't know why everything suddenly gets all complicated when there's no need.'
'It's people. We're complicated.'
'I'm not complicated. I'm frickin simple.' Jude raised his eyebrows. 'Alright, perhaps I'm a bit complicated, but even so.'
'All I know is that it's just nice to meet someone who gets where I'm coming from for a change. Who feels like I do and for that Lauren, I'm pleased that fate has brought us together.'
'Ah fuck fate, it's just chance. But sometimes the odds just swing in your favour.' She finished off the dregs of her drink, slammed her glass down, stood up and grabbed Jude's arm. 'Come with me, I want to show you the river.'

Star was getting drawn further and further in. These words. They were the ones she'd imagined him saying to her for the past six weeks. Now she was really hearing them. She was sure the air in the room had changed. The whole thing felt vaguely cinematic and stylised. As if someone had scripted this for them. That Kyle was reading from an autocue. The words were right, the delivery almost flawless but something about the whole thing felt unreal. Forced. Brought about not by real feeling but by the demands of the narrative. Kyle was playing a part. Should she play one too and if she did would it lead to happily ever after ?

'I've just been really, really stupid doll.'

He called her doll. He knew she hated that. Whatever. At least he was admitting he was stupid.

'I just can't get you out of my mind. I don't know why I did it. I keep asking myself why.'

You're not the only one. Actually why did he do it ? What was that all about ? Premature mid-life crisis or something ?

'I just got my head turned.'

Head turned ? By something so shoddy. Jude said that Kyle leaving was symptomatic of something deeper, that it only happened because of failings in the relationship. Failings that Jude had seen for years and which primarily lay with Kyle. Mind you, it takes two to tango.

'Remember that time we went clubbing to Nottingham, and you lost your shoes. You'd taken them off because you couldn't dance in them and someone must have picked them up and wandered off.'

She knew this story. They left the club with her barefoot, but he scooped her up in his arms and carried her back to their B&B. It was meant to be a cut-above the run of the mill guest house. Kyle's treat. But the owners vision of upmarket seemed to resemble a cut-price version of a twee Country Living interiors spread from 1991. It was all pot-pourri and carved wooden wildfowl. She'd feigned being impressed so as not to hurt Kyle's feelings or to spoil the moment. Not that there had really been one come to think of it. Not for her anyway.

 He remembered that night as being one of fantastic sex, she remembered it as being a bit average and slightly embarrassing. He was always coming out with that same story. She tried to imagine someone carrying her cousin. It didn't seem very likely. She was too tall for starters. You'd have to be six foot five to even attempt it. The absurd image of someone attempting to romantically sweep Lauren off her feet made her chuckle inwardly, forgetting that she was meant to be listening to her former partner's big apologetic moment.

'So, if you'll have me Star, I really want to move back in. Give it another shot.'

'Oh I…' Now what ? Her stomach churned with an unpleasant knot of possibility. She wanted it. Yes, she wanted that. Not to be alone. But then, wouldn't that be a backwards step ? Oh god. Where are you Jude ?

'I can come round tomorrow if you like. Discuss it a bit more.'
'The thing is…'
'You don't want to. I understand why you wouldn't but I think I've really learnt something you know.' So he's been on a voyage of discovery has he ? Kyle's very own little Marco Polo moment. Aww bless. The tosser.
'No it's just I'm not…'
'You're not ready. Ok, that's fine. I'm staying at my dad's at the minute. We could see each other again for a bit, go out , talk things through, see where it leads. No pressure.'
'Look Kyle, the thing is…'
'You don't want to ?'
'No, I..' she didn't know what she wanted. 'I'm not in Newtham at the minute.'
'Oh. Where are you ?'

She noticed a change in his voice. Surprise definitely. His blustery confidence had immediately dissipated. She wasn't where he expected her to be. Sitting at home in the flat, waiting for him to call. As she had been for the past six weeks.
'I'm in York, with Jude. We're at my cousin's place.'
'I didn't know you had a cousin in York, what you doing there ?' He didn't seem very happy.
'It's a long story Kyle can I call you ? I need to think.'
'You do ?' She could tell that this wasn't how he imagined this particular script playing out.
'Yes. I do. I'll call I…'

But the phone at his end had gone dead. Star looked at her mobile and wondered how she felt. It wasn't immediately easy to pinpoint. Not how she imagined she would certainly. A couple of weeks ago if this had happened she would of broken into tears and almost bitten his hand off at the offer to come back. Now she wasn't quite so sure. Something was happening. Could she be moving on ? She'd text Jude. Just as soon as her hand stopped shaking.

Millie who had been listening from behind the front room door popped her head into the front room as her curiosity got the better of her.
'Hi babes..is it all OK ? You guys back on ?'
'Erm..no, it's complicated a the minute. I'm not sure I…'
'Oh alright.' Boring then. No big romantic reconciliation. 'Might take myself to bed before psycho-madam gets in. Not sure I can be doing with her madness at the minute.'
'OK, sleep tight.'

Star sat back down. Home alone again. Not that it really mattered did it ? This felt significant. Coming here was a good thing. She was sure of that, if for no other reason than it reasserted a little of her lost independence. The freedom she felt was positive. It was easy to forget that when you tie yourself so tightly to the emotional life of another you inevitably lose something of yourself in the process. If you gain more from being tied than you lose, then the sacrifice is worthwhile. If it's not then surely it's better to retain that emotional self-determination until the right circumstances and a person worthy of it come into your orbit. Tonight she was no longer sure Kyle really was that worthy. He could stew for a while whilst she tried to decide.

Jude and Lauren walked out of the pub into the night, continuing down the barely lit St.Martin's Lane and out into the now desirable terraced streets of Bishophill. They had undergone something of a makeover during the past decade and now modest undeveloped two-up, two-downs sold for the same price as sizeable semi-detached properties out in the leafier suburbs. Lauren liked it. It was handy for The Ackhorne but since stepping off the career ladder any remaining ideas of ever owning a place of her own had been put to bed.
'Mills and I looked at a place down here earlier in the year. To rent.'
'Not what you were after ?'
'It was dead nice, small but alright. The thing was it was right opposite one of Millie's ex 'this man is all I ever wanted' boyfriends and his new partner. She had a baby on the way as well and it was too much of a case of 'look at what you could of won' for Millie's comfort. It was like when they wheeled on the sit on lawnmower top prize at the end of Bullseye when the contestants were only going home with a shitty looking decanter.' She drew on her cigarette.
'Oh sorry, not offered you one.'
'I don't smoke.'
'Very wise.' She blew smoke in the air. 'It's a filthy habit. Although…'
'Yeah ?'
'You do have to admit it does make me look pretty damn hot.' Lauren grinned mischievously. It was the alcohol bringing out her playful side. That and the presence of a pretty attentive boy. She wanted to grab him, push him against the wall and snog his face off. But she resisted.
'Haha ! Yeah.' Jude blushed and pushed his fringe out of his face self-consciously. Did she know what he was thinking? 'You are sex on legs.' Whoops. Now she did. That had just popped out.
'Bloody hell mate you must have low-standards.' She tried to give his comment a matey brush-off but was trying hard to hide her pleasure at his words. People just didn't say things like that to her very often. Apart from Barry of course, but he was just a big fat beardy old perv who could get away with murder. He said stuff like that to everyone - old women on buses,

lollypop ladies. Actually, the lollypop lady near where he lived got so freaked out by his regular over-friendly flattery that she reported him to her employers. Lauren was convinced Barry was about to end up with a restraining order. And about time too.

They fell into an awkward silence as they both tried to work out what the other happened to thinking. Were they both feeling the same way and if they were what happened next ? These moments were as difficult as they were electric.

Soon they reached the river down by Skeldergate bridge where they joined the lit towpath that ran in front of once desirable eighties flats that were now beginning to show their age. A fat, fluffy pedigree cat in a window was stretched out in a hammock. It had one eye open and was keeping a sleepy watch on what passed. Lauren wondered if it ever ventured outside.

The lights flickered on the river. It was so quiet, the occasional car across the bridge not really breaking the silence but instead providing a little gentle background fuzz. The row of houseboats, the steam rising from their little hot air vents looked cosy and inviting. They walked on, past the entrance to Rowntree Park.

'It's beautiful down here.' Jude finally spoke.
'Glad you like it. I come down when I need to think. You can walk for miles along the banks.' She grabbed hold of his arm. 'Don't worry, I'm not going to make you walk miles. Just have a wander to clear my head before we go home.'

Lauren sat down on a bench overlooking the water and Jude joined her. There was more silence. There wasn't a millimetre between them but they gazed out at the water, not speaking, not making eye contact. After what felt like hours, but was in reality only a couple of minutes, Lauren turned and stared for a second at Jude's soft round cheek lit by the light.
'Where did you come from ?' She smiled at him.
He seemed slightly startled and unsure. 'Er..well from just up the road from where you come from.'
'No, not that. I mean, where did you come from ? I had no idea you existed this time yesterday now you're staying at the flat and I'm sitting with you on a bench watching the river. Life's weird. It throws stuff up when you least expect it.' Lauren continued to look at him but he seemed a little lost as to how to respond. 'Sorry I'm being a bit sixth-form poet aren't I ? I'm not good at profound.' She snapped a twig and threw it into the water.
'No, no, you're good. You're right. I know what you mean.' Jude paused. 'To be honest, you were not what I'd been led to expect.'
'And what was that then ?'
'Well Star seemed to remember you being a bit grumpy and withdrawn or something, and your auntie reckoned you were a lesbian.'

'Haha ! She wouldn't be the first.' She drew on her cigarette then blew smoke into the night air. 'Just to clarify I'm not a lesbian, although I have been tempted when faced by what most of the male population has to offer. I wouldn't say I'm grumpy either but I am definitely withdrawn. Anyway, I thought you were gay when I first set eyes on you.'
'That's what usually happens.'
'That's cool. Gay blokes are generally much more attractive. To me anyway. It's either the unobtainable thing or it's the streak of the feminine in them. I'd have loved to have been a gay man if I'm being honest. I'm hoping I get reincarnated as a notorious Swedish homosexual.'
Jude laughed. 'Why Swedish ? That's very specific.'
'They're frickin gorgeous. It's a question of cheekbones I think. Have you seen that woman from The Sounds ?'
'Cheekbones ? Lauren, yours are amazing. You could slice paper on them babies.'
Lauren smiled in a way you might call coy if Millie had done it. 'Yeah, but there's always room for improvement isn't there ?'
The silence returned. Lauren finished her cigarette. Jude eventually turned to her.
'Lauren, look I think I…'
'Don't say anything.'
'What.'
'Just don't say anything.'
She leaned into him and gently kissed his lips. He placed his arms around her and they hugged.
'Lauren…'
'You know this can't lead anywhere don't you.'
'But…'
'I really like you and everything Jude and I hope we'll always be friends but I just don't think I'm in the relationship business.'
'Oh right I…'
'If I was I could think of no better person than you to be in it with, but I'm just kind of OK with where I'm at. Does that make sense ?'
'Yeah it does. Kind of. I think I'm the same.'
'I thought you were. That's why I kissed you. Wanted you to see that I felt something. That you were worth it.'
'Thank you.'
'No, thank you mate. You've turned my night around. I don't fess up to much about myself with many people. It's rare I meet someone I think I can trust.' Jude let a big natural smile overwhelm his face. Lauren returned it and touched his nose playfully. 'Come on, let's get back home before I start getting cosmic again.'

Bright new morning…

Lee had risen early. He had found a real motivation to get out of bed and to try and make something of the day. It was a feeling he hadn't experienced for some time. To cap it all, the sun was shining. He opened the window of his bedsit to allow a little fresh air in. Mum would be pleased. She was always wandering into his room when he was a teenager to open his little top window. He loved that room. It was only a box room, Keeley got the larger one and you could barely see the wallpaper for Formula One posters. He wondered if mum had ever found his wank mags. He had a great hideaway for them, under the mattress. No wait a minute, mum used to change his sheets once a fortnight. Of course she'd seen them but never said anything. His stomach turned over a little. He thought of his mum rifling her way through 'G-String Grannies'. He'd got that off Graeme Hollis at school. He was a bit of a porn aficionado. His dad had loads in his garage and Graeme would nick them and swap them at school for tapes. Lee had swapped an AC/DC cassette and couple of rare Marvel Comics for G-String Grannies. It was a special edition. Not that the women in there were technically grandmas they were just a bit older than your usual glam mag fodder. Milf's if you like. Mothers I Would Like To Fuck. There were so many ways of categorising the opposite sex wasn't there ? Must be quite flattering for a woman who was knocking on to get called a Milf. He'd seen some of them had put it on their Myspace profiles. Their way of showing they still had it in them. That was the right idea wasn't it ? Have a lark, take the compliment, play along with it. Didn't mean anything. It was only mixed-up fuck-ups like Cassie who spent too long reading the Society pages of the Guardian that took offence at that kind of thing. Cassie had done Women's Studies before she trained to be a social worker, or as his old student mate Porkloin used to call it 'Dykes and Bag-Ladies anonymous.' Bag ladies because you had to put a bag over their heads whilst you were fucking them for fear their faces might put you off your stride. Cassie was alright though. She was quite a looker. He was drifting off into might-have-been melancholia again. Stop that right now.

No, he was definitely off older women now. They came with more baggage, more strange ideas. He was going younger. Naïve, stupid and pliable. Someone who'd look up to him and who he in turn could treat properly. Buy stuff for, take to new places. That kind of thing. Again, this was natural wasn't it ? Men were programmed to desire younger women, and women were programmed to want an older more clued up and together bloke. It was always the way. You only stored up problems for yourself if you went against it. He'd been deceived by modernity, by all these nonsensical ideas that had confused us as a species over the past few decades. Now he was getting back to basics. Back in touch with his core masculine energies and the result was fantastic. He'd not felt so alive for years. It was like the energy he had as a ten year old playing war on a long summer evening on the waste ground. He could feel it again. That essential pulse that made a man. Back then it was a flicker of what was to come. Or the growing seed that could see him shipped off to foreign parts a rifle in his hand in times of national crisis as he came of age.

Lee picked up his camera and switched it on. He held it at arms length, pointed it at himself and snapped. Looking at his image on the display window he wasn't too horrified. He didn't look half bad. Something was changing for the better here. Like Thom Yorke he had an art. Photography. It was so fucking obvious it bugged Lee just how long it had taken him to realise. What was wrong with you boy ? Authenticity. Naturalness. Being what nature meant you to be without complications. He was sure the streets would fit him better today. He looked out of his window and smiled. This was his world. He felt alright.

Lauren was working the morning at Ainsty Antiquarians, the little second hand bookshop down the road from the flat that provided her with part-time employment whilst she attempted to write her novel. The shop was run by a tall thin man with a full head of messy white hair that made him appear older than he really was. Lauren knew him only as Mr Lindacre. He wasn't the most talkative of people. He had a bookish, dusty air that seemed too Dickensian and appropriate to be true. But it was true. In Lauren's experience, York was full of exactly the kind of people you'd expect to find in a cathedral city. Owlish men in leather elbowed jackets flicked through slightly foxed old volumes on church history, awkward unfashionable young men leant their bikes outside the shop window before popping in to furtively finger their way through highbrow Victorian erotica, intense young women picked out books of literary criticism. All of which Lauren impassively keyed into the cash register, barely giving them a smile as she did so. More often than not she'd sit behind the counter and read her own current book. At the minute she was enjoying an old history of York. She'd read countless of these in the past, but each one of them told her something different. There was so much to know.

Working at a bookshop was fantastic. She was able to borrow things off the shelves without Mr Lindacre's knowledge, then return them in a few days when she'd done with them. Mr Lindacre seemed far too otherworldly to notice. But he couldn't be that dim. Ainsty was a thriving little business with an excellent local reputation. Oftentimes it was empty for hours, then suddenly it would fill up with eager single-minded bibliophiles handing over large amounts for rare volumes. It was a good place to work. Far better than Accent Advertising. Anything was better than Accent Advertising. She shuddered as she remembered the mind-numbing tedium, the dodgy air conditioning, Barry's post lunch earth quaking farts followed by cries of 'oooh scuse I.' She was grateful to at last be free of it. Also the freedom that came from stepping off the rat race escalator. There comes a point where you realise that a career as such is not really what you're about. That all you want is to earn enough to pay your way and have plenty of time left over to pursue what really interested you. In her case it was reading and writing. Even if it never really went anywhere, she was certain that she was doing what she was meant to be doing. It was where her joy lie. She was following her bliss.

Life had a certain easy logic to it at present. Things seemed to fit even if she sometimes wondered where she was ultimately heading. She had concluded from hours of pondering these questions that it was the question itself which was the problem. The idea that life had to make some kind of linear sense. Couldn't it just be lived and experienced from day to day, following interests and developing ideas and relationships with an open mind as to where that might take you ? That was a much more appealing way for her to think than by comparing herself to her peers. Thirty-something women with settled relationships, or high-flown careers, or a couple of sunny kids, the ones she saw on Myspace who lived locally but with whom she knew she could never be friends. Her life was too alien, her lack of desire for the conventional, her feeling that what passed for success in the terms of most of her contemporaries was empty. When Lauren clumsily attempted to define her own vision of success it was usually framed in terms of time for thinking, for growing as a person, for being true to who she felt herself to be without too much reference to what popular culture told her she should be as at this stage of her life. She didn't need to belong either to a man or to a family and the potential role of mother left her cold. There was not an ounce of her that desired that now, whereas previously she'd gone along with the lazy unquestioned assumption that one day she might. Having actually engaged with the question, then put it firmly to bed she felt liberated. A person again, not just a gender on a treadmill. Fair dues if that was what you wanted but how many people really sat down and questioned if it was what they wanted ? How many women got steamrollered by partners, by breeding peers, by their families into having offspring of their own ? Likewise with relationships. Single (largely) straight woman must require single straight man for mutually frustrating misunderstandings mixed in with generally unsatisfactory sex, supermarket shopping and a couple of holidays a year. The thought terrified her. The ugly normality of the masses. Intelligence and the ability to stand back and examine usually untouched assumptions was her strength. It was good at last to be Lauren Seymour. To finally be moving through the world in a way which honoured her deepest motivations. She had a room of her own. A computer, an income to cover her modest expenses and a vision of what life should be about. For her. Not for anyone else. They could work out their own salvation.

Which was one reason for her reticence about taking things further with Jude. A relationship was a complication. It would demand things of her. It would mean she had to do things she perhaps didn't want to do. Her freedom would probably be encroached upon. Add to that the fact he lived a hundred miles down the road through some of the most suicide inspiring flat desolate countryside in England. Any relationship would have to be conducted largely by telephone and weekend visits. Wet weekends in the East Midlands nowhere of Newtham was not what Lauren had in mind for the coming months. Even if she would be spending it with a lithe gorgeous boy with eyes you could swim in, who seemed to instinctively understand her and in whose company she felt totally at ease. She gazed at the floor of the shop and sighed. Pretty, pretty, pretty boy Jude. Where had you come from ? They'd walked home together the previous night, sat for a while in front of the TV and had a cup of tea with Star who had appeared a bit preoccupied. Jude and his best friend were planning on doing a spot of sightseeing today.

Just then the doorbell of the shop signified a customer. Or more likely a browser. They tended to major heavily on the browser front. York was a city built over the centuries specifically it would seem for the desires of ambling browsers. Lauren secretly wanted to punch them in the back of the head when they got in her way

'Good morning my anti-social friend ? How are we this fine day ?'
'Yay ! Franny you big fat queen ! How are you mate ?'
'None the better for seeing you I'm afraid.' He was doing his, I'm trying to display anger but really I'm just a bit indulgently amused face. It didn't convince anyone, but its marshalling let Lauren know something was not as it should be.
'Why ? What have I done ?'
'I've popped into the flat.'
'Oh god. Here we go.' Lauren rolled her eyes and shook her head. 'What's madam been telling you ?'
'Just that you had a bit of a hissy fit at the Opera House and proceeded to embarrass her. Did you know she's so ashamed she's phoned in work sick today ?'
'So ? That's her problem. I've done nothing wrong.'
'I think you know you have. Have you apologised to her ?'
'No I haven't ! Get off my case, she was in bed last night when I got in, and I

dashed off this morning before she was about.'

'You're going to need to speak to her.'

'Why ? Never gets us anywhere. She just needs to cool the jets and get over herself.'

'You are one of the most self-centred, unthinking people in the world when you want to be Lauren Seymour.' Francis folded his arms across his chest and shook his head.

'Fuck off ! I'm dead empathetic. You've said so yourself.'

'You are but I think you've got an on/off switch and you only turn it on when you feel like it.'

'If I let my emotions rule me Francis I'd be a complete wreck. I've been there, I know what I'm like. I've got to batten them down at times just to try and keep some sense of order in my life. I'm not just an unthinking bitch you know.'

'I know that. You know that. But does Millie know that ? You two are still feeling your way as housemates. You might have been friends for years but living together is a very different kettle of fish. I've had twenty years of lodgers, including this one lanky sullen anti-social woman who rarely came out of her room. Couldn't get rid of her. She hung around for years, but in the end I couldn't imagine living without her. Millie must be a dream to live with compared to you in the early months. Talk to the girl. She's meant to be your best friend.'

'I will, I will. Just give me a day or two eh ?'

'OK. I trust you to do the right thing.' Francis rubbed her shoulder and smiled. She'd come good. Of that he was certain.

Francis felt like family to Lauren. The difference being it was family that she actually got on with. When she moved in with Francis nine years earlier she had been the stranger. He had advertised for a housemate in the local paper and his was the third house she'd traipsed round to visit. The first one she'd seen was with a driven young woman who worked at Norwich Union in an immaculate flat on Skeldergate, the second was with an immediately lecherous musician and his girlfriend off Scarcroft Road. Then there was the Francis big gay palace. Or the big gay two-up, two-down in a shabby state of repair inhabited by an over the top, very effusive fat man who made her feel instantly at home. So she plumped for the room on Diamond Street. Not that she was in any way certain that she'd done the right thing. For a long time she confined herself to her room, keeping out the way of her landlord, until time gave her more self-confidence and their bond started to grow. The first visit Millie made to the new house was a roaring success. It ended with a drunken Francis and Millie serenading each other with songs from the Sound Of Music, and her best friend declaring that Lauren had found 'the best possible housemate ever.'So that was that then.

'Did you see our guests ?'
'Ooh yes. So I did. I thought initially it was two girls and you'd invited a lanky clone of yourself to stay for a bit of moral support, then I realised one of them was a pretty boy. Where *did* you find him ?'
'Dunno. Mate of my cousin's.' Lauren sighed. 'He's nice isn't he ?'
'Only really said hello. Millie collared me in the kitchen so I didn't get chance to say much. Something in your tone of voice tells me that you think he's rather fine though.' Francis raised a suggestive eyebrow.
'Yeah, no point hiding it.' She threw a resigned arm in the air. Everyone had rumbled her. 'He came round and found me in the pub last night. Had a good chat. We got on really well.'
'Excellent !' Francis clapped his hands together. 'So what's the problem then ?'
'Oh I don't know Francis. He's not going to be around for long is he and I'm not sure I need a relationship right now. It's not the right time.'
'It never is though is it.'
'Well, no, but I'm used to things as they are. They've taken a while to settle down, I'm not sure I need all that potential heartache.'
'Heartache ? Why does there need to be any heartache ? It's not compulsory you know.'
'You always get some.'
'Tony and I don't.'
'That's different.'
'Why is it ? Because we're both blokes ?'
'No, I didn't mean that it's just…'
'You're making excuses. My advice to you is give this boy a chance. You don't know what you might be closing the door on if you don't.'
'No, I've decided. It's too big a risk. I'll enjoy him being around whilst he is and try to keep in touch.'
'Well, as long as you know what you're doing. You shouldn't slam doors in the face of opportunity. You do have a bit of a habit of it.'
'It's not that, it's just that I'm happy. I'm alright you know. It's good being me.'
'That's something I'm pleased to hear because it's always been good to know you. You're a one-off Lauren Seymour. But I can't hang about. I've got to meet Tony at the theatre in ten minutes.'
'Send him my love. I'll pop round in a day or two.'
'You do that. We've not seen you at our place for a while. And remember.'
'What ?'
'Millie's your best friend. Talk to her.'
'Ok, Ok.'
'Ciao beanpole.'

'Bollocks fat boy.'

   Jude and Star strolled down Stonegate, a cobbled street of overhanging medieval timber framed buildings. It was all a bit different to the grey concrete 1960s High Street of Newtham, but neither of them appeared to be paying much attention to their surroundings.
'Why didn't you say earlier ?' Jude asked.
'Didn't get chance. You were a bit preoccupied with my cousin if I remember rightly.'
'Oh god, sorry sweet cheeks, I feel a bit awful for that.'
'Hey don't worry,' Star waved it away. 'It's allowed. No, I just hadn't found the right time. This is the first I've got you on your own properly since it happened. I didn't want to tell you just before bed last night as we'd of sat up into the early hours talking about it.'
'Thing is though, I couldn't sleep last night. My mind was whizzing.'
'Mine too.'
'So what have you decided ?'
'I don't know, I really don't know.'
'You know what I think about it all. He's bad news.'
'I know that, but…'
Jude stopped in the middle of the street. He grabbed Star by both shoulders and turned her towards him, looking directly into her eyes. 'Star, he's not a nice guy. He dumped you for a bimbo. She's bored with him and he wants to crawl back to you. You'd never be able to trust him. You've got to move on.'
'Oh I know that Jude, you just can't help your feelings.'
'Sometimes though they can't be trusted and in this case, you need to think more and feel less.'
'Easier said than done.'
'Well yes, but sometimes you've got to do the difficult stuff.'
'Says the person who runs from every relationship or job at the first sign of trouble.'
'That's not fair Star, it's you we're talking about here.' Jude looked mildly offended.
'OK, OK.' Star looked down Stonegate towards the Minster. 'Lets head there shall we.' She pointed in the direction of the huge gothic cathedral. 'See if we can find a bit of spiritual enlightenment.'

   Lauren was trying on a pair of oversized sunnies she'd picked up from a bargain bin at the second hand clothes shop just down from the flat. It was run by a blue-eyed shaven headed lad with a gentle bearing and a slight lisp. He seemed nice. Millie thought he was hot but then she would. This wasn't the season for sunglasses but they were only a pound and she could save them for next year. She was glancing at her reflection in the shop window immediately behind the counter when the shop-bell rang again. It was Mr Lindacre. He paused and looked at her slightly confused for a moment. It was a different confused expression to his normal everyday look of mild bewilderment doubtless caused by the decade dysphoria that had seen a man from 1862 forced to live his life in the early twenty-first century. Mother nature was a cruel random bitch at times. She never thought these things through.

'Oh Lauren it's you. I didn't see you behind your glasses.'

Lauren took them off, looked at them, folded them and placed them in the old school Dunlop bag Millie had bought her for her birthday from a little retro shop on Goodramgate.

'They're not really me are they ?'

'I don't really know much about these things.'

'No, of course not.' Did that sound too presumptuous and dismissive ? Away from work Mr Lindacre might be a fashion icon. Although it was perhaps more likely he kept the dismembered bodies of missing schoolgirls under the floorboards. 'How are you today ?'

'One has been better.' He brushed his hair which had momentarily drooped down over his eyes, back across his head with his hand. 'I've had a degree of difficulty with a noisy neighbour. Kept me awake most of the evening with, how can I put it.' He glanced towards the heavens for inspiration. 'Carnal noises.'

'Right.' Lauren shifted uncomfortably from foot to foot. Best not pursue this line of enquiry.

'I came very close to knocking on their door and requesting they desisted, or at the very least restrained their ejaculations.'

Lauren made her eyes wide, and strangled an emerging guffaw, trying to maintain a note of decorum in the presence of her bonkers employer. Had he really just said the word ejaculations with a completely straight face ? 'But you didn't ?'

'No. I decided against it.'

'Probably for the best.' She smiled and made a nervous chuckle. Mr Lindacre looked at her as if she were a disembodied vital organ in a Victorian specimen jar. It was beginning to freak her out.

'Miss Seymour. May I ask you a question ?'

'Sorry to be pedantic but it's *Ms* actually. But you can call me Lauren you know. That's kind of my name.'

'Good. Yes. I was thinking that maybe you would like to join me one evening for dinner ?'

'Oh.'

'Yes. Nothing fancy of course. Just something at my small cottage off Marygate. It's a bit of a bachelor pad I'm afraid, but I try and keep it homely.'
'Oh right. Erm..yes, er, of course. That would be nice.' Actually she hadn't yet had time to try and digest what the hell it might be.
'I don't get many visitors.'
Oh my god. Where had she heard that one before ? Neither did she, but she didn't get visitors in a perfectly regular and well-balanced kind of way, whereas Mr Lindacre probably didn't get visitors in a 'he was a bit of a loner' say the neighbours about man just convicted of his killing his mother kind of way. No mustn't think like that. He's probably just another introvert. Like her. One of the anti-social brethren. Why did they all have to be so frickin weird though ? Or was she just kidding herself when she thought that she was perfectly sane ?
'No, OK then. When did you have in mind ?'
'I don't have any suitable foodstuffs in my larder presently, so we shall have to make it in a day or two's time which will allow me opportunity to purchase the necessary provisions. Is there anything you prefer ?'
'What ? As in foodstuffs ?' God, she was at it now. This archaic speak was definitely catching. Too long spent in Ainsty Antiquarians and she'd be freely using words like 'verily' whilst discussing the ins and outs of Big Brother. It wasn't a totally happy prospect.
'Yes, as in what kind of fortification would you favour ?'
Now this was clearly just taking the piss. No one really spoke like that. Apart from Chris Eubank and he had issues. Great big fuck-off truck with no reverse gear size issues at that.
'Erm…Italian..that's always nice.' The first thing that came into her head.
'Good. I will acquire some fresh pasta, sauce and meatballs from Marks and Spencer. Then maybe you could arrive by around 8pm on Thursday.'
'Sure.' Lauren was completely flummoxed by the whole conversation. Buying in M&S food especially though. In Lauren's book that definitely ticked the box marked 'classy.' If she'd have been entertaining she'd have wandered to Budgens last minute and bought a couple of packets of pre-packed sandwiches and a big bag of kettle chips. What the hell was this invitation about though ?
'You won't have any problems digesting meatballs ?'
'I'm sorry ?'
'Meatballs. Can you eat them ?'
'Erm…yeeessss..' Lauren was now giving him a look that said 'you're weird Mr' but Mr Lindacre appeared to be too otherworldly to ever possibly notice.
'Good. I wondered if you might be vegetarian.'
'No,' she laughed again. 'I just look ill because I don't eat properly.' Actually, her diet was almost vegetarian, but this wasn't an ethical or moral stance. Just

that she ate a lot of snacks.

'You don't ? Do you have some kind of disorder ?' He seemed slightly concerned.

'Oh, god no. Well not properly. Don't worry about it.' She wanted to draw this awkward conversation to a close. 'Eight on Thursday. I'll look forward to it.' Would she ? Would she really ?

'Yes. Good.'

With that he turned sharply on his heels and headed through the shop into the back room. Lauren watched him with a wide-eyed quizzical look as he disappeared through the long narrow gaps between the crammed bookshelves, and through the door into the rooms that lie at the back of the shop. She hoisted herself up onto the small swivel chair in the window of the shop and fired up the cash register. Frickin freaky weird shit. Please someone just make it stop.

Camera obscura…

Lee didn't look up very often. Now he was wondering why not. Everything was immense today. This place. It made you gasp at times with its antiquity and its sheer goddamn beauty. You just took it for granted usually didn't you ? Any length of time living here and it became like everywhere else. It was only when you stepped back and really clocked the place proper that you saw it wasn't like anywhere else. Just how many other places had the largest gothic cathedral north of the Alps slap bang in the middle of town ? Well, none actually. He stared up at the great West End of the Minster. It was disorientating. It seemed to reach up forever. Pointing to the heavens. How must it have looked to people when it first went up ? They would have felt as if they were in the presence of something mighty and unreal. As if god really did live there. Maybe god did live there. He might be looking down on Lee now. Smiling at him. 'At last', he'd be saying to his divine self, 'that Canning lad has really got it sorted. Nice work fella.'

He lifted up his camera which he'd strung around his neck to let people know that he was a photographer, put it to his eye and clicked. Not bad. He'd just taken a photo of where god lives. Good sense of perspective and height. Might make it black and white on Photoshop when he got home.

He began walking around the perimeter of the Minster towards the statue of Constantine the Great. He wasn't looking where he was going and a middle-aged cyclist who had been furiously ringing his bell to signal his presence had to swerve out of his way. Lee remained oblivious. Too lost in the possibilities of his new start.

There were a group of Japanese tourists taking photographs of themselves and making John Lennon style peace signs in front of the statue. Lee thought this was a strange thing to be doing seeing as Constantine was such a warrior. Read your history folks. He snapped at the statue and noticed on the edge of his photo he'd inadvertently captured one of the Japanese girls. She looked quite cute. They dressed a bit weird though didn't they ? As if they'd just wandered out of one of those Manga cartoons. Not to worry, she was definitely better to look at than a camp looking statue of a Roman. He retreated a little and glanced to where the Japanese group had moved to. They were standing on the steps by the door to the Minster, milling around wondering what to do next. Lee pretended to be taking a photo of part of the architecture but in reality he was capturing the image of two of the girls. They were talking to each other and smiling, one threw her head back as she laughed and pointed at the other. He wondered what they were talking about. For a moment he imagined them kissing. Two girls. How hot would that be ? He took the photo quickly then began to move away. One of the robe wearing stewards on the Minster door had noticed him and was casting something of a suspicious look in his direction. Best not hang around. He stepped backwards and clattered into someone.
'Watch it !'
'Sorry I...' Lee turned sharply. It was the girly-man from yesterday. With him stood the cute girl.
'Hey, it's you who showed us where to go yesterday.' She spoke to him and smiled. The girly-man looked on with what Lee took to be a pleased with himself grin. Fecking idiot.
'Yeah. Hi.' Lee was embarrassed. He could feel his earlier confidence seeping away, leaving him feeling increasingly naked and a little foolish. It was the girly-man's presence that did it.
'Thanks so much for helping us out.' Lee couldn't speak, he just smiled. The girl noticed his camera. 'What you up to ?'
'Oh, just taking a few snaps.' He picked up the camera held it to his eye and quickly snapped them both, then grinned. The girly-man raised his eyebrows at the girl who looked on open-mouthed for a second. 'I'm a photographer.' There, he'd said it. He was as well. It hadn't sounded stupid. It was his new career. That's what all this was about.
'Gosh, a photographer Jude. That's great.' The girl looked back at her disbelieving friend who didn't appear to be very impressed. Had the girl just called him Jude ? That was a girl's name. There were a few bloke Judes, like Jude Law for instance but he was almost a girly-man himself. What did women see in these soppy freaks ? Jude Law had been out with Sienna Miller for god's sake. Lee needed to find some words.

'I could take some photos of you if you like. You'd be a great model.' Ha ! Stick that fucking girly-man. That's how a real man goes about things. No fucking about, just straight in there.

'Oh I…' The girl seemed a bit embarrassed. That's natural maybe. Bet she's flattered though. She's bound to be. Every girl secretly wants to be a model. I bet even Cassie quite liked the idea underneath all that feminism shit. Girls want to be pretty. It's why Argos sell shed-loads of Barbie dolls. Something for them to aim for.

The girly-man took hold of the girl's arm and began moving her away. The cheeky bastard. Didn't like it up him did he. Actually, he probably did seeing as he was dead cert bender. You didn't need a gaydar to spot that.

'Well it's been lovely seeing you again.' The girly-man spoke. 'But must dash. Bye.' He grabbed the girl by the arm and pulled her away. Yes thought Lee. Freaked the fucker out. Who's laughing now eh ? He knows that girl liked being told she was attractive. In not so many words. And now he feels fucking threatened. Serves him right. The smug effeminate little bitch. Fucking Simon Redburn all over again. Lee could teach the sly little twat a thing or two given half a chance. Remind him of his place in the pecking order.

Lee quickly turned and snapped at the back of the couple as they moved off. He then looked at his two photos. There they were. Trapped in his camera. The girl had a beautiful mouth. Really full lips. He imagined what it must be like to kiss them, to feel them tracing a moist line across his body. As this thought began to spread uncontrollably through his eager grey cells, he felt the first stirrings of arousal further south.

But the girly-man was in them as well. Looking at him, judging him, laughing at him. Standing there with his failure on display as if it were something to be proud of. Photoshop would sort him out. Remove him from the picture. Delete him from Lee's view.

He would take some more photos of the Minster. Maybe he could sell the prints to tourists ? Then he'd wander into the Museum Gardens. See if there were any young women he could capture in his viewfinder from a distance. The zoom on this thing was quite handy. Really powerful for such a little piece of kit. Then it would definitely be time to go home. Lee Canning. The photographer. Captor of people. The numero uno of his own little digital universe. He was doing alright. He impressed himself.

'Ohmigod what a weirdo.' Jude was slightly incredulous about what had just happened. 'Just taking our photo like that ?'
'Aww leave him alone. He seemed quite sweet. Just a bit awkward.'
'No way ! He's a mentalist. You can tell. All that stuff about you modelling for him. Weird.'

Star slapped Jude's chest playfully. 'Shush Jude. Leave the poor guy alone. You know nothing about him. We'll never see him again.'
'Wouldn't be so sure. He liked you.'
'Don't.' She shuddered. 'You never leave things alone.'

'Millie are you in ?'
Lauren shouted down the hallway as she slammed the front door of the flat behind her. Her morning had flown by. There had only been a trickle of customers and her own mind had been whirring with all kinds of randomness. What she was going to say to Millie ? How had Dimitri Montage come up with that stuff. And Jude. Especially Jude. Try as she might she just couldn't force his pretty face from her mind, even if his eyes and lips in her mental image kept wanting to merge into Millie's. And she really didn't fancy her flatmate. Honest. She'd decided this was the case years ago and it was definitely remaining that way.

There was no response from her friend. 'Mills, I know you're not working today and you had nowhere to go. We need to talk don't we ?' Still no sound from her friend, the woman who usually bounced down the hall talking ten to the dozen whenever she heard Lauren return. 'Are you in your room ?'

Lauren knocked on the door to Millie's. No answer. She put her ear against it but could hear nothing. Opening the door, she tentatively peered inside. There was no sign of her flatmate.
'Millie ! Where are you ?' She shouted down the hall, walking in to the front room but again finding it bereft of anyone. She flung her bag down on the sofa, sighed and went into the kitchen to put the kettle on. On the little bistro table in the corner there was a note. Lauren picked it up and read it :

Lauren,
I've gone out. Don't know when I will be back.
Millie.'

No kisses, no Millie flourishes, no flower doodles in the corner. She was obviously still fuming. Lauren made herself a mug of tea, wandered back into the front room and retrieved her phone from her bag. Time to break the habit of a lifetime. Dialling Millie's phone she waited for it to start ringing. It didn't, the click of the voicemail service immediately fired up.
'Oh hi Mills, it's me...er...Lauren that is. But you probably knew that already. Just wondering where you were that's all. Could you give me a bell chucky-egg ?'

Ten minutes passed. No response was forthcoming. This was starting to bug her. Millie was always immediately available. Making another attempt at trying to read yesterday's paper failed. Down on the street a young man in an oversized ill-fitting suit was hassling a young woman in a skimpy dress. It must be the races or something. Maybe that's where Millie's gone ? No don't be stupid, she's probably not even aware of where the racecourse is. She put the TV on and flicked through the freeview channels. Half of them weren't working again. QVC briefly engaged her. She was wondering if the waist of the perma-tanned presenter's trousers could get any higher before it got classified as an astral object. No it was no good. She wandered listlessly into the kitchen. There on the work surface was a box of Nicorette Patches. Millie had bought them for her a couple of weeks ago and Lauren had briefly gotten the hump with her 'fucking nannying.' It had passed though and giving up smoking had never been mentioned again. Lauren picked them up, read the back of the box and sighed. It was no good. She needed to get out.

Lauren stood flicking through the racks at HMV with her earphones in as she tried to zone out to The Concretes on her MP3 player. She'd been forced to use HMV following the closure of her beloved Track Records, a long standing York institution that had recently bitten the commercial bullet. She didn't know what she was after. Nothing really and to be honest her mind was too busy with wondering where Millie was and why she wasn't communicating with her. It was quite unlike Mills to sustain anger for any length of time. Her blow-ups tended to be brief and temperamental. She was nothing if not fickle. This was deeply unsettling.

Lauren hated arguing with her best friend. Millie was a certainty. Lauren had precious few of them. Nothing must endanger that. Despite her best intentions she couldn't concentrate on the CD racks, so she walked back up Coney Street, nipped in the newsagent bought a Guardian, a chunky Kit-Kat and another packet of cigarettes. Handing over a tenner she shoved them in the bag and gave a sneery grin to the unsmiling young man behind the counter. Today was going to be one of those days.

Finding herself a spot on a bench in the Museum Gardens she enjoyed the weak watery sunshine. At least it wasn't raining. An attempted read of the paper came to nothing. Half way through reports she'd realise that she'd taken none of it in. So she'd stop go onto something else, before giving the whole thing up as a bad job.

'This is ridiculous.'

She took her ciggies and lighter out of her bag, drew out a tab and looked at it. Putting it back in the box again she shook her head and sighed.

'Millicent Croft you sneaky little minx.'

Out of the corner of her eye she noticed a man, probably about her age, perhaps slightly older. He was a bit dishevelled. He had a vague smile on his face that Lauren immediately slotted into the box marked 'three sheets to the wind.' A camera was strung around his neck and he was staring at something. She followed his line of vision and saw three young women. Students probably. Pretty, busy girls in skinny jeans and ballet pumps. They were talking animatedly. Lauren looked back at the man. He was pointing his camera at them. The zoom was extended. Weird. She kept watching him discretely. Now he was looking at the display window at the back of his camera. He must of sensed someone looking as he glanced in her direction. Lauren quickly looked down at her newspaper. He was unsettling. She was sure he was taking a photo of those girls. That wasn't right was it ? Or was she overreacting ?

The article was something about negotiations for a treaty to tackle global warming over which the US was dragging its heels. Same old, same old. Should she bothered by this ? She did recycle her rubbish and her carbon footprint as a non-driving singleton who largely worked from home must be pretty minimal. But she couldn't get that exercised about it all. When the waters start lapping she might have to learn how to swim a bit better. Fuck it. She looked awful in a swimsuit. And as for a bikini, you just don't want to go there. Try Miss Anorexic Ladyboy 1997 during the swimwear round as a mental image and you wouldn't be too far wrong.

She turned the page then briefly looked up. The man was pointing his camera directly at her. It clicked. He removed it from his eye, looked across at her and smiled. That just wasn't on. She jumped to her feet, threw her paper to one side, sending pages flying across the grass, and stormed across to the man who retained his eye contact, and maintained his grin.
'What the fuck do you think you're doing ?'
'Oh, sorry love.' He grinned. 'I'm a photographer. I was just taking your picture. It's for an exhibition.'
'I'm not your love and I think you'll find it's polite to ask permission first.'
'Well the thing is you see, if I did that then you'd start posing and the shot would lose it's naturalness.'
This threw her. Maybe he was a photographer. Deep breaths Lauren. Think. Come on. Think.
'What is the exhibition about then ?'
'Oh, it's called The Women Of York. It's a little tribute to all the ladies who live here or pass through.' He had a clearly false tone to his voice. Like that fella from the Gold Blend adverts in the 80s. It was crap school of charm at work. He looked her straight in the eyes. 'I want to capture something of their beauty.'
This was creepy. It didn't feel right. He was clearly talking bollocks. 'Can I see my picture please ?'
The man smiled and shook his head. 'Oh no, I couldn't allow that. I'm an artist you see.'

'I really need to see it.' She made a grab for the camera but he pulled it away.
'Now don't you start getting difficult sweetheart.' His voice changed, non-specific northern with a hint a menace. 'There's no need for that.' The guy was definitely a creep. Of that Lauren now had little doubt. 'I'm not sure I'll be using yours' anyway.' He chuckled to himself. 'To be honest I wasn't really sure if you were a boy or a girl until I got you in the zoom. Then of course I saw you had breasts. Small breasts.' He leered at her chest. 'You should make more of an effort love. You're not top draw but you're not dog rough either. You wouldn't be my first choice but I doubt I'd chuck you out me bed if I found you there.'
'You cheeky fucking bastard.' She grabbed hold of him by his anorak collar and lifted him to his feet. 'Show me that fucking photo or I shop you to the nearest copper alright ?'
'Calm down you mad cow. It's only a photo.'
'It's a photo of me which I don't give you permission to have. I own this face alright.' She let go of him and pointed at herself. The man was still grinning and occupying her personal space, even though he could now move back if he wished.
'Are you a dyke ?'
'What ?'
'Are you a lesbian ? You look like one. If you are could you tell me what it's like ? Two women. I've always wondered.'
'Right. That's it.' Lauren was incensed, she made another grab for the camera, this time making contact and ripping it from his hand.
'Give me that back.'
'You can have it back when I've deleted my photo.' The camera was similar to her own and she had no problem finding how to display images on the little window at the back. It immediately threw up the last shot that had been taken. It was of her, sitting on the bench, the zoom at close quarters meant her head and shoulders almost filled the shot. She hated looking at her own image anyway but this was just creepy. She quickly hit the delete frame as the man started trying to reclaim his camera. He made a lunge at her. She dodged out of the way and then started to run down the grass bank to where the three girls were standing. Hearing the kerfuflle they broke their conversation and looked towards her running figure.

'See that bloke.' She pointed at her pursuer. 'He's been taking photos of you.' The girls looked at each other startled and then looked towards the man. Lauren paused by them and looked at the camera. There on the display was the photo of the girls. The man stopped running and walked towards her with his arm stretched out.
'Give me that fucking camera.'
   Lauren quickly scanned the images. They were full of close quarters shots

of young attractive women. Wait a minute. There was one of Star and Jude. What the hell was that doing on there ? Did he know them ? There was definitely something not right here. She hit something on the camera and a message popped up on the screen :

Delete All Frames

Immediately she hit the OK button and sent the whole lot of them into nothing. She looked up.
   'Here you go fella.' She chucked him the camera and began walking off, giving the man a little backwards wave as she did so. He caught the camera, and anxiously tried to see if his morning's work was still etched on the memory card. It wasn't.
'You fucking bitch ! You mental fucking bitch !'
Without looking back, Lauren gave the guy the finger and carried on walking, her heart beating double-time in her chest as she did so. She wasn't going to run though. She'd keep a steady, consistent pace and not get freaked. He wouldn't dare try anything on would he ? Not when town was so busy.
   The man incensed began furiously snapping at her moving away from him, photo after photo, after photo until she was no more than a dot on the screen and a message popped up that his card was now full.

Seriously snapping...

Lee was perched on his bed. His mind was raging. How dare that dykey boy-woman do that ? Who the fuck did she think she was ? She had no right to delete his photos. HIS photos. No one else's. He was the photographer. He was the artist. No one had any right to tell him what he could or couldn't take photos of. What had happened to the right to free expression ? It was all being eaten up by the endlessly politically correct minority who tried to police perfectly normal, perfectly reasonable behaviour. It wasn't if he was hanging around playgrounds taking photos of kids was it ?
   The world was full of freaks today. Stroppy dykes who accost you for no reason, and weird girly-men who want to take the piss. The whole place had gone mental. At least he had some photos of the boy-woman in his camera. He'd load them up to his computer. Take a look at them. See if they gave him any clues as to why this had happened.
   The photos didn't help much. Just the back of the boy-woman as she

walked away, although the more he looked at her and thought about it, the more her frame seemed familiar somehow. He was sure he'd seen her about. She was tall for a girl. Taller than him at least and he was five foot ten. She must be pushing six foot. Her bag seemed familiar. It was one of those Dunlop retro looking shoulder bags. Like kids used to have for school back in the day. That was it. He knew now. She walked up and down this street. He'd seen her sitting in the window of the second hand bookshop. The silly bitch. She hadn't banked on him knowing where she worked had she ? Might have to pay her a visit. He couldn't just sit back and passively take stuff anymore. That was what had landed him in so much trouble previously. He needed to take hold of life. Assert his own agenda for a change. He plugged in his computer printer and heard it whirr itself ready. He filled it full of paper and started printing off images of the boy-woman. A dozen in total which he then preceded to blu-tack onto his walls. He would of rather they had been images of all the different girls he'd been snapping but that silly bitch saw to it that he couldn't. So for that crime alone, she would be forced to be stuck to his wall. He stood back and admired his handiwork. Oh yes. He'd got her now.

Lauren decided it was time for a nerve steadier. She wandered into the Wonky Donkey aka The Three Legged Mare, a York Brewery Pub with a strict no-children policy that gave her a frisson of vindictive delight every time a flustered anorak clad tourist couple complete with miniature versions of themselves attempted to gain entry. One of the bar staff would rush across and shoo them away. It shouldn't give her pleasure of course, but she was grateful that at least some places offered a bit of sanctuary from the breeders. Not that she had anything against them of course. Some of her best friends were parents. No, that was a lie. She only had two friends. One was a gay bloke, the other couldn't find a man willing to hang around long enough to inseminate her. Her parents were parents though and they were alright in small doses. Which reminded her. When was the last time she phoned them ? Must be about three weeks now. Best see what they're up to before too long. They'd given up phoning her as she never answered the thing. And wasn't she a child once ? She must have been, although she always did used to find other children annoying now she came to think about it. Whatever, she'd have a bottle or two of nice cider, kick back, read the paper, see if she could get hold of madam.

It was amazing how quickly she managed to recover from freaky disturbances these days. Once upon a time the encounter in the Museum Gardens would have unsettled her for days. It was like the time a bald middle aged man with a dodgy French accent and a dank smelling ragged wool coat sat down next to her in the pub one night and informed her he had a bomb in his bag. Turned out he was just spinning some elaborate yarns - stuff about his wife being dead, being a lecturer in European Literature at Montpelier University, about having his money stolen from him. She'd not known whether or not to believe any of it at the time, but she'd emptied her pockets of change and let him have it. For the next few days she'd thought of little else than this unsettling encounter. Today though, the perv in the park barely bothered her. She was pleased with herself for deleting his photos. He didn't have any right to go round snapping women he didn't know like that. Doubtless he was back buzzing around town filling up his memory card again but at least she'd made a stand.

Out of the corner of her eye she saw two figures walk past the pub on the street outside. She recognised them. One was the slender elegant figure of Jude. He was arm in arm with Star. Lauren felt a small twinge of jealousy. She knew that it was nothing more than close friendship with those two but the sight of someone else being intimate with that beautiful boy made her heart ache a little. She sighed and tried to concentrate on the newspaper. Seconds later she became aware of being watched. Two faces were pressed right up against the glass of the pub window squashing their noses and distorting their features.

'What the fuck !' Lauren jumped up alarmed. The two faces removed themselves from the window and started chuckling. It was Jude and Star. They must have seen her. Soon the door to the pub was swinging open and in they walked.

'Did we make you jump then ?' Jude teased with a grin on his face.
'You frickin did ! Nearly had a heart attack. This isn't the day for nasty surprises.'
'Ooh why not.' Jude unpeeled his coat and Star followed suit. They sat down opposite her at a table in the window of the pub.
'Had this weird encounter in the Museum Gardens. Saw this guy taking photos of these girls I didn't think he knew, then next time I look he's pointing his camera at me. Then it gets really weird.'
'Why ? What happened ?'
'I went across to him, told him I didn't appreciate having my picture taken without being asked and I grabbed the camera off him.'
'You didn't ?' Star was open mouthed.
'I did. And I deleted my photo, then looked through the rest. All pictures of attractive young women just wandering about. Really freaky.'
'Urrghh. The creep.' Star made a little shudder.
'There's more. One of the photos was this close quarters shot of you two.'
Jude looked at Star. 'That was that bloke from earlier !' He jabbed Star in the ribs. 'I told you he was a perv.'

'Does that make some sense then ?' Lauren looked at them.
'Yeah, it does. We bumped into the guy who we asked for directions to your place yesterday. He was a bit odd with us, then all of a sudden just pulled out his camera, shoved it in our faces and took one.'
'Weird.'
'And he asked Star to model for him.'
'Really ?' Star nodded. 'Nutjob by the sounds of thing. Not that I mean you couldn't model of course. You clearly got the looks in our family. In fact you look nothing like mum's family at all ? Suppose that's a blessing.' There was a reason for that of course but Star wasn't sure whether or not Lauren actually knew she was adopted and who her real mother was ? That story could probably wait for a bit. Lauren finished her cider. 'Are you two stopping then ? Shall I get in another ? '
'Yeah go on then. We've no place to be in particular. We're on a road trip.' Star relaxed into her seat. Jude gave Lauren a little smile of acknowledgement which gave her a tremor that Millie would of recognised. It momentarily unsettled her which was more than the creepy camera guy had managed.
'Excuse me a sec. I think I just need to nip outside for a fag.'

    Lauren stood on the step of the pub dragging on her cigarette and gazing upwards so as to prevent herself from glancing in the direction of Jude and Star sat at the window seat inside. What was happening to her ? Her feelings were getting out of control. She couldn't help herself.
    The cigarette was helping calm her nerves but it was no good. She couldn't resist glancing discretely over her shoulder into the pub. Jude was standing at the bar handing over a tenner. He was smiling. It was a beautiful, engaging smile. Her heart was melting. Deep breaths. Finish off the fag. Stop being so frickin rubbish and get back inside. Talk to Star. Catch up on old times. Lauren stubbed her cigarette out in the bucket of sand provided and wandered back inside.
    'What's your plans then. How long do you intend on hanging around ?'
'Oh god sorry Lauren we feel awful about just turning up and expecting to kip on your floor, it was dead cheeky of us. We'll head off tomorrow. I think we should go home.'
'Star ! No. We've only just come away.' This was the first Jude had heard of this.
'Where are we going to go Jude ? Neither of us have any ideas, neither of us have much money. It's done me good to get away for a couple of days but I think we should head back. There's work I need to catch up with.'
'Sure it's not Kyle you want to catch up with ?'
'Kyle ?' Asked Lauren.
'He's Star's ex. They split up a few weeks ago, but now he's sniffing about

again.'

'But you're not interested ?'

'She is, but she's not to get in touch with him as he ran off with someone from work who must have got bored with him.'

'Jude ! Let me answer for myself.' Star took a gulp of her drink and gathered herself. 'It's difficult Lauren, I loved him and we lived together for so long. We had a lot of good times together.'

'But ?'

'He just suddenly took off with someone from work, came right out of the blue, told me one day it was all over and that he was leaving. It knocked me sideways.'

'It almost killed you Star.'

'Don't exaggerate Jude. It wasn't that bad.' She pushed the memory of herself sat on the edge of the bath with a razorblade in hand to one side.

'Exaggerate ? Moi ?'

Lauren smiled at Jude who returned it.

'What do you think Lauren ? We talked on the phone last night. He seems dead sorry about everything. I think I should probably forgive him.'

'Bollocks !' Lauren almost shouted her response.

'What ?'

'Bollocks to what you're saying about forgiving him and bollocks that belong to the twat that you should probably remove given half a chance. The sleazy arse.'

'Hahaha !' Jude started laughing. 'Told you that's what she'd say.'

'Oh.' Star looked disappointed.

'You can't take someone back who does that to you. It'll happen again. You can't let people treat you like that. I'm hardly the most traditional person on the planet but monogamy in my book means monogamy. He's a loser. You're better off without him.'

'But you've never met him. I used to see…'

'Yeah, yeah, a different side to him and all that. You've told me all I need to know. He walked out on you for someone else, now he wants you back, which gives you the perfect opportunity to tell him to fuck right off.'

'I see.'

'You know it really, you just want to hold out the possibility that he might have changed and that he still loves you. You've got to get your self worth from inside though, not from whether or not some dodgy wandering bloke likes you or not. Jude loves you don't you mate.'

'God yeah, I love her to bits.'

'But it's different ?'

'How is it ? You don't need people in your life who fuck you about, it's better to have fewer people who you can rely on rather than a load of them who screw you over. Significant other's included. That's why I stay single and don't have many mates. I keep myself intact and content.' This was less advice, more Lauren's philosophy of life. It was good to get the opportunity to articulate it now and again. Millie would never buy it, and just occasionally Lauren needed to hear herself say it to remind herself that it was what she was about.

'Is that enough though ? Don't you get lonely ?' Star asked.

'Course I do. Now and again, but then so do people in relationships. Some of the loneliest people in the world are those stuck in loveless couples, or who have tons of mates but none who really know them that well.'

'I suppose you're right.'

'You know she is.' Jude stroked her hand. 'Let me have your phone.' Star rummaged in her bag and handed it over. Jude flicked it on and found the address book. He found Kyle's number then handed it to Star. 'Here, delete it.'

'I can't.'

'You can. Go on.' Lauren added her own encouragement.

Star looked at Jude, then looked at the phone, her finger hovering above the button that would send her ex partner's number into the nothing. Then she did it. Sat back in her chair, looked at Jude, then at Lauren and smiled. 'I did it.'

'Yay ! Big hug.' Jude threw his arms around her.

'This calls for a celebration. What we all drinking ?' She stood up and left the two friends to share a potentially significant moment. She'd helped facilitate this hadn't she ? A bit of her philosophy had helped someone else take a step forward. Her stomach sank for a second. That was quite a responsibility. What if she'd just pushed Star to make a big mistake ? She glanced at Jude. His face was beaming. He'd seemed quite certain. She'd just have to trust that pretty face was right about Star's relationship wouldn't she ? A relationship she'd never herself seen in action. She'd put faith in the idea of Jude having the right perspective. Why ? Because he's Star's best friend ? What idea about her own relationships would people have if they listened to Millie ? Lauren didn't like this train of thought. She picked up their empty bottles and headed back to the bar. Trouble no one, be troubled even less. Had she just broken her own cardinal rule ?

Princess diaries...

'What was it you said you wanted again flower ?'

Francis was busying himself in the kitchen as Millie slouched on the futon in the little two-up, two-down terraced Groves house. She'd taken up his invitation to escape the flat for a while. To talk things through. He always had such a good listening ear. Like a wise-headed older brother, or a father figure even. Completely different to her own dad whose idea of comforting emotional counsel didn't run much further than handing over a twenty pound note from his wallet. He doted on Millie enough, just struggled to put his feelings into words. Francis was like a big gay dad who understood what you were going through. Everyone should have a big gay dad. Millie didn't know how she'd managed prior to discovering her own.
'Oh, I don't know. I think I'm off my food.' She sighed in her ordinary over the top fashion, but somehow it seemed more full of feeling than usual.
'Now don't start getting like that. You'll be as bad as lanky-madam.'
'She never eats.'
'No but you always think carefully about your food. Tell your Auntie Francis what you'd like and I'll knock you something up.'
'Salad ? Can I have a salad.'
'And a baked potato ?'
'And a baked potato. Oh with grated cheese please as well.'
Francis smiled at her. 'Of course you can princess.' He turned on the oven, quickly washed a potato and threw it inside, took off his pinny and carried two mugs of tea into the front room. He sat down next to Millie and took a sip.
'I'm fed up Francis.'
'I can see that sweetheart, you're normally like a little bundle of sunshine. What's come over you ?'
'It's the Lauren thing. And the Damian thing. I'm feeling a bit unloved.'
'Awww, I love you.'
'Thank you.'
'Lauren is difficult, we both know that. She can be a complete mare at times, but you two have been friends for years, you'll come through this. Just chat with her.'
'She's not an easy person to talk to always. I think she thinks I'm a bit silly and giddy.'
'She loves you to bits. She just never tells you. It's the differences which make you work, but they might sometimes mean you misunderstand one another, even after all these years of being joined at the hip.'
'Maybe.' Millie didn't seem convinced.
'And what's the deal with Damian ? I thought you two had the perfect relationship. He's a lovely boy.'
'He's just gone a bit quiet on me. Don't know what's wrong. He seems dead off-hand on the phone and every time I try and arrange to go see him or him

to come over he makes an excuse. I've not seem him for over a fortnight. That can't be right. I thought he loved me ?'
'Oh dear. I'm never sure what goes on in young men's heads half the time.'
'Has Tony mentioned anything ?'
'Noooo…he's not really one for the relationship thing, he wouldn't mention if he had. He's a simple man of simple tastes who minds his own business. A bit like beanpole for that actually.'
'Really ?' This was an interesting and unexpected insight..
'Oh yes. They're quite similar. I'm sure a therapist would have a field day with that wouldn't they.'
'You and Lauren would have made a lovely couple.' Millie giggled.
'Don't even joke about it. Imagine that ! Living with her ! Wait a minute, I think I did for the best part of a decade.'
'Aww bless her. She means well really.'
'She does, she's a one-off.'
'Where is Tony anyway ? I though he was off work ?' Tony was meant to be retired. He spent his days baking bread, doing his watercolours and tending to the gardens of a few elderly less mobile friends.
'He is, just nipped to the doctor's.'
'Ooh he's not poorly is he ?'
'Oh no, just man things.'
'Man things ?'
'Examinations that gentlemen of a certain vintage have to be subjected to.' Francis raised his eyebrows, pursed his lips and turned his head to one side.
'Oooh I see.' Millie winced.
'Don't worry, we have it easy really. No periods, no smear tests, no childbirth, no having to suffer the purgatory of bra buying. Someone fiddling around for your prostate now and again is hardly anything to cry about.' He sipped his tea. 'Actually, come to think of it. Some men pay damn good money for someone to do that for them.'
Millie laughed. 'Yeah but all your hair falls out and your choice of clothes is shit.'
'True.'
They both fell into silence.
'Francis.'
'Yes sweetie.'
'I really want a baby.'
'Pardon.'
'A baby. I want one. I think it's the right time.'
'Is this a proposition, because if it is….'
'No silly', Millie slapped his leg. 'I want a baby with Dee-Dee.'
'Golly right. You are one for the surprises aren't you.'

'I'm not getting any younger. I'm 34 next birthday. Always presumed I'd be a mother by now. It's not fair.' She was getting animated.
'Do you think being in such a hurry for the whole marriage and kids thing might possibly of worked against you ?'
'How do you mean ?'
'It's just you do have a habit of rushing headlong into relationships, making these sudden declarations of lifelong love to people who you haven't really had chance to get to know.'
'Do you think I scare them off ?'
'Maybe, but I was thinking more along the lines of you giving your affections too easily to people who don't really deserve it. You're a special person young lady, any man who got you should be very grateful.'
'Awwww Francis.' Millie hugged him. 'You'll make me cry if you talk like that.'
'Do you think there's any truth in it ?'
'Well I am pretty special I suppose.' Millie beamed. Bless St.Francis. He always had a way of making you feel good about yourself. Equally, he was quite nifty at shining a blinding, sometimes uncomfortable spotlight on your failings.
'I'm glad you think so.'
'And I do have a habit of making disastrous relationship choices. But at least I actually have boyfriends, not like Ms 'I don't need no-one' humpity-oompity 'oooh I'm so independent and together.'
'Oooh speaking of which.' Francis tapped her knee with back of his left hand. 'Has she got a thing for that pretty young thing staying with you currently ?'
'Oh gosh she has.' Millie put down her tea and made a fluid gesture with her hands. It was hard for her to speak without being able to use them to emphasise her point. 'She fancies the pants off him. It's quite funny.'
'I asked her about it earlier when I popped into the shop. Said she didn't want to take it any further because she's happy on her own.'
'Oooh that makes me mad.'
'What ?'
'He's clearly ideal for her and he's just turned up at our flat. That just doesn't happen normally does it. What's more he's interested. Where's the problem ?'
'I think we both know actually don't we.'
'Matt ?'
'I think so.'
'Poor Lauren.' Millie looked thoughtful and sad.
'You go talk to her.' Her touched her leg again. 'You're her best friend.'

Lee needed to get out. His room was stifling him and the sight of all those printed off shots of the lanky boy-woman were just irritating. It made his tiny room feel even more claustrophobic than it was already. She'd got the better of him. He might have her photos all over his wall, but she was only there because she'd killed all his other girls. All those attractive, pretty normal girls who didn't steal your camera. The ones who liked having their photos taken. The ones who would of looked so lovely above his bed. They'd of brightened the place up.

He had to get some more images. He wouldn't be beaten by a mad woman. The light was beginning to fail but he had a flash on his camera. If it got the attention of the people whose photo he was taking then that didn't really matter. He could run quite quickly, and actually, wouldn't they secretly be flattered by the attention ? Of course they would. They might pretend to be annoyed, but really they liked it. He was doing them a favour. Even the lanky boy-woman was probably into it.

'Shit !' Lauren had lost track of time.

'What ?' Jude jumped to attention, almost choking on his cider as he did so. She kept doing this to him.

'It's nearly five. I'm meant to be meeting Shrimp.' Lauren began trying to find the arm of her bomber jacket.

'Shrimp ? A small shellfish ?' Asked Star.

'Haha, yeah. No, er..she's a friend. Sort of. Small chav girl, works in M&S.' No time for chatting, needed to get off.

'Oh right. Didn't have you down as a friend of chavs.'

'She's not really, a chav I mean, and er..it's a long story. Must dash, seeya at the flat later yeah ?' Lauren shot to her feet and grabbed her bag, pulling it over her shoulder as she left the pub and made down the street.

'Er yeah..bye.' Star waved and looked back at Jude who shrugged his shoulders.

'Time for another drink ?' May as well make themselves at home.

People were beginning to make their way home from work, ambling themselves into Lauren's impatient way as she moved at double quick speed. Occasionally she broke out into a brief run as she moved down Stonegate. A Big Issue seller gave her eye contact, to which Lauren mouthed a 'sorry' and looked away guiltily, before heading up along Parliament Street towards Marks & Spencer. The shop was closing. It had that slightly, unsatisfactory tail-end look about it. There standing to the right of the main doors was a small figure with her hair tied back in a ponytail wearing a company jacket and trouser combination, looking effortlessly composed and together despite a day on her feet on the shop floor. It was Beth. She examined her nails,

hitched her sliding bag up onto her shoulder and then sighed. Lauren seeing her smiled and quickened her pace into a slight jog. She often thought that Beth must be a natural aristocrat. All the more truly blue-blooded for it being so unlikely. She had a real stately air. Millie recognised that as well but called her 'The Chav Princess' and couldn't really understand what Lauren saw in her. Lauren put this down to jealousy. Millie was so used to having her best friend all to herself, any new friendship Lauren struck up was immediately seen as a mild threat. But Lauren persisted in liking Beth's feisty-ness and determination. Her actions ultimately came from a good place. She was a good kid at heart despite the shit she'd been dealt. Mental, foul-mouthed and likely to beat you to a sorry pulp for looking at her a bit funny as well, but we all had our faults. Lauren had written her reference for the M&S job. She'd claimed that Beth had worked as her 'voluntary personal assistant.'
'What took you so long.' Beth gave Lauren a frosty disapproving stare.
'Oh god sorry Beth, I got delayed.'
'You stink of booze. You been drinking ?'
'Er yeah…one or two.'
'Lauren yer tool, you shouldn't be supping in the day, you're meant to be writing your book aren't ya ?'
'I am.'
' 'ow many times I told yer about not getting yer head down ? You've only yersel to blame if it all goes tits up.'
'Don't you get nagging Shrimp, I'm 'aving enough trouble with Mills at the minute.' Lauren tried to shrug this off. She knew she shouldn't. That her procrastination was an act of self-sabotage.
'Don't drop your aitches either!' Beth jabbed her in the ribs. 'You shouldn't pick up my bad habits, I'm trying to talk all refined now I'm working.'
'And how's it going ?'
'It's alright. I just have to wander around asking if anyone needs any help, then I sit on the checkout for a couple of hours, then I eat me sandwich, then I drink some tea, then I wander about a bit more and then I go 'ome. I get a discount as well but the clothes are all dull shite made for grannies so I doubt I'll ever use it.'
'True. Millie swears by M&S undies though you know. Mind you, so does my mum.'
'I've seen her. Millie not yer mam. She didn't see me. Or she pretended not to see me. I know she thinks I'm common.'
'Aww it's not that Beth.'
'Don't lie.'
'Sorry…I…look, Mills is a bit like that at times. She doesn't mean any harm.'
'Nah, she's alright. Bit clueless like but alright.' Beth shrugged her shoulders, paused then looked Lauren up and down. 'Don't suppose you ever need to

take advantage of our free bra fitting service do ya ?'
Lauren looked down at her chest grinning. 'It's never really been an issue shrimp. I'm not the most mammary gifted bird on the planet. In fact...' She prodded herself. 'I think you'd struggle to find my gifts in the dark.'
'You should be happy. I 'ate buying bras.'
'I've heard it can be difficult.'
'Too fucking right it's difficult. You should be pleased you're half-way boy. They get it much easier. Just find themselves a tracky in the right size at JJBs and wear it until it falls apart. Me mate Gobber Carrol's stinks of piss. Everyone's too scared to tell him though as he's mental. They don't want him to beat them up as he's only just come out of youth custody and if he twats them he'll go straight back inside.'
'That's very thoughtful of them.' Lauren smiled. Beth's world had a strange morality and code of honour to it. The only problem was, it wasn't really one that any else really recognised. 'Anyway, I'm dead pleased for you. About work I mean. You're doing well. It's a good gig as well.'
'Don't be daft it's only Marks's.' Beth looked embarrassed. She wasn't really used to praise.
'You'll be running the company in ten years.'
'Ah fuck that, I'm going to be running me own company in ten years.'
'What doing ?' This was news.
'Clothes. Good clothes for pregnant women. They're all shit in there.' She gestured behind her at her workplace.
'Sounds like a great idea.'
'Of course it is, it's my idea innit. Bound to be sound.'
 Lauren looked at her watch. 'Where do you want to eat.'
'Normally I'd say Maccy D's but I'm trying to avoid Hughesy at the minute, and I know he's likely to be in there with Jugs throwing gherkin at the exchange students.'
'Hughesy ? Jugs ? I don't think you've ever mentioned them.'
'Hughesy is a lad who used to go out with Kaz Barker, from upstairs at the flats. 'Cept she dumped him for some reason.' Lauren nodded, she thought she might of met Kaz once. Pretty girl. Scary. All Beth's friends were scary.
'Well, he were out the other night with Kieron Tomlinson, and Knobhead Fisher.'
'Knobhead Fisher ?' Lauren chuckled. 'How did he get his name ?'
Beth gave her a perplexed look. 'Well he's a Knobhead obviously.'
'Oh yeah, sorry.' Stood to reason didn't it ?
'Anyway, they were out, I were out, I bumped into Hughesy and to be honest we were both off our faces, so I snogged 'im cos I'd fancied 'im since year nine, but everyone used to think he were a bender. He's not, and it were alright.'

'And the problem is what exactly ?'
'He's going out with Jugs.'
'Jugs ?'
'Debbie Jugs. It's not her real name or owt, well Debbie is, but she's called Jugs because…'
'She's got big boobs ?'
'No, she's got nowt, it's sarcastic like. She 'ates to be called it and she's dead hard. She put Kerry Janley in hospital for looking at Hughesy. Got off with a caution cos she were pregnant at the time, except she weren't really, it were all a fat one. She'd just put a load of weight on cos she'd been working at Farmfoods and kept nicking frozen pizzas.'
'Sounds a bit fierce.'
'She is. Mam says she's a bit touched and always used to be mental as a toddler but it were because they pulled her out her mam's fanny with forceps. So it's not really her fault.'
'Right.' Lauren winced. That wasn't a pleasant mental image. Childbirth. Difficult underclass childbirth at that.
'I don't want to talk about her anyway. Lets go Pizza 'ut.' Then Beth's phone kicked into Lady Sovereign. She immediately began fumbling in her bag.
'Soz Laurers, scuse me.'

Do the bump…

    Lee pressed his way up Fossgate. He was a little out of breath as he turned the corner onto Pavement. He briefly glanced at the menu board of the fast food chicken takeaway and promised himself something nice for tea. Breaking into a jog and dodging a bus he headed onto Parliament Street. He'd sit by the fountain, see who was about.
    He was anonymous tonight. People were too concerned with getting home to be bothered to do more than glance. This was a good thing for a photographer concerned with realism and authenticity. Blending into the mass, he would be able to capture life at its most unexpected. Female, feminine life.
    He scanned the street. There were two teenage girls with sloping emo hair and lots of black eyeliner chatting. Get out the camera, point it vaguely in their direction, then move it quickly as possible to where they were standing. Flash, click. Got them. Stand up, move on and look as if nothing untoward had happened. Because of course it hadn't but for some reason he was feeling guilty. Don't be a wuss Lee, he chastised. Why should a conscience

get in the way of art ?

As he entered Newgate Market he paused, displayed his latest image and looked at it. Not bad at all. You could make out the full lips of one of the girls. She was quite a looker. Her mate was a bit plain, but passable. They'd do first off. The autumn light was failing, the streets were buzzing with busy shop girls, busy office girls, places were closing, doors were being locked, folk hummed about and Lee felt alive in it. He'd spent too long moping. His existence had been reduced to his dreary four walls.

There used to be a time when he held down a job, had a girlfriend, sat on the leather sofa in the open plan living space of their laminated flat and ate take-away pizza whilst watching Friends DVDs. Then he'd vigorously shag his girlfriend. Sometimes more than once a night. Crazy, crazy, halcyon days.

A fleeting sorrowful thought for what he'd lost flitted into his mental vision. It made his stomach recoil. Get rid of it immediately, grip your camera, point it, capture someone, then move on.

He wandered back down Parliament Street in the direction of the planned to be demolished toilets known locally as 'the splash palace.' They were a stinking subterranean hole in his experience. For a second he imagined bumping into the girly-man whilst he was down there. Yuk. He'd definitely fear for the sanctity of his arsehole if that were ever the case. It was obvious the girly-man fancied him. He was sure all gay men probably fancied him. They fancied anyone with a knob didn't they ? Always fucking at it. It was one of the most compelling attractions of the gay lifestyle as far as Lee could see, the sheer amount of action you'd get. No temperamental female sex drive to deal with. But you'd have to mix with mincing tossers like the girly-man which would undoubtedly be a headache. Thank fuck none of this applied to him.

He might lean up against the entrance to Whittards and snap women as they went in and out of the loos. That would be an interesting study. Could do a before and after style thing, see if their expressions change. Did women feel the need to piss the same as blokes ? Now that was an interesting question wasn't it ? Seeing as the plumbing was so different. Cassie used to get dead irritated and did a little impatient dance when she needed to go and wasn't near a toilet. He'd never felt the need to do that. Men and women clearly felt pressure differently.

There's a girl in a navy blue suit and name badge talking on her phone by the post box. If he got the zoom in close enough he'd be able to read it. That was a lovely little bonus. When she was on his wall he'd be able to talk to her and address her properly. Looking at her from a distance he guessed she might be an Emma. There were loads of Emmas knocking about. Everyone knew an Emma. Fuck it, she's turning away. He better move nearer. There, that's loads better. Right where he needs her, in goes the zoom and…

'Excuse me mate, what do you think you're doing ?'
Someone tapped him on the shoulder. He turned abruptly. It was that lanky boy-woman again. The bitch. What the fuck did she want ?

It must be the alcohol. She was definitely feeling bolder and seeing that freaky perv eyeing up little Beth through his viewfinder was not something she was willing to just sit back and watch. The guy had some cheek didn't he ?
'Fuck off.' The man turned and spat. 'It's none of your fucking business.' He clutched the camera close to his chest like greedy treasure, and hid it from her grasp.
'You were perving at my friend. I think it's my business.' Lauren stood, making her shoulders wide, one hand placed firmly on her hip. The man by way of contrast seemed to cower. This emboldened her.
'All I'm fucking doing is taking photographs, it's not a big fucking deal.' He was sounding exasperated. Passers-by were starting to look on. Beth finished her phone call and walked across to where Lauren was standing. It looked like intrigue. Beth was never one to shirk from intrigue.
'What's the matter 'ere ?'
'This bloke was taking a photo of you.' Lauren pointed at the horrified looking man.
'What fer ?'
'He's been doing it all day, taking photos of women. I caught him earlier in the Museum Gardens doing the same.'
'Weird. 'Ey mate, are yer some kind of perv ?' Beth moved closer and jabbed him in the chest.
'Shut your ugly fucking mouth and mind your own business.' This was humiliating. A girl and the lanky boy-woman teasing him in public.
'Let us have a look at your photos then. Like you did earlier.' Lauren grinned at him. His discomfort was plain to see. He was far too easy to upset this one. Doing so made her feel slightly cruel. But only slightly. He *was* a perv. He *was* out of order.
'No way, fuck off. Leave me alone. You're not fucking stealing my girls again.'
'Your girls ?' Lauren widened her eyes and looked incredulous. Any doubts about what she was doing evaporated. 'You're mental pal. Give me that here.' Lauren made a grab for the camera.
'I SAID LEAVE IT !' The man backed off and shouted at the top of his voice. Lauren and Beth looked at each other open mouthed.
'Ok, ok, cool the jets. Sheesh.' Lauren shook her head. The man started to cry.

'Now you leave me alone before I do something I regret.' He looked at them earnestly, wagging his finger, and walking backwards away from them. Suddenly he turned on his heels and started to run. Lauren and Beth looked at each other, silent for a second. Finally the senior of the two spoke.
'I think we should go to Pizza Hut.' She took Beth's arm and purposefully crossed the road.

His heart was threatening to beat itself out of his chest. He tore at an uncharacteristic speed up Whip-Ma-Whop-Ma and onto Colliergate, he didn't know where he was going but he knew he had to keep moving. The obvious thing to have done would have been to have turned back down Fossgate and head for home, but somehow his direction had been set for him and he knew it was too late to turn around. They might be following him. They could have told one of those crappy pretend police community officers what he was up to.

He kept running into people who bounced off him and shot him dirty impatient looks, or muttered something about looking where he was going. Others were assigning him looks that suggested they knew what he was about. They were the hardest to deal with. But he wouldn't stop running until his legs became physically incapable of carrying him. As he dodged his way down Goodramgate, the sweat starting to pour, he could feel his will beginning to falter. He was so badly out of shape. He was really feeling this. Couldn't even run for five minutes. What a disgusting fat waster he'd let himself become.

He couldn't just stop here though. Not with all these people around. It would look awkward and everyone would stop and look at him. They might ask questions. He needed to get somewhere where there would be less folk, gather himself, try to look a bit tidier and more together. Then he could just carry on snapping and put this whole nasty episode behind him. The world was full of vile people. People like the lanky boy-woman, but there was no accounting for lunatics, he must not blame himself. And anyway, lightning striking three times in a day was just so unlikely.

Evening snapping. There'd be less people around for sure but it would be darker and he might look less conspicuous. There would be more shadows to hide in. It was ceasing to be an interest this. He now knew he *needed* to get these photos. There was a void in his life into which all these images should go. This was important to him, if only people could realise and accept that. There'd be less hassle then. It wasn't unreasonable to dedicate so much time to something that was going to make you feel better about yourself was it ? That was the problem with the world. Everyone was so caught up in their consumerist dreams that they couldn't allow for those of an artistic temperament. All those years of wondering what he was about, trying to find motivation to get out and on with life and here was the truth. He just wasn't like other people. He was creative. He was an artist. They lived by different rules. This was his vocation and no weirdy freaky boy-woman who was clearly stalking him was going to spoil that.

He could feel his energy, already fairly drained, dropping further as the noise of a premature firework made him start. Everything was so alert and alive within him. This was painful but liberating in equal measure. He looked upwards , a shower of golden sparks illuminating the huddled medieval buildings, but all the time his feet kept moving.

'Arrrrggghhh.' A shocked, female scream.

He'd run into someone. They had bundled each other onto the pavement. It was a woman. She was lying there in the street, moving herself slowly back to her feet, looking dazed and confused as to what had just happened. 'Ow.' She started rubbing her elbow.
'Oh god, sorry love. I wasn't looking.' He held his hand out for her to take hold of it. She looked up at him, her brow furrowed, her expression slightly aggrieved. After a second's hesitation she took it, finding her sense of balance and proper orientation. Her expression immediately softened. It became apologetic.
'Don't worry, thanks, I should have been looking myself. I was miles away.' She started brushing her coat down, and leaned down to pick up her knitted beret off the pavement. 'Don't think I'll wear that again until I've washed it.' She made a little giggle. She was quite beautiful. Huge green eyes, masses of brown curly hair, a great face engulfing smile. And her smell. Whatever it was it was enchanting. She was enchanting. A proper princess. It definitely made a change. She looked at him quizzically.
'You OK ? You been crying ?'
'Oh it's nothing.'
'And you're dripping with sweat. I think something's wrong.'
'No, it's nothing really.' Come on Lee, find the words. This is an opportunity.
'You can tell me you know. I'm a great listener. Are you feeling sick or something ? Or is it girlfriend troubles ? Gosh no, sorry.' She held out her hands. 'That's far too nosy of me. Forget I said anything. But are you OK ? You don't look OK. I mean…I…'
'No I'm just a bit off colour.'
'Aww poor thing.' She rubbed his arm. She touched him. She actually touched him. 'Well why don't you let me buy you a cup of tea or something and you can tell me all about it ?' Her face was hugely sympathetic. Caring. Special. He'd randomly run into a special person. The gods were on his side after all.

Jude and Star decided it was time to leave the pub. They'd stayed long enough. Lauren had given Star a spare key to the flat so they could come and go as they pleased.

'Do we have to leave tomorrow Star. I think I'd like to see what happens.'

'Between you and my cousin do you mean ?'

'Yeah, it's not very often I meet anyone.'

She took hold of his hand in both of her own and rubbed it.

'I suppose we could hang around a bit longer. Listen why don't you suggest doing something with her tomorrow ? Have a bit of time together, see what happens. She said she wasn't working.'

'Oh god, I'm not sure what she'd...'

'You don't know until you ask. My intuition tells me she'd probably jump at the opportunity.'

'But she told me she just didn't want a relationship at the minute.'

'That may be so but it's down to you to show her that you're too good an offer to refuse isn't it ?'

'I'm not though. I'm gender confused dole scum.'

'Shush.' She placed a finger on his lips. 'Less of that kind of talk. You're not at all confused. You just confuse other people but that's their problem. If they can't handle a bloke who isn't a dickhead then so what.' She was getting animated, she hated to hear her best friend getting down about his difference. The difference that made him who he was. Why should he ever have to feel that he should neatly fit into other people's narrow little stereotypes ? ' And, you're the prettiest person with a penis I have ever set eyes upon Jude. She thinks the same. Just go spend some time with her whilst you can and see where it leads. It might be nowhere, or on the other hand it...'

'Might go tits up after a couple of weeks like all my other relationships.'

'It might, but then if you don't at least try you'll never know will you ?'

'I suppose not.' Jude looked pensive. 'But what will you do if I go swanning off with Lauren all day ?'

'Erm..thought I might check out the Art Gallery, maybe pop in the Castle Museum, wander about have a bit of an explore. Have some time on my own for once.'

'I think that might be good for you. You need to value your own company more and not feel you need some twattish bloke by your side constantly to keep you happy.'

'Whereas you need to learn that sometimes your life can be improved by the company of the right person.'

'I found her in 1982 when I ran into you.'

'Yes, you're my twinny, but you need more than what I can give. Romantic love.'

'Is that real though ?'

'You'll have to find that one out for yourself Jude. I'm damned if I know the answer.' She linked his arm. 'Come on, let's get back.'

Millie made to sit down in the window seat of Habit but the stranger didn't appear to want to acquiesce to her choice of table.

'Can we sit further back. Less conspicuous.' He was looking out through the glass anxiously.

'Ok. No problem. You find a nice comfy spot and I'll get us some drinks. Tea Ok is it ?'

'Yes. Tea.'

The man stood awkwardly for a while seemingly unsure of what to do with himself and then headed for a small table at the very back. A few minutes later Millie joined him with a tray containing a pot of tea for two, a small jug of milk and two cups.

'Well this is an unexpected little pleasure. I don't meet new people very often.' She placed the tea tray down on the table and held out her hand. 'I'm Millie by the way.'

'Oh.' He looked at it then tentatively took it. 'Lee. That's me. Lee.'

'Hello Lee.'

'Hello.' He didn't immediately appear to be very talkative. Never mind. Millie was sure she could help him warm up. He started fiddling around in his coat pocket and after a few moments produced a small camera.

'Can I take your photo.'

Millie was surprised and slightly confused, but smiled at him.

'Oh, gosh, yes if you like.' She giggled and started messing with her hair, shuffled in her seat and composed herself. 'Off you go then.'

Lee snapped a photo, the flash momentarily blinding her, then another, then another. He then looked at his handiwork on the screen at the back.

'Are they any good ? Can I see.'

'No !' The man raised his voice a little and looked slightly alarmed, protecting his camera with his hand. Millie was thrown again. Was that peculiar ?

'Oh, sorry. No, probably for the best. I look awful in photos.' She lied. She looked around the room, then gave him another little awkward smile whilst trying to find conversation. 'Well this is nice isn't it ?'

Jude and Star let themselves back into the flat. The place was in a silent darkness.

'No Millie then ?' Star fumbled for the light in the front room.

'Doesn't look like it ? What do you make of her ?'

'Don't know really. Seems quite sweet and friendly but I'm not sure how genuine she is.'
'Oh I think she's quite genuine, just a bit superficial. Nice girl though. Pretty.'
'Totally not your type Jude, and anyway she's got a boyfriend.'
'Oh god I know that. I don't need anymore complications.' He waved her line away dismissively and sighed.
'Aww poor Jude.' Star took hold of his arm. 'You're feeling it aren't you.'
'I fucking am. It's not good. It's not right.'
'Ha ! It is good. I'm glad you're suffering. That's attraction, that's starting to feel something for someone. I bet she's feeling the same.'
'Well I don't like it.' He paused, giving Star an anguished and confused look. 'No I do like it. Ah, I don't know.'

'We've got my cousin and her friend staying over at the minute.'
   Lauren was just finishing her last slice of pizza, and trying to pick out the cherry tomatoes from her salad bowl.
'Blokes ?' Beth spoke with her mouthful.
'My cousin's a girl, called Star and her best friend is a bloke called Jude, but he looks very slightly like a girl. He's quite girly with it. In a nice way.'
'He's got a lasses name as well. Is he a bender ?'
'Apparently not. And try not to use that term B. I know you don't mean anything by it but still.
'Sound. Yeah. No more benders. Do you fancy 'im then ? Sounds like your type. Like that fella you showed me on your shitty old music video.'
'Brett Anderson ?'
'Aye, that wer 'im. He were alright looking but his tunes were shite. But then all the stuff you like is shite.' Lauren laughed. Beth looked her straight in the eye. ' So do yer ? Fancy 'im I mean ?'
Lauren swigged from her Diet Coke and hesitated a second before answering.
'Er..to be honest I...'
'You do then.'
'No..I..'
'Yes you do. I can tell by your face. It's gone weird.'
'My face is always weird shrimp and yes,' Lauren sighed, 'I think I do fancy him. Quite lot. Oh dear.'
'Does 'e fancy you ?' Beth remained as poker-faced and clinical as ever. She'd gone into her interrogation mode. Lauren often thought she'd make a great detective.
'I think so.'
'Nice one. Have you copped off yet ?'

'Pardon ?'
'Snogged, have you snogged him.'
'Well we had a kiss by the river but I…'
'Why is everything so complicated with you ?' Beth grinned and shook her head dismissively.
'What do you mean ?'
'I mean you always go around the 'ouses, rather than getting stuck in there.'
'It's not that simple.'
'Don't see why not. I'd mek a move before he leaves.'
'I know you would but…'
'I get loads more action than you.'
'I know that, I'm just not as bothered as…'
'Bollocks. You just tell yourself that cos you're not getting owt.'
'Arrghh…Beth. You drive me up the frickin wall, you never leave things alone.'
'That's me job innit ?' She leaned back in her chair and started rocking it defiantly. 'I'm your gobby little shit'ead of a mate. I was sent to earth to irritate you into doing stuff.'
'But you're not going to succeed in this one alright !' Lauren finished eating, pushed herself back into her seat and crossed her arms. 'I'm happy single, I'm staying single. I don't need Jude or anyone else for that matter.'
'Whatever.' Beth yawned, glanced out of the window, then pushed her plate away. She looked back at Lauren with a mischievous grin across her face.
'Can I have cheesecake ?'

'Have you lived in York long Lee ?'
Millie was stirring her tea. She elegantly placed the spoon down on her saucer, every gesture fluid and together. She was attempting to engage her companion in eye contact. He just looked down self-consciously, as if her gaze was too honest and unsullied for comfort.
'Er…been here a while. Came to Uni.' He mumbled half-heartedly in return.
'Oooh gosh. I was at the university ! History.' Millie seemed to bounce into life.
'I went to St.Johns.'
'I once had a boyfriend from St.Johns. Tom, erm Tom Mac something or other. God I can't remember his surname ?' She giggled. 'How terrible must that sound ? Met him at the student night at Toffs on a Thursday. Did you ever go Lee ?'
'Yeah. Now and again.'
'It was great for the first few months when it was all new, but by the end of

the second term of the first year you got fed up of dancing to the same records in the same order, seeing the same faces, week in week out. Me and Lauren stopped going.'
'Yeah. Who's Lauren ?'
'Oh, she's my flatmate. My best friend, we've known each other for years.'
'Have you got a boyfriend ?'
Millie was mildly taken aback by his directness, but decided she'd overlook it. He seemed harmless enough. A bit odd but then weren't we all in our own way ? 'Erm..yes I have. Dee-Dee, sorry I mean Damian. Dee-Dee is my pet name for him. He's lovely actually, although I've not seen him for a while as he's busy. Sometimes I wonder if he still wants to go out with me.'
'Sorry.'
'Oh don't worry about that. These things are never straightforward in my experience. Do you have a girlfriend Lee ?'
'No. I used to but she dumped me.'
'Aww gosh, I'm sorry to hear that.' She touched his hand, pushed out her lips and tilted her head to one side with look of total understanding. 'What happened ?'
'I don't want to talk about it.' Lee hung his head again.
'Oh god, I'm so sorry. I'm terrible. Of course, you don't have to tell me. Do you work in York ? I work at the Opera House. Box Office. You get to meet quite a lot of people actually, famous people I mean. The other week I bumped into Joe Pasquale. I couldn't believe it. His voice doesn't sound as high pitched and annoying in real life. Lauren just laughed when I told her, she's got dead snobby and artsy since she got the job in the bookshop, she's always been that way, but she's definitely got worse of late. I wonder sometimes if we've still got much in common. What was it you said you did again ?'
' I didn't. Bookshop ? Which bookshop ?'
'Oh erm..Ainsty something or other. On Walmgate. Second hand books and things. I've been in once to see her but it's dead dull. Really dusty and boring. Not my cup of tea. She loves it, definitely in her element in there.'

It was her. The smiley pretty girl was talking about the lanky boy-woman. The fucking stroppy freak. That bitch who had spoilt his day, scuppered his relaunch, poured cold water on his new career. Women were definitely the problem. Not this one. She just seemed a bit stupid and pretty. She had a degree though so she couldn't be that thick, but remembering back to his own university days he was sure attractive girls got letters after their name by smiling sweetly at the lecturers. They had different rules didn't they ? It was so unfair. Fucking Cassie was as bad. She wasn't that pretty but her head was definitely full of shite. He didn't like to imagine what was in the lanky boy-woman's head. Not what should be there that's for sure. At least this one was sweet, amiable and feminine. A proper girl. Being in her presence made him feel more certain about his own place in the world. What was required of him.

He'd been so confused in the past. Desperate to be the nice guy, wanting to be the friendly generous face around the place. But girls just didn't go for that even if they said that they did. They just took advantage. Held you in contempt whilst secretly longing for someone to come and master them. Dominate them. It was the shits who got laid. The macho fuckwits .All those alpha-male movie heroes had women throwing themselves at them. They wouldn't have been beating themselves up about a single solitary slap. He'd made the decision to get off his knees and start asserting his masculinity. The slap hadn't been a disaster. It had been a catharsis. He'd reconnected with his true animal self and that was very potent. Cassie was probably too dykie and fucked up to realise but the smiley pretty girl could certainly see it. She was eating out of his hand, she'd bought him a cup of tea, she was asking him about his life. She was absolutely gagging for it, boyfriend or no boyfriend. The poor gimp. He wouldn't have any idea that someone was making a move on his female.

This was Darwinian though wasn't it ? The survival of the fittest. The dogs fighting it out amongst themselves for the bitch on heat. And this one was almost certainly on heat. And what a perfect way to get back at the lanky boy-woman. Shagging her best friend. That would fuck with her head. That would show she had no right to speak for women on whether or not they wanted their photo taken. Secretly he was sure they'd all be flattered to be his wank matter.

Forget that though. Tonight he was going to have the real thing. His cock was definitely pussy bound. All the signals were there. It was just a case of biding his time.

'Oh god, look at the time.' Millie glanced at her watch. 'I must get off.'
'Oh I thought…' Lee looked at her slightly taken aback.
'It's been lovely though.' She jumped to her feet, wrapped her long scarf around her neck and pulled on her coat. Something about her companion was beginning to get unsettling. Her default view of humanity was largely trusting, She generally felt most people were essentially benign, that if you left them to their own devices they'd no more do you harm than they would hurt themselves. If you gave people a chance they could well turn out to be someone important in your life, that serendipity could throw an opportunity in your path that you'd only miss by being closed off to experience. But something here just didn't feel right. And she trusted her instinct more than

she trusted herself. Even if it did occasionally let her down.

This had probably been a bad idea. Lauren would tell her off if she knew what she'd done, but she could hardly have left the poor guy in a sweaty teary heap in the street could she ? With hindsight, perhaps she should of. He looked at her oddly, and the photo thing was definitely peculiar wasn't it ? He grabbed hold of her hand.

'Well can I have your number then ?'

'Sorry, I.' She pulled her hand away. 'Er…no..I.' Her heart started beating a little faster. That was out of order. Must try to remain calm and together. Don't get him irate.

'Please.' He made another grab for her hand but she quickly pulled it away.

'No, look. I really must be off.' She grabbed her bag, slung it quickly over her shoulder and dashed out of the café. Lee jumped to his feet and followed behind.

Millie hurried down Goodramgate towards the centre of the city, Lee was only ever a few feet behind but if she was aware of him, she never looked. He maintained the distance, and occasionally lifted his camera to his eye to take a photo of her unawares. She turned down Colliergate, strided across Whip-Ma-Whop-Ma, breaking out into a little jog as she went, and down onto Fossgate. Lee smiled. She must live near him. Then she paused outside the girly shop that he'd taken the pretty girl and the girly-man too the other day. She rummaged around in her bag for her key, pushed open the black wooden door into the snickleway at the side and was gone from his sight. That must be where she lives. With the lanky boy-woman. Lee took photographs of the heavy black door, then pointed his camera to the window above the shop. He could see curtains and ornaments in the window. That must be their flat. He smiled to himself. So much information, but what would he do with it ? For now he'd go home and see what delights were contained on his memory card. They had to be better than the ones currently bothering his grey matter memory. If only they could be so easily deleted.

No mates…

Lauren watched Beth's pixie-esque figure climb onto a bus outside the Stonebow, a huge 1960s monstrosity of a building that dominated this unpromising section of town. Lauren had read somewhere that it had been meant to resemble a ship. Although that was hard to see now. It looked grey and incongruous alongside the jumbled architecture of the buildings below. In the basement was the sweaty teen skank-dive of Fibbers, which she still occasionally popped along to when a band came up who she fancied seeing. It was getting less often these days. She was definitely getting older. She pulled her Ipod earphones out of her jacket pockets and placed them in her ears, flicking her player into life as it randomly threw up a Tegan & Sara track.

As the bus pulled away, Lauren waved, Beth smiled, stuck two fingers up and then blew her a kiss. Lauren shook her head, smiled to herself and wandered back towards the flat. What a curious day. The alcohol was beginning to wear off and she had the beginnings of a headache. Then she remembered she had visitors. Her heart sank a little. Not that they weren't pleasant people and one in particular certainly brought a bit of sunshine into her life, just that she didn't feel like talking to anyone. The day had seen far too much sociability already. She knew what she'd do. She'd rustle up some tea for her guests, be polite, suggest they go out for the evening then take herself into her room and mess about on the internet for a while. Dimitri Montage was making her curious. She was certain he was an oily cheat, she needed to Google his name and try to find out some background on him. Could make for an interesting article. Maybe this could be a new line of work. Rumbling quacks, pretendy psychics and show-me-the-money mystics. The world was probably littered with them.

When Lauren got in she found Star, Jude and Millie sitting with trays on their laps watching TV and eating what looked like chilli. Millie had been doing the hostess thing she was so good at. This shouldn't have annoyed Lauren. Mills had saved her a job, but for once in her life she was actually looking forward to cooking something for someone. Whatever, doubtless Millie would do it a lot better. As she entered the room, Millie glanced up, pretended not to notice her and went immediately back to watching TV. Lauren allowed her bag to drop on the floor to try and get people's attention. Star looked up at her.
'Hi Lauren.'
'Hi' she sheepishly responded. This was embarrassing. Everyone knew her business.
'There's some chilli left if you want it.' Millie spoke dispassionately, not even turning her head to look at Lauren, who immediately picked up on the extension of her earlier frostiness.
'It's alright. I've eaten.'
Millie said nothing.
'Did you have a nice time with your friend ?' Jude finally looked at her, his gaze immediately feeling both more at home and more unsettled. She was out of sorts because she knew she couldn't just stride across the room and wrap her arms around him. God he was so perfect, why didn't she

just…..stop that right there.'
'Yeah it was alright.' She felt awkward standing there. Didn't know what to do with herself. 'I'm just going to go to my room for a bit.' She pointed to the hallway with her thumb backwards over her shoulder. 'Got a headache coming. Are you two OK ?'
'Yeah we're fine.' Star waved her hand dismissively. 'We might pop out to the cinema later if we feel like it.'
'Oh, good right.' Lauren hesitated for a second. 'Right then, I'll go shall I.' She turned, scurried down the hall and entered the sanctuary of her room. Turning on the light she collapsed backwards onto her bed and sighed. Placing her hands over her face she tried to block out the emotional mess she felt she was making.

'Jude ! Now's your chance.' Star jabbed her best friend in the ribs.
Jude turned sharply to look at Star. He'd been engrossed on a news items about the Japanese intention to go whale hunting on scientific grounds.
'Sorry ?'
'She's on her own in her room. Knock on her door, ask if you can pop in for a chat.'
'Star, she's having some time on her own. She doesn't want me bothering her.'
'It's a perfect opportunity Jude.' Millie chipped in. 'Although I haven't got the slightest idea what you see in the obstreperous cow.'

  Jude made a slight apologetic knock on Lauren's door. He wondered precisely what he was doing although he was in little doubt that he wanted to. That he wanted to be in her presence. There was no answer. He tried again. 'Yeah ?' A slightly impatient voice sounded from behind. He opened the door tentatively and poked his head round.
'Is it alright if I come in for a chat.'
Lauren lifted her head from the bed. 'Er yeah. Tell you what though. You couldn't make me a cup of tea first could you ? The bags are…'
'…in the biscuit tin, we found them earlier.' He smiled. 'Back in a sec.'
'Aww nice one. What a good boy.'

  A few minutes later Jude returned with two mugs of tea and Lauren shifted herself up, so that her back was leaning against the headboard. She banged the mattress next to her twice in quick succession with the palm of her hand, gesturing for Jude to sit down. He handed one mug to her, placed the other down on her bedside table and climbed alongside her. She took a sip of her tea then smiled at him.
'Well this is very cosy.' She had the hood of her hoodie pulled up, it pushed

her fringe down over her big brown, heavy kohl defined eyes, and he was sure her full lips were definitely pouting.

'I hope you didn't mind me disturbing you.'

'How could anyone mind you disturbing them eh ?' She looked him straight in the eyes and he seemed to blush slightly. 'Course not.' She rubbed his knee reassuringly, sending an electric judder up through his body.

'Good day then ?'

'Not bad. You ?'

'Yes.'

They fell into an awkward silence.

'What you doing tomorrow ?' Jude finally asked.

'Nowt planned as yet. Might go for a wander by the river, see what's happening. Sit on t'internet, might even pop along to see my big fat gay friend Franny.'

'Oh right, you're busy then.'

'Nah not really. Why do you ask ?'

'Oh I was just sort of wondering if…'

'Yes ?'

'Well, if you fancied spending the day with me.'

Lauren appeared to be slightly surprised. 'With you ?' She pointed at him. Jude nodded. 'What about Star ? Would she mind me tagging along ?'

'No, erm, Star wants to go off do some stuff on her own. Thinking and things I think, about you know, erm. I'm going to…'

'Be on your tod. I'd love to.' She smiled.

He relaxed. Relieved. 'You would ?'

'Course. Be nice. Don't expect too early a start though will you. I like a lie in on my day off.' She chuckled self-consciously. This was almost a date. With someone she actually fancied. They then both sat drinking their tea largely in silence. 'Although we'd better find a few more things to talk about by then otherwise it could be a very long day.'

After a few awkward minutes Jude made his excuses and left the room. Lauren was clearly flagging and needing a bit of a re-charge. He had her all to himself tomorrow. He shouldn't be greedy of her time. As he paused for a second perched on the side of the bath after visiting the toilet he noticed his hands were shaking. This was weird. This was different. There were no previous moments in his life he could ever recall feeling quite like this, but what it was all about he had little idea. Then he thought of her. The few inches that separated their lips moments earlier seemed so suggestively nothing, yet almost an impossible barrier at the same time. He ran his fingers through his hair, then grasped his head making an expression of powerless frustration. Someone please help him out. This was impossible.

Lee was busy printing off his new pictures. They weren't bad. The random few he took in the street were a bit sketchy. It was the failing light at the time, you couldn't really make out their faces which was a problem. Never mind. It was a start and even with undefined features they were miles better than the backside of the lanky boy-woman. There was nothing about her from the rear that suggested she were a girl. She could easily just be a skinny boy. The thought made Lee feel unpleasant. That he could have pictures of a boy's backside next to his bed.

He started to rip her photos down off the wall. Something about that woman unsettled him but he couldn't figure out what it was. It was something similar to the disgust he felt towards the skinny girly-man. They were just ineffably wrong in his eyes. They didn't fit into his tidy mental categories. But they seemed to fit quite well into the world and it was him, with his normality, who was having problems coping with life. He was regular, he was ordinary, they were undeniably freakish. Yet they wandered around grinning to themselves as if all was well in their sick world. Something was definitely wrong somewhere. It wasn't right that people like that should be getting in his way, interfering in his life. They were bad news.

Previously he'd been so tolerant of difference. Not that he actively thought about how he felt about these things, or that he could ever really befriend anyone who wasn't in their own way fairly regular, just that he knew he was cool with stuff. That had been part of the problem in the past. Dad had never had time for shirt-lifters.

Now that Lee thought about it, actively considered it rather than just presuming, he knew he didn't like them either, nor proper lezzers. The ones in jizz mags were OK as they looked like regular porn models and were just straight girls acting up. Which was fine. You knew what they really longed for was a bloke to see them right. But proper mad boyish dykes who didn't, like the lanky bitch were fucking freaky. They were kind of women that ran charities and refuges for beaten women. A lot of them were just stirrers weren't they ? Encouraging normal wives and girlfriends in perfectly satisfactory relationships to report the occasional slap. Or to paint their other halves as violent thugs when all they were doing was attempting to assert the proper way of things. That was probably where Cassie had got it from. She was a fucking social worker for god's sake. She'd mix with mad bints like the lanky boy-woman all the time.

It was a clear undeniable truth. Men had to be men. Women had to be women. That was how the world had worked for centuries. Blokes could be no other way and it was what women secretly wanted. We were from Mars and Venus. As different to each other as chalk and cheese, but get the chemistry right and it would work. If we struggled to communicate in words, we could at least communicate through the biological impulse. That was it all it came down to at the end of the day, there was far too much confusion abroad these days. That had been his problem in the past. Trying so hard to be a nice, modern, understanding guy when all women really wanted was a well-hung wealthy brute with cheekbones. People like the lanky boy-woman and the girly-man were going against nature. Things might not be totally perfect for him now but at least he wasn't attempting to defy the natural order. With his beer paunch, lazy dress sense, pasty skin, rambling eyebrows and nasal hair, accompanied by his compulsive masturbation addiction, prompted by his ceaseless thinking about sex, he was definitely working with the grain. The girl he'd met earlier, Millie, with all her smiley feminine loveliness was doing likewise. There was a perfect symmetry there wasn't there ? Adam and Eve almost. They must be made for each other. He bet she had a perfect womb. A lovely warm little nest for all his future children.

Except she might not think that. He remembered she mentioned she had a boyfriend. What was he like ? If her best friend really was the lanky boy-woman then her head might be full of nonsense. Her fella could be one of those preening pretty-boys who messed around with moisturiser and talked about their feelings. That couldn't satisfy a woman like Millie over the long term though. He was certain of that. Give her time and she'd see the light. He had faith in her to reach the right conclusions. Particularly if he gave her a helping hand or two.

Ideally he'd like to see his two tormentors exterminated, taken out of the picture, the way left clear for proper people like him, and Millie, and the pretty girl. It would be doing both women a service to liberate them from the influence of the freaks. He looked again at his three photos of Millie. She really was breathtaking, far too nice just to be wandering about round here. Her huge natural smile in itself was breathtaking. Like something a film star would have. One of those old school girl-next-door style ones. It made you feel so good about yourself just looking at it. Imagine what it must be like waking up to that every morning.

Then he had an idea. He'd stick her at head level next to his bed and every morning when he woke up that was precisely what he'd see. He could even pretend she were his girlfriend. She soon would be of course and the need to pretend would be no more. She might even move in. No, fuck it. What was he talking about ? He couldn't move Millie in here. The place stank of takeaways. He'd have to get himself a job. A proper job. A graduate job for once that would earn him enough to support them both in a nice place in town. Wait a minute though, don't get ahead of yourself Lee. If you're in too much of a hurry you might fuck it up. Let's face it, it has been known.

The signals were clearly there in the coffee bar though. Sure he didn't have her number yet but he knew where she lived. He could call round. No, wait a minute. He'd have to be sure that the lanky boy-woman wasn't there. That shouldn't be too difficult. He could easily identify what she looked like from the back from all his photos, so all he had to do was make sure she was sitting in the window of Ainsty Antiquarians. Then it would be safe. Lanky boy-woman would have to be dealt with properly in the long run though. She'd only get in the way otherwise, but firstly he needed to re-acquaint himself with his little angel. He lay back on the bed, placed a kiss on the lips of his bedside photo and slowly allowed his hand to head crotch bound. Moments like this made being a man all the more worthwhile.

Lauren heard Jude and Star leave the flat. They must be going to the cinema like they said. Wonder what they were going to see ? Was that jealousy she was feeling ? Maybe. Very slightly. No, stop that. Let them have a lovely night. They're such special friends those two. You could hear it in the way they talked to each other, looked at one another, made little gestures. It was a rare thing to find. She thought that so much of what passed for friendship was really little more than a vague bit of socialising now and again played out with a surface niceness that never really allowed for true connection. Jude and Star seemed to have that instinctive connection. If she were the religious type she might call it spiritual. Actually, no she would still call it spiritual. The word needed to be reclaimed and given something solid. Not because she thought that it possessed anything supernatural or written in the stars about it, just because it seemed to transcend the sum of its parts, made the lives of those involved more whole, more human. Gave people the purpose that the universe was blind to. One friend like that was a worth a thousand vague associates.

A bit like she and Mille used to be. Lauren sighed. Poor old Mills. What was happening with that boyfriend she wondered ? Maybe she should go and have a chat with her. Whilst she was deciding whether or not to venture out of her room and actually initiate a rambling Millie conversation, she started to hear the bath water running. Millie's baths were legendary. They usually involved candles, expensive bottles of highly scented bubble bath and Millie singing unselfconsciously throughout. They also seemed to last for ages, any moment Millie would be calling to ask…

'Laurers !' Millie hollered. 'Do you need the loo before I get settled in the bath. Speak now or forever hold your pieces.'
'Coming.' Lauren dashed to the bathroom, passing Millie in the hallway. They both embarrassedly continued to avoid eye contact.
'Number ones only though remember.' Millie spoke to her, stopping Lauren in her tracks. 'I don't want to be lounging in the bath having to suffer your smells.' She smiled. Lauren returned it. Her best friend. Her lovely specialest bestest ever friend. How could you not love her forever ?

'You have my solemn word.'

I'll be there for you…

   Millie lounged in the bath. The room full of steam, the water up to her shoulders, scented bubbles everywhere, the only light coming from rows of flickering candles of all shapes and sizes. Heaven. Except she was finding it hard to relax. The encounter in the coffee bar had been unsettling enough. That had been stupid of her. What kind of trouble could she have been inviting ? It's nice to be nice, but sometimes it's better just to mind your own business. Lauren had a point on that one. Had that been him following her ? She was certain someone had been behind her and the one furtive glance she made over her shoulder as she walked down Colliergate seemed to suggest he was there. But it was dark and her imagination could have been playing tricks on her. She had been unsettled by the encounter, her mind was ill at ease with the whole Lauren thing. As much as she wished she could rise above arguments with her best friend, she knew she couldn't.
Being on bad terms with Lauren made her worse than Damian's current diffidence. They had known each other so long, been through so much. Her friendship couldn't just be allowed to die. She envied those people who were hitched to partner's they considered their best friend. It was rare as well as special wasn't it ? You always knew it when you saw it though. They just fitted together like pieces of a jigsaw, always seemed to delight in the other's company, got each other's jokes, finished each other's sentences, had tons of conspiratorial secrets and together seemed like a total team Just like she always used to have with Lauren. But she'd never had that with a man. At times she wished that Lauren had been a boy, then it would all have been different. Would she even have been Lauren's type though if she were a boy ? She used to think she would. Now she wasn't so sure. How do you assess the type of person someone would be attracted to if they were the opposite sex from their current taste *in* the opposite sex ?

   Jude was definitely Lauren's type as much as she had one. She knew she liked sensitive pretty blokes. Blokes who didn't seem particularly bloke-ish. The problem was that they were so rare. Just how many men like Jude are there walking around ? How many women were there like her best friend ? Millie couldn't think of any other's that she'd ever known. She hoped Lauren would see what a potentially good thing had just fallen into her lap. Maybe she and Jude could be one of those best mate couples ? The thought momentarily made her feel sad. Her concern for Lauren's well-being wanted her to be happy, at the same time as her heart recoiled at the thought of losing her. Surely one day though that was precisely what would happen ? What then ? Lauren helped her make sense of the world in a way no-one else could. She had a handle on how men thought, saw how the average woman responded, yet didn't seem to think particularly like either. She looked into the heart of situations in a way that Millie couldn't. Or did, just in a different way. There was something special and different about her. Something which Millie couldn't contemplate sharing without a degree of jealousy. Jude reminded her of Lauren, and even though he was a boy, she didn't feel any attraction. If Lauren were a boy she would be like him, and still they'd only ever be friends. But friends was enough wasn't it ? Why was so much importance given to that romantic or sexual relationship, when a true friendship was the basis of everything we were about ? It was more dependable and possibly supportive. True instinctive friendship attached to romance and sexual attraction - that was the holy grail. Millie wondered if she were just too much of a girl, and wanted too much of a boy for her to ever find that kind of happy combination and instinctive understanding. Lauren just didn't seem to think like any girl Millie knew. Not that she thought like a boy either. It was if she was above all that, as if thinking in those terms just made no sense to her. Not for the first time she found herself pondering the mysteries of how her enigmatic friend really ticked. After all these years of friendship, she still wasn't totally sure and Lauren didn't give much away.

But Millie's heart *was* aching for a real boy. Another let-down, emotionally difficult real boy who she had yet again allowed herself to fall for. She'd sent him another text this morning and had no response. Where was he ? Something wasn't right. If you said you loved someone and they messaged you, then you immediately got back to them. Well she did. Their relationship was still only months old. It wasn't as if they were an old bored with each other couple. Things seemed to be going fine. The last time she was over at his place in Leeds they'd barely got out of bed all weekend. But that was starting to feel like a long time ago. He never wanted to talk to her. This couldn't go on. She reached her hand down out of the bath, grabbed her towel, wiped her hands, then picked up her phone which she'd perched by her head at the side of the tub. She found the number she needed and dialled it before her hesitancy prevented her from acting. One of her candles burnt out, a small plume of smoke twisted towards the ceiling as death made it fizz in the hot damp of the room. Millie glanced at it sharply as the phone rang twice. Then it was answered.

'Hello'. A well-spoken male voice. It made her heart sink.
'Damian, it's me. I think we need to talk.' But she pressed on anyway.

Lauren was sitting at her computer. Myspace for a while she thought.

Logging on, she wasn't really expecting much. She spent hours on there that would be better put to reading or writing. It very rarely interested her, yet for some reason or other she repeatedly found herself staring at it blankly. Or searching for new bands, or reading the profiles of people she would never add. There were some she wished she dared she could, but it just seemed rude somehow. Some random woman barging into their life asking to be their friends. Far too needy. Best leave them alone.

Oooh two new messages. Don't get excited. One from a local band asking if she'd be going along to their gig at the Junction. She quickly visited their page. They sounded like sixth formers tuning up to play Kooks covers. That'll be a no then. The other was from her unlikely cyber-friend Connie. Lauren had nothing in common with the forty-five year old mother of eight born again Christian from Michigan, but she'd been so surprised to hear from a real person she immediately approved her friend request. Ever since she'd been deluged with sickly sweet comments, and bland biblical references, as well as repeated assurances that she was being prayed for. Connie must have missed that bit on her profile that said she was an atheist and that all religious believers were a greater threat to mankind than Crocs. But only just. Plastic shoes made global warming look like a kid's picnic. They were frequently worn at kid's picnics. Lauren had an image of herself as a well-scrubbed yummy-mummy alongside slightly chubby husband and fresh faced child at a sun-lit picnic somewhere idyllic. All of them wearing Crocs. With those charms inserted. She shuddered. What a truly desperate (and unlikely) prospect.

She didn't have the heart to delete Connie, although it was hard to know what to talk about with someone who only listened to Christian and Country music, thought George Bush was the saviour of civilisation, and whose favourite books were all works of spiritual guidance. Connie kept telling how she'd understand what she was talking about 'when she became a mom.' As if this was as written in her bible as what god did to the town of Sodom. Never mind, Connie was bearable and well-meaning. Generally she tried to stick to what the weather was like in England in her replies to Connie's lengthy dispatches about her children's ailments and what was happening in her local town. Hopefully one day she might get bored, but sadly that didn't seem to be the case just yet. She only had four friends, and Lauren was her top one. Why, she had no idea. Such was the random nature of these things. You made the most curious of connections. She wondered if Jude had a Myspace page. It would be interesting to take a look if he had. Sadly she didn't know his surname. Come to think of it, she wasn't really sure of Star's. They might be cousins but it was on the maternal side, so Star was probably not a Seymour. Couldn't be too hard to find a Star though could it?

She hit on the search function, put in the name Star and an NG

Nottingham postcode, add a radius of twenty miles, hit search and hey presto. There she was. The one and only. It was a lovely photo of her. Black and white and very arty looking. All soft focus. She was amazingly attractive, very natural and almost model-esque but not up herself at all. What a nice young woman. It had been a pleasure to meet up with her again. Taking a look at her profile, it didn't really say much. No fancy background, not much in the fields. She hadn't been on for a couple of months. There in her top friends as her numero uno, was Jude. He was in a club or a bar somewhere, a bottle of lager in his hand, pouting at the camera. Lauren chuckled and took a look at his page. Immediately she was hit by a Blondie tune, and a flashing disco background. By way of contrast with his friend his page was full of random information, pictures of equally ambiguous pop stars from the past few decades, long lists of music and films and TV shows. Bit thin on the books front, but she'd soon kick that into touch. Wait a minute, what was she talking about? There'd be no kicking of anything into touch. She'd probably never see him again after he and Star head home and out of her life in couple of days time .Lauren wasn't going out with him or anything. He was just a random person who'd wandered into her flat, sat on her bed and made her feel dead special. She sighed. No, this wasn't good. These thoughts had to stop. The ones that saw them together, arm in arm walking by the river, larking about in the pub, wrapped in each other's arms in front of the TV. God no. She wouldn't send him a friend request, she would stop looking at his page, she'd move on. Her cursor hit on the X shutting down the page. He was gone. Looking at the screen, now showing nothing more than her Belle & Sebastian wallpaper and a list of never used programme icons a sense of emerging sadness started to bubble up. Her bottom lip instinctively pushed itself out and her posture in the chair started to slump. Then there was a knock at the door. Lauren jumped to attention and spun around in her computer chair, the door opened and a little face appeared in the gap. It was Millie. She looked as if she'd been crying.
'I've done it.' She sniffed melodramatically.
'Done what sweetie' Lauren jumped to her feet and headed towards the door, which pushed open and in walked Millie dripping water from her huge white towelling robe.
'Damian. I've finished with him.' She wiped her eyes with a screwed up tissue.
'Oh god no.' Lauren couldn't quite believe what she was hearing. She never finished with anyone. Every relationship was almost certainly the special one which would propel her to a life of roses round the door, doting husband and a host of easily dandled cherubic babykins with ringlets. This was Millie facing reality. She started to cry again. Big heaving sobs. Lauren walked across to her, and wrapped her arms around her tiny frame and pulled her

close. She allowed her right hand to reach up and stroke her best friend's hair.

'Sssshhhhhhh. Come on princess.' After a few minutes, Millie finally spoke.

'It wasn't working Lauren. I can see that.'

'But I thought it was perfect.'

'No, I was just kidding myself. It was all lies. I was hiding from reality. He just didn't have a lot of time for me.'

'Why not eh ?' Lauren looked at her, and pushed some of her friend's hair out of her face and lodging it behind her ear. 'You're lovely and beautiful and kind and considerate. Anyone should count themselves lucky to get you.'

'Oh Lauren. You're the nicest boy I've ever met. I only wish you were.' She looked up at Lauren, her eyes full of tears, her face red from crying and her brow deeply furrowed. Lauren smiled, and kissed her forehead.

'To quote Franny at this point, I think it might be time for a cup of tea.'

Millie returned her smile and let her best friend go. Everything was going to be alright.

That evening they sat crossed legged on the floor , talked, drank tea, ate biscuits. Just like they used to. All they were missing was a nice juicy fat spliff to round off the proceedings. Lauren had lost contact with their dealer, a shady waster who somehow bumbled his way through a chemistry course, slept with half the population of their halls of residence, and went missing for three months, which if the rumours were true, were due to a forceful invitation to spend some time at her majesty's pleasure. Shane 'Drugsy' Malone was his name. Nice boy.

Otherwise it was like rolling back the years. They were no longer thirty-something women beginning to diverge, but two 18 year old soul mate freshers thrown together by chance, or fate, or serendipity, or synchronicity ,or the vagaries of the university clearing system. They were proper friends again. Everything the other said made perfect sense. For the first time in ages they were talking about the future together. How they'd always be there for the other. If no one else came along then it didn't matter. Their friendship was special. It would never break. That was what they'd promised back in 1992, now they were reaffirming and re-discovering it.

To Lauren, it felt like a huge privilege. She must never underestimate her flat-mate. Beneath all that pronounced feminine giddiness and mannered innocence, behind those big beautiful soul searching eyes, and huge ever-ready smile was a sharp mind and a heart as wide as the River Ouse. Just like the river, it occasionally got so full it couldn't help but burst its banks. Millie was a lovely force of nature. The kind that took your breath away and reminded you why you bothered with life. How could anyone want to hurt her ? It didn't make sense. Then she remembered the little drama she had initiated the previous night. It wasn't just Millie who could do drama queen was it ?

'Mills, I'm so sorry about yesterday you know. I was completely out of order.'
Millie smiled. 'Thank you babes. Don't worry, it was difficult for you. It must have been so uncomfortable.'
'It was. But still.' Lauren made an embarrassed shrug.
'And how do you feel about the whole thing tonight ?'
'What ?' Lauren shifted uncomfortably. Her natural reaction at this point was to immediately nip this developing conversation in the bud. But no. That would be going against the spirit of the evening. She'd be open. 'It just stirred up lots of things. It was all weird. Hearing that guy talk about Matt as if he were talking to him. I mean, how could he be ? Why would my Matt talk to a man like that ? It makes no sense and rationally it's preposterous.'
'I don't know. It was unreal. How he knew that stuff, got your name right as well.'
'It has to be some kind of hoax. Or lucky guess or fishing for information or something. These people are crooks.'
'You don't know that for certain though. Maybe he really was talking to Matt. Maybe Matt did want you to move on.'
'Do you think ? Not that he was really there, I'll never believe that, but that he would want me to move on ?'
'Lauren, I've thought that for years but found it so hard to say anything. He was a lovely bloke but you don't know how the whole thing would have panned out over the years. He was damaged. I thought he was spot-on for you from what I saw of him , but you just don't know.'
'I find that hard to accept though. He was my soul mate.'
'But he's not here anymore. You never really got chance to find out did you ? I think in your mind you've turned him into this perfect figure. You might be an atheist but in your head you've created this untouchable saviour who you want to keep yourself chaste for. In a way you're like a nun.'
'A nun ! You're frickin joking aren't you ?'
'No, I'm not. Look at it this way, you've sworn your life away to this invisible vision of perfection. He's your Jesus.'
'Matt was no Jesus.' Lauren laughed.
'Precisely. He wasn't. He was a flesh and blood bloke who fell in love with you. He then left your life in dramatic unexpected circumstances and you've never been able to accept that and move on.'
'But I have in lots of ways. I don't spend all my time thinking what might have been.'
'But you never allow yourself to fall in love in case something like that

happens again. You're terrified of suffering. Whereas my problem is…'
'You fall in love too easily.'
'That's about the extent of it.' They were silent for a moment before Millie spoke again. 'In the absence of a spliff, can I nick one of your fags ?'
'You've not smoked for years, I should say no but…'
'You could do with the company on the back landing.'
'Yeah, come on then.'

   Out on the landing the October chill was made manifest by the lack of a cloud in the sky. The stars twinkled vividly, as above the roof tops steam appeared to be rising from boiler flues and bathrooms of top floor flats. Millie dragged on her cigarette.
'God, I'd forgotten how good that is.' She looked at the lit ciggy between her fingers.
'Don't go getting a taste for it again. It's a filthy habit.'
'Does help take the edge off things though doesn't it ?'
'No ! Only if you're not used to it, after a while it only ever takes the nicotine withdrawal induced edge away.'
'So why do you keep smoking then ?'
'It's part of my character isn't it ? I'm a chain-smoking androgynous singleton with a mouth like a sewer.'
'Well only one, maybe two of those characteristics are non-negotiable you know. You could be a healthy living happily in a relationship, androgynous bird with a mouth like a sewer.'
Lauren drew on her cigarette. 'Too many whats, ifs and maybes Mills. I know what I'm about. I don't feel any need to change.'
'If I can go from being a passive victim of a bloke's whims and dump my first ever boyfriend at the grand old age of 33 then you can change too you know.'
'Are you saying I need to change ?'
'No, you don't *need* to, but it might do you good to be less set in your ways occasionally.'
'Maybe. I should ditch the ciggies. They're shit aren't they ? And expensive.'
A cough tickled her throat right on cue, but luckily didn't develop into one of those disturbing morning hacks that regularly got her scurrying onto NHS websites for advice as to how to give up. Then she'd change her mind an hour or so later when the very first tendrils of withdrawal started promising to make life difficult.
'Well yes, but that wasn't really what I was thinking of.'
'I know you've been on a 15 year mission to get me into frocks and mincing about in uncomfortable heels but it just 'aint going to happen.'
'Oh bloody hell no ! I've long since given up on that one. Anyway, you'd

only look like a tranny. No, I was thinking more about the singleton thing.'
'Wait a minute…' Lauren attempted to put her hand on Millie's mouth.
'Listen, don't try and shut me up.' Milled dodged her friend's hand smiling mischievously and determined not to be silenced. 'Jude. He's perfect, even if the mental image of you two together confuses me a little.'
'How do you mean ?'
'You're practically identical aren't you ? I'd never be sure which was the boy or the girl.'
'Haha..me neither.' Lauren drew on her cigarette and blew smoke into the night sky. 'But that's not necessarily a bad thing. We'd both be a bit of both.' She arched an eyebrow suggestively. 'Ooh. Nice one.'
'So. What's the problem ?'
Lauren sighed. 'Oh Mills, it's difficult. He doesn't live here does he, we'd have to go through that whole distance relationship thing, wondering what each other is up to. Also, I'm just in a really good together place at the minute. I'm scared of endangering that by throwing my heart away.'
'OK'. Mille tapped her arm.
'OK ?' Lauren had been expecting a little more arm twisting. Hoping for it as well maybe. Wishing someone would really twist her arm into giving their visitor a try.
'Yes, that's OK. You know your own mind.'
'I do ?'
'You do.' Millie sensed Lauren's slight disappointment at having got away with it so easily. Reverse psychology. It could well do the trick. 'Clearly. I'm just glad you were able to talk to me about it. Like you used to.'
Lauren smiled. 'Do you know what ?'
'What ?'
'So am I. Come on, let's go inside. I'm freezing my tiny boy tits off out here.'

   They talked for a little longer, but both were feeling exhausted and needing the healing only their beds and sleep could truly offer. Lauren gave Millie another huge hug in the hallway before going their separate ways. 'You've done the right thing you know.' She stroked her hair out of her face then placed her hands on her shoulder as she looked directly into her eyes and emphasised her point.
'I know. It's a relief.'
'So what's next then ?'
'Me time. Definitely me time. Thought I might book myself a holiday somewhere. City break or something.'
'That sounds perfect.' Lauren smiled. 'Hey I could come to. Properly this time, no stalling.'
'Really ?'

'Yeah really.' For once she thought she meant it.
'Good night then.'
'Good night.'

    Jude and Star were sitting in a window seat in the City Screen bar watching the lights play on the river.
'This is a beautiful place.' Star was gazing at the water as it gently passed by. Jude finished the last of his lager. 'I could live here.'
'Make a change from bloody Newtham,' Star sighed.
'I know. Don't make me think about it.' He put his head in his hands despairing at the prospect of a return to his tormentor of a hometown, and more awkward hours with Carly. Life needed to change. Star started playing with his hair.
'Move then.'
'What ?' He looked up.
'Move. Take yourself to University. Get that degree you missed out on.'
'God no I couldn't…' The idea was both exciting and appalling at the same time. Actually taking the leap he'd always promised himself he would, but knew in his heart of hearts he was probably too scared to ever realise.
'Why not ? Doesn't have to be here, could be anywhere. Could be London, or Leeds or Edinburgh or even abroad.'
'Star noooo…I'd miss you too much.'
'The last thing I want for you Jude is to see you growing old and unhappy in a shit-hole like Newtham. You're too big and beautiful for it. You need to move on.'
'I guess. I have wondered you know.'
'I know you have. I want you to do it as well. Not because I want rid of you, just because I want what's best for you. I'd miss you like crazy, but I'd never stand in your way.'
'No ?'
'Course not. Anyway, I'd be coming to stay with you before you knew it.'
'You could come with me !'
'Eh, now…don't let's get ahead of ourselves here. Let's see what happens.'
'But it's a possibility ?' Jude was like an E-number fuelled child when he got an idea into his head.
'It's a possibility.' Star smiled. Non-committal but secretly thinking that her best friend was once again making perfect sense.
'Yay ! We're moving !' He shouted a bit too loud. The people around them glanced in their direction.
'Don't get excited just yet.' Star hushed her voice, hoping Jude would follow. 'Keep a lid on it.'
'Oh, Ok then.' He smiled and put a finger on his closed lips.

You and me song…

Jude woke with a slight headache. He could hear someone busying around in the kitchen. It must be Millie. She was working today. Star was on the sofa, her left arm hanging off, her mouth slightly open, a light sheen of dribble seeping over her chin as she made a slight snore. Fast off. He smiled and put his head back down, closed his eyes and tried to go back to sleep. He was drifting off into a satisfying shallow snooze, when the sound of the heavy front door slamming shut made him jump up. That would be Millie on her way to work.

It was no good. He had to get up. Yawning, and stretching, he saw Star begin to stir. She opened one eye, saw her friend standing there and smiled.
'Aww morning babes. Cup of tea if you'd be so kind.'
Jude shook his head. 'Oh darn it. I thought I'd got away with it this morning.'
'No such luck. I'm like a coiled python me ready to pounce at the first sign of movement.'
'Cereals ?'
'They're not ours though J. We should ask first.'
'Lauren said help yourselves.' He shrugged.
Star sat up from under her coverless duvet 'Did you see in her cupboard yesterday ? Biscuits, pot noodles, crisps, and Kit-Kats. No proper food at all. She's worse than me.'
'Ooh Kit-Kat for brekkie !'
'Actually, that doesn't sound too bad. Go on then. Lauren won't mind. I'll replace them when I go out.' Star giggled then laid back down with her hands under her head, examining the ceiling.

Jude took himself into the kitchen. His stomach was already in knots. He was spending the day with Lauren. His weird mirror-image woman with whom he knew he was falling. Falling into what exactly he couldn't really tell just yet. Whatever it was it made him feel alive, yet unsettled. Oh god. What was he going to say to her ? Normally conversation wasn't a problem but just being in her presence turned him near jelly. Then he heard her bedroom door open and a heavy footed pound pad its way down the hallway. Jude turned around knowing what this meant. There she stood at the door to the kitchen in a huge oversized Sonic Youth t-shirt, barefoot, her hair falling messily over her face, lifting an arm to eyes that were barely open. She yawned, then handed him a dirty mug.

'If you're making one…ta.' She turned and started to head back towards the hall, pausing for a second at the doorway to speak again. 'Oh and help yourself to a breakfast Kit-Kat. Just the ordinary ones in the multi-pack. I save the Chunkies for dinner as they're more substantial.'

She then made a slight sleepy groan, stretched her arms, and padded flat-footed back down the hall and into her room. Jude's mouth hung open. Even first thing in the morning she looked gorgeous. Shabby with it admittedly. She was one of those mysterious people who seemed to make zero effort, always looked vaguely dishevelled, but absolutely beguiling and together with it. All her clothes were spot on for her. They fitted her personality. She wore them, not the other way round. You found it hard to ever imagine her making an outrageous fashion faux-pas along the way. Cool was the word. She was definitely cool. He looked at his hand as it reached to open her cupboard door. It was shaking.

Tea bags. Biscuit tin. Concentrate.

Star, Lauren and Jude had sat watching the breakfast news, eating Kit-Kats and drinking tea, before Star had made her excuses, taken herself into the bathroom, got dressed and said her goodbyes. It was Jude and Lauren. Together. They were perched awkwardly on the sofa. Each struggling to find the right words. Finally, Lauren thought she should take the initiative. She was just being silly. It wasn't as if he was her boyfriend or anything. They were just hanging out together for the day. That was all.
'What do you fancy doing ?' She asked.
'Don't know really.'
'That's a help.'
'Sorry.'
'No worries.' She tapped his knee. 'We could go for a walk. It's not raining.'
'That would be nice. By the river ?'
'By the river.' Lauren nodded and got to her feet.

Down on the tree hung footpath along by the River Ouse, conversation was still hard to come by. Lauren was beginning to think this was a bad idea. She just didn't make new friends. Never knew what to say to people, never felt much need to say anything. Jude was clearly nervous. She was trying not to be but every casual glance at his soft features made her stomach turn over with mixed longing and dread at acting on her feelings. It was all just too uncomfortable. It reminded her why she didn't do romance and was grateful that what sex drive she had didn't compel her into situations like this on a regular basis. She'd walk to the ends of the earth for a brilliant, life-changing book or a breathtaking bit of Swedish indie pop, but a shag was nothing to get too excited about. Not unless you really meant it. She felt a bit sorry for people who were so driven by their biology that it became the imperative that ultimately dominated their lives. Dumb climax junkies. The culture was so sex soaked wasn't it ? Lauren didn't feel any kind of prudish disapproval towards it, just a mild boredom and a little bewilderment. No, make that bemusement. All these people randomly following their most animal instincts. It was just funny. Clever, thoughtful people rendering themselves as stupid as the kind of slavering idiots who beat themselves off to the Daily Sport or dodgy satellite wank channels. Yuk. She liked to think herself more evolved, and well, just better than the herd. Conceited ? Well yes. But she had plenty of reason to be conceited. She was sorted. She rocked.

Maybe there was a natural aristocracy ? Her heroine Virginia Woolf had asserted as much. It was made up of smart, gender-transcendent people like her and Jude. The ones who didn't reduce themselves to clichés, who just weren't that driven or defined by their biology. The ones who could be any number of things dependent on where their interests took them. Who felt no need to be one of the girls or one of the lads, but instead were happy to just be one of the species. The ones who didn't reduce themselves to sex-games, the kind of people who when they mated did so as much with the intellect, and the inner-person as they did with the body. The kind of people for whom the culture's ideas about what was or wasn't meant to be attractive held little real attraction. In short, people who thought for themselves. Like her. Like Jude. Free-will, not being a slave of your anatomy, self-determination. These were the true marks of the more evolved. Those ahead of the herd. They were the future.

Jude on the other hand was considering more melancholy matters. The story of Matt. The ex-boyfriend ghost who had spoken to Lauren. What was he like ? Was he really her soul mate ? Was he a proper bloke ? The kind of bloke that Jude just couldn't be ? Was he going to fail to connect properly to her because of this, was she looking at him as a friend not as a potential partner ? Where was the difference when most of your mates were girls anyway ? There had been countless times when women he'd really liked had regarded him as nothing more than one of the girls, whilst going off with blokes who he felt were clueless insensitive beasts. The kind of men who took the piss out of him or laughed at what they saw as his failings in the masculinity stakes. Stakes that he had never understood or seen any reason in which to compete. Then something disturbing troubled his mind. What if Matt were watching them now ?

'Do you think there's an afterlife ?' He finally spoke.

'No, not really.' Lauren looked at him a little confused. 'Where did that come from ?'

'Don't know really. Sometimes your mortality just hits you doesn't it and you wonder.'

'I guess. I think death is just like falling asleep. I like sleep. I can't see it being too much of a problem.'
'I wish I felt the same. Death scares me shitless.'
'I think it does most people. I've seen too much of it of late.' She bent down, picked up a stick from the cycle path and threw it over arm into the river.
'Do you mean that guy you were going out with ? Tell me to shut up if you don't want to talk about it.'
'Nah, you're alright.' She shrugged and looked nonplussed.' I don't mind. There's that and there was this other thing earlier in the year. But I really don't want to talk about that.'
'No worries.'
'Look Jude.' She stopped and took hold of his hand. 'I'm not some emotional screw-up because a past boyfriend probably took his own life you know. It's made me more cautious, but I'm not a fuck-up.'
'I never thought you were.' Jude shook his head. He really hoped he hadn't offended her.
'Good. I know what I'm about and I think I'm a pretty good judge of character.'
'So what do you make of me then.'
She smiled. 'I think you're a lovely human being who seems to get what I'm about and in whose company I feel good about myself. There. Satisfied ?' She looked away, her cheeks starting to redden. Her outward composure, for once, was beginning to be betrayed.
'Gosh I…'
'You don't have to lie. I know you don't feel the same.'
'No, god, I do. I do feel the same. You're amazing.' He took hold of her other hand and looked directly at her. She tentatively started to turn her eyes towards him, fixing his gaze. A gaze that made her feel both uncomfortable and alive, but from which she was finding it difficult to disengage.
'I'm many things Jude, but I'm not amazing.'
'To me you are.'
'Oh. Ok then.' They paused staring at each other, the mood pregnant with expectation. 'Suppose we better kiss again then.'
'I guess.'

They moved in close and their mouths slowly locked. It had felt like an eternity but it was over in a matter of seconds. They moved away simultaneously, their synchronicity glossing over their reflected awkwardness. Their arms fell around each other and they held one another oblivious of their surroundings. They stood together in silence for a moment before Lauren finally looked at him.
'Shall we head back to the flat ?' She whispered.

Jude smiled. 'I think we should.'
She took hold of his hand and led him swiftly back along the footpath.

Lee was enjoying the new day. He had a spring in his step. It was so nice to see the sun again. It had been rare for him to get out and about so early of late. For the best part of the last 12 months he'd been living in a strange sterile dream world, never fully able to control himself. Locked in a cycle of underachievement and lethargy, what passed for his existence slowly being reduced to a small bedsit, a mental health diagnosis and no sense of really fitting. Now he felt as if he were becoming part of the world again.

It was love that was doing it. And his photography of course. Art was giving him life. He'd realised in the night. Sleep had been difficult. His mind had been far too active, his stomach tied in knots. He couldn't stop looking at the photos of Millie. She was so perfect. It wasn't just lust, although the thought of her naked on all fours before him wouldn't leave his head. No this was definitely L.O.V.E. That four letter word was so potent. He used to be cynical about true love and happily ever afters, but something had clicked in the coffee bar. He really felt something for this girl. He was almost fairly certain she'd feel the same.

Down along the riverbank, he'd paused and allowed himself to take some photos of the ducks and geese who were gathered by a houseboat grooming themselves. Nature photography. Not his true direction admittedly but he was sure they'd look nice enough. Good to get some diversity in your portfolio. Whilst he was crouched at goose level talking to wildfowl, two people in matching shoes hurried past, far too bound up in each other to notice anyone, never mind Lee's insignificant stain of a presence hunched in concentration.

Back at the flat they could barely contain themselves. Lauren and Jude locked in a passionate embrace in the hallway before she pulled away and led them both into her bedroom. She stuck the 'Do Not Disturb' sign she'd nicked from a Travelodge on the door. It was a slightly tongue in cheek attempt to protect her privacy from Millie's random intrusions into her space. Not that she minded. Not really. Except now of course. This was different. The last thing she wanted was Mills bustling in as she was making the beast with two backs with Jude. She was at work so it shouldn't be an issue, but you could never totally relax in shared accommodation could you ?
As they stripped off their clothing, layer after layer of self-protection and denial, together they started to feel as if their bodies could make some sense of what they were starting to feel inside. As if the biological urge had a point after all. In these circumstances it did. Connection that was it. In the perfect midst of it all it didn't matter who was doing what to whom, or which was

boy or girl, as such arbitrary distinctions dissolved in the moment. They were simply conjoined souls, together in their otherness. Lost in something bigger than the sum of its parts, they became whole in each other's arms.

So this was what sex was meant to be ? Not just a casual and debased exchange of fluid, but a deeply layered, meaningful joining of souls. In a godless universe, it gave you a glimpse of the divine. Neither had felt anything like it before.

As they lay together in silence stroking one another's hair and gazing in meaningful distraction at the cracked dirty cream woodchip on the ceiling, the sublime sense of peace they found was all embracing. They could hear voices outside, the noise of the traffic, the comings and goings in the shop below. They could stay like this for hours.

Jude was the first this time to break the silence. He needed to step out of the prescriptive over-cautious box into which he'd placed himself. Something was starting to bug him. If they didn't talk, they could lose this. And he didn't want to contemplate that. This was unreal. This was perfect.
'So what's next ?' Courage finally opened his mouth. His nerves reminding him that despite the intensity of what they had just shared, they were still relative strangers. Lauren sighed.
'Don't Jude.' She gently placed a hand on his full beautiful lips.
And then they were silent again.

Party of one…

Star wandered out of the City Art Gallery. It had been mildly distracting, but without Jude's ever present company she was feeling oddly self-conscious. She was alone wasn't she ? Not only in the relationship sense but in life. She was going to die alone one day. Wasn't that the nature of our reality ? We came into the world on our own, we die on our own. No, that was a stupid self-obsessed saying. It was undoubtedly conjured up by a man. You were accompanied into the world by your mother, a midwife, flesh, blood, agony and ecstasy, and when you leave it unless you're a misanthrope of the highest order you're missed by someone. We all made connections. We all left some kind of stain, be it fair or foul. So in the crowd of anonymous faces, she wasn't really alone. None of us were, and in her solitude she could allow herself to feel part of everything and nothing at the same time. There was freedom in this, and she became conscious of her slowly returning smile as she headed back towards the centre of the city.

What had surprised her most over the past few days was just how far she had healed. Kyle's absence was no longer a pain and even if it wasn't yet a relief, it certainly wasn't a life-ending matter. Not something so mundane as all this. What a waste of melodrama that would be. No life should be wasted on a loser like Kyle. It would be paying him the ultimate compliment. No utterly predictable, utterly ordinary man was worth that kind of sacrifice. None of them were.

Had she really been seconds away from slicing that razor-blade across her wrist ? The thought made her shudder. No, of course she hadn't. It was self-pitying mannered posture. She wasn't her mother. And anyway, her guardian angel would never have allowed it to happen. She wondered how that angel was getting on. She hoped he was doing alright with her cousin. Although what would happen if he got seriously together with someone ? It had always been Star in the relationship, Jude the ever present single friend who could be relied upon to provide a listening ear whenever it was needed. She was the one who'd gone to ground with boyfriends in the past, or temporarily distanced herself when some clueless bloke got shirty about their relationship. Kyle had never liked it but by the time he came along Star had been determined never to allow any man to get in the way of their friendship. If they couldn't handle it then tough. As time went by she realised it wasn't necessarily Jude's sex that boyfriend's objected to, but his lack of male clubbability. He just wasn't one of them. Didn't share their jokes or their perspective, or if he did it all felt a bit forced. That was what unsettled them. Jude just didn't fit in the narrow confines of straight male identity. Not that it seemed to bother Jude overly. But other men did get freaked. The few who didn't were sound but in the minority. In future a man's reaction to Jude would be her character bell-weather for potential boyfriends.

She mused about Lauren too. There was something equally other about her. Perhaps that was why the attraction between her and Jude seemed so instant and apparent. They recognised something in one another and it was like a light going on. They both existed in a space between or beyond genders, as if the arbitrary accident of their bodies was an irrelevance. They both could have gone either way and in each case their personalities wouldn't have been any different. That they just weren't rooted or defined by their physical nature.

This thought unsettled her slightly. What if the connection was so great it superseded what she and Jude had shared over the years, what if this was some kind of homecoming for Jude ? He had talked clumsily about these kind of things in the past but she'd never really understood. How could she ? There was no way she could ever fully get her head around something so profound, key and personal to his identity as that. If this was to be a homecoming she couldn't help but feel happy for him but hoped that Lauren wasn't about to displace her in his affections.

According to Millie, Lauren was a real loner, had only a handful of friends and felt little compunction to be with anyone, never mind a significant other. How could you be like that ? Most people wanted or needed someone, even if they grew used to being single by circumstance, but with Lauren you got the impression it really wasn't any kind of posture. Was this because she never really fitted either ? Star could well imagine what growing up would have been like for a girl like her. Tall, a bit gangly, looking pretty but boyish and unconventional, not really being that girly or approachable. She would have stuck out like a sore thumb. Friends would not have been that easy to come by. The dyke accusations would have been flying, and the boys would have avoided her as well as they tried to attract and find favour with the more conventional girls who made her life a misery. Star's early school years had been difficult, but as she grew she found herself able to merge with the crowd. Find middling anonymity among her peers. She had known girls like Lauren, and had stayed silent as the group ostracised them. Remembering that now she felt slightly ashamed, but it had been done out of self-protection. Girls like Lauren had taken the heat off girls like her. Without them Star herself could easily have been the one who everyone turned against.

You perhaps needed to be a loner to survive. Which came first though ? Lauren's introversion or her exclusion ? Maybe if you were someone who needed validation from other people that kind of isolation from your peers would have been unbearable. If you were someone like Lauren who seemed blissfully content in their own company it was probably easier to put up with. This was just surmising though. Perhaps Lauren had been a popular extrovert at school. Somehow though, Star doubted it.

This musing would have to be put on pause for a short while. She needed to buy Kit-Kats.

Millie had been unable to resist. The previous night on the back landing had reminded her of the relief that only nicotine could bring. She'd bought a ten pack of Benson & Hedges from the newsagent. Not knowing what brand of cigarette to buy or how many, she asked for the first pack she saw. And a packet of disposable lighters.

She stood outside the front door of the Opera House, inhaling deeply, loving the illicit thrill of it all. It felt naughty, and a bit anti-social. She'd changed over the past few years. For the worse as well. She'd definitely allowed herself to get boring. Danger, excitement, being a bit more herself, not what she thought she should be. Sod men. Sod being neurotic about good health or a few extra pounds. Sod thinking that she had to conform to what everyone expected of her. She'd been too good at that. Now she was going to embrace a little of her flatmate's F-You attitude and see where it leaded her.

The cigarette was helping take the edge off the awkwardness she was currently feeling. Her colleagues had seen what had happened a couple of nights earlier, and guessed the reasons for her absence the morning after. None of them had mentioned Lauren's little scene, but the cautious way they were talking to her suggested they knew all about it. It was deeply uncomfortable. Then she saw him. The strange awkward guy. Walking up the other side of the street was the man she'd literally ran into the day before. Did he say his name was Lee ? He had his camera around his neck again and seemed to be snapping random passers-by. Weird. Mustn't let him see her.

Millie hung her head and examined her ballet pumps. They were looking a bit shabby. She definitely needed a new pair. Would nip to New Look after she'd done here. They had loads and they were dirt cheap. She glanced up. Ohmigod. He'd seen her. He was looking towards her, smiling, his face slightly manic. She looked away and quickly started stamping out her cigarette. As she turned to go back into the building she felt a restraining hand upon her shoulder.

'Millie ?'

It was her. His new love. There she was, waiting for him. It was like something from a dream or a film. He'd come for her. It was like the fulfilment of something. Tying up the ends of the plot. He was here for her. He was going to rescue her.

God, she was still just as perfect, although he was disappointed to see that she smoked. It was a filthy habit and even more unbecoming on a lady. Cassie smoked. And her doubtless lezzer friends. Knocked back the black coffee and always had a fag on their bottom lips. Disgusting.

Never mind. Soon put a stop to his new love's habit. She seemed quite pliable. He'd be able to mould her into something worthwhile. She made nervous little jump when he touched her. It was quite becoming. It must be because he was just so damn masterful these days. Like that Heathcliff fella from that Bronte book he'd never read.

'Yes. Sorry. Hi.' She turned and looked at him. She looked at him. She was looking at him.

He looked dreadful. A real disgrace of a man, but totally unremarkable and like so many of his peers around a similar age. What happened to men that made them turn from attractive hotties who made an effort in their early twenties to these smug paunchy careless freaks in such a short space of time ? His face was drawn, his eyes red raw from what looked like sleeplessness. He was wearing a long-sleeve grey t-shirt that stretched over his defiant belly, it was stained and there were clear ring marks expanding from underneath his armpits. It couldn't just be poverty that was making him look so shabby. Neither she nor Lauren had much to spare but they still looked half-decent in their own very different ways.

He wore no coat despite the autumnal chill in the air. He stank as well. Stale sweat and food. He looked even more disgusting than he had the previous day. Then his camera clicked again. She looked shocked and surprised. He just grinned.

'Would you mind not doing that please.' Millie was annoyed.
'Doing what ?'
'Pointing that thing at me.' Millie gestured toward his camera.
'What this ?' He lifted his camera to his eye and took another snap. He wasn't about to be told what to do by his new girlfriend. She'd only just met him and besides, she was probably only teasing.
'Please don't do that.'
'What…' he started to lift the camera towards his eye. His subject matter was irritated. She instinctively hit out, slapping the camera, stopping it's upward movement and in the process dislodging it from his hand. It crashed onto the pavement, the batteries immediately pinging out. They began to roll down the slight incline of the street and away from Lee, who turned his panicked head back towards Millie.
'You stupid fucking cow !' He spat, his fury immediately displacing his creepy smile.
'Sorry I just didn't want…' Maybe she shouldn't have done that. Now he was angry.
'You silly, silly little bitch.' He was shaking with rage, his face contorted and animalistic.
'I'm sorry, but I'm going.' Her heart was beating fast in her chest, this was awful. What a nutjob, she quickly made to go into the Opera House, but before she could a hand was gripping hold of the white collar of her work shirt.
'You're not going anywhere.' He whispered aggressively into her ear. She tried to pull away but couldn't. There was only one thing for it. Scream. Very loudly.
'Aaaaaaarrrrrrrrrrgggghhhhhhhhhhhhhh' An ear piercing high-pitched bawl. Passers by who until now had been vaguely aware of something not right going on across the road, broke from their studied indifference and stopped in their tracks. A male colleague darted out of the theatre.
'What's wrong. Millie ?' It was Dave, a young stage hand. He was affable and polite. A nice boy. He'd been leaning against the box office counter chatting with Hannah, a fellow young employee for whom he'd long held a torch, but who had shown not the slightest interest in reciprocating, when the scream had made him nearly drop his coffee. This was a chance to impress his love

interest.

'She's mine !' Lee was wide-eyed as he saw Dave appear.

'Now calm down fella.' In turn, Dave just looked bewildered.

'Leave us alone. She's mine.'

Millie was shaking with fear.

'Look I don't know what the problem is but…'

'Call the police. Quickly !' Millie shouted at her colleague. 'Or get more help. Get more help.' She was wriggling, slowly losing a grip on what remained of her composure, in the process beginning to look hysterical. This gave her attacker chance to twist how the scenario was playing out to bystanders. People on the opposite side of the road slowed down, or stopped completely rapt by what they were seeing.

'Police ? What the fuck are you on about ? They're not going to get involved in a domestic.' Lee shook his head and laughed to himself.

'Sorry Millie, is this your boyfriend ?' Lee's behaviour was doing enough to start to sow seeds of doubt in the young stage-hand's mind. Inexperience maybe was getting the better of him.

'No he's not my fucking boyfriend. For god's sake look at him.' Millie couldn't see any real reason for hesitation.

'Sorry. Who is he then ?' Dave had lost his earlier dynamism. This looked too complicated for him to get involved.

'I've no idea, he's a lunatic.'

'Lunatic ?' Lee's grin threatened to explode out of the confines of his face. 'I don't think so my darling. That's not what you told me last night.' He attempted to kiss her cheek, pulling her closer. Millie kept moving her head but eventually he landed his lips on her. She contorted her face into an expression of complete disgust.

'I don't think I should get involved.' Dave started to back off, a sight which just incensed his captured colleague further.

'David. This man is attacking me in the street.' She raged. ' He's a stranger. I think you SHOULD get fucking involved.'

'Don't listen to her mate, she's clearly raving.' Lee was enjoying this. He'd gone into casual blokey bluster. It seemed to be working. 'Stopped taking her medication, she's all over the place.' He made a little screwy gesture at the side of his head with the pointed forefinger of his free hand.

'Millie is this ?' This was too much for one so young to deal with. And all that business the other night at the psychic thing. That had been a bit weird hadn't it ? Maybe Millie was having some kind of breakdown. He didn't really know the woman.

'No it's not true. It's not fucking true, just do something.' She stamped her feet, and violently tried to pull herself free.

'Don't listen to her mate.' Lee continued. 'I think we need to get her some medical attention pretty sharpish before she hurts herself. You know how hysterical women can get you.'

Lee was in charge, he was on top of his game, this was too good to be true. He'd got his lady. Sure she was resisting a little and making a bit of a scene of things, but he'd handled it well so far hadn't he ? The scene in itself had been an opportunity to assert a bit of dominance. A bit of order on the world. It was good to hold his new girlfriend and if anything the wriggling was a turn-on. The young lad didn't suspect anything. And if he did he'd cut him some slack. There was a man thing going down here wasn't there ? Then he felt a tap on his shoulder.

'Oi mate. How's this for hysterical ?'

A flying left hook hit his head and sent him reeling. He immediately lost his grip on Millie's collar and wobbled across the pavement, dizzy and confused, his cocky confidence rudely shattered.

Lauren stood there smiling. Then she examined her knuckles. 'Ouch.' She turned to see Lee glaring at her from his semi-prone position. 'Don't mess mate.' She grinned and shook her head. He'd definitely had it coming. Generally she was a pacifist but some people just took the piss didn't they ? 'You ! It's you.' He pointed at her. He was hysterical.

'Yeah it's me' She put her hands on her hips and broadened her shoulders. 'And I've had about enough of your perving pal. See that pretty thing over there.' Lauren pointed across the road to where Jude was standing talking into his phone. 'He's just calling the police.'

'Gosh Lauren. How did you know ?' Mills was straightening herself off and stood mildly in awe of her best friend. What a star. What an absolute life-saving fucking star.

'Just call me your guardian angel Mills. I've special powers. ' She smiled at her flat-mate. 'And I brought you your pack-up. You'd left it on the kitchen table. Can't have you living on Kit-Kats and crisp sandwiches you know.' They hugged briefly, but as Lauren moved away she made to sniff Millie's hair. 'Have you been smoking ? You really reek.'

Lee sat alone in the cold of the police cell. His head in his hands. That punch. It had done something. Knocked some sense into him his dad would have said.

How had this been allowed to happen ? What had he been thinking ? The intense mental charade of the last few days was making itself painfully scarce. He was being confronted with the reality of what he'd been doing. His mind was finding its way back to proper perspective and the part he'd just been playing was starting to look disturbing. Had he really been doing that ? Lee Canning. The good boy. The nice modern guy. Wandering around taking photographs of random women, working himself into a frenzy of hate for people who differed from himself, finding weird justifications for appalling behaviour.

And it all ultimately sprang from one thing. That slap. That stupid fucking slap. Or maybe that slap had sprung from something deeper. The straightjacket of his identity, his failure to really come to terms with himself, his constant need for easy, straightforward answers. The desire to fit in, to just be one of the lads, the fear of complexity, the sense that he might not be all that he should be. A way of living in the world that sought to remain unexamined for fear of what probing might discover. That covered up its insecurities with bluster and the anonymity of the herd. He remembered Simon Redburn. That poor, poor boy. What they'd subjected him to. The living misery they must have made of his life. How utterly shameful. He felt himself to be a coward for not speaking out. For going along with the meatheads.

That moment he'd lost it and delivered the slap, the second he'd allowed himself to become an angry bloke-ish cliché. A subject for a problem page letter, a 'can he ever be trusted' feature on a low-rent daytime telly discussion show, an 'it all begins with a slap' warning to the world. He'd transgressed a cardinal rule, but he'd so easily transgressed it because he had never asked what the reasons for not doing it were, or why it was seen as a great act of self-control not to. He had felt powerless in a place where his upbringing, his peers, his own subconscious had told him he should remain powerful. Incapable of dealing with the shame he felt, he had reacted with a targeted nuclear strike. Then had come meltdown. It wasn't the insignificance or otherwise of a half-hearted open hand to the face that had been the problem, but what it symbolised. The charade of his nice guy image hid complexity upon complexity, that remained fearful of being found out. The camera strung around his neck of the last few days, accosting a woman he barely knew, these were all part of the same problem. He had failed as a human being by reducing himself to an angry little aggrieved man. The taunting he'd received had been intense and pointed, but that in no way excused his response. He had been unable to handle the situation, he had been incapable of finding the words, the emotions to defuse her anger. He hadn't been able to act as a rational, emotionally literate human being. Instead he had chosen to take the intolerant 'how dare you speak to me like that' road of the pathetically, angrily emasculated man. The kind of men who feel the only way they can assert what they feel themselves to be is through fists, bruises and broken bones.

The position he was now in had some logic to it. A man who feels it acceptable to hit his partner should experience a cold cell. Even if it was just a slap. A thorough kicking or a red-glowing hand mark on a woman's face. They all sprang from the same set of unquestioned assumptions, the same bad attitude.

He now needed to admit he was wrong. He needed help. He needed to root himself in something or someone good. A steadier. A moral compass. He needed his best friend. He needed Noah. He had one phone call. He'd better not fuck that up as well.

Don't get me wrong…

Millie had insisted on going back to work, so after ensuring she was alright, Lauren and Jude had found themselves in the café at the Theatre Royal eating jacket potatoes. Millie was determined that despite everything that had happened, she wasn't about to be freaked out, nor did she want to get in the way of the last chance her best friend and the clearly made for her visitor would have to be together and to come to their stupid, stubborn senses.
'That was impressive you know' Jude was smiling.
'Oh god…' she batted it away. 'Thought I might be a bit rusty as I've not done it in ages…well not that I can remember.'
'No it was some punch.'
'Punch ?' She had a fork-full of cheesy potato suspended half-way betwixt plate and open mouth. 'Oh sorry, I thought you were talking about the sex.'
'Noooo.' Jude blushed and hid his face behind his hands. Finally peering from behind one, he looked at her. 'But that was pretty special.'
'Awww cheers dude. You were pretty hot yourself. Now change the subject before I die of embarrassment.'
'But it was on your mind though.'
Lauren shoved Jude in the chest. 'Jude. Shut up !'
'Ok, Ok'
Then the silence returned. It was awful. There was so much they wanted to say to one another but couldn't. Lauren felt the need to take this whole thing in hand. Arrest her scatty chain of thought. It had been a lovely special interlude. He was a good mate. Now they'd got over the attraction thing it would all be simpler. She would make the effort to keep in touch. When she got in she'd send him that Myspace friend request. Now and again they could probably meet up for a drink. Probably with Star and Millie in tow. Friends. That was a big enough word to contain their relationship. Good friends maybe. Time would tell.
'Are you off home tomorrow then ?'
Had she really just asked that ? It had taken an act of will and doubtless sounded awful. As if, having had her wicked way with him, she was now eager to shuffle him off. She sort of hoped he might think she was asking

because she didn't want him to, even if that was the opposite of her intentions. It pained her. It *really* pained her. But she needed rid.

'I'm not sure. Why ?' His face was distrustful. Not knowing quite how to respond, as if its owner was beginning to fear the worse, but was attempting valiantly to hide the fact.

'Oh no reason. It's just.'

'Yes ?'.

'I think it might be for the best if you probably did.' Concise. Crisp. Lacking emotion. Androgynous android. Nothing was given away. Despite the fact her heart was beginning to break at what her rationality was now making it suffer.

'Oh I thought...' He looked as if his world had just fallen apart. Lauren felt like a bitch. The worst kind of bitch.

'Jude, don't take this the wrong way or anything, you're dead special.' She took hold of his hand. 'But I've already explained that this can't go anywhere. If you hang around for too long I think it might not be good for either of our sanities.'

'So you do feel something for me ?' He was so hurt. She could see it all over his achingly beautiful face. He looked like he was going to cry. Those eyes. They were filling. She'd made those soulful windows well-up. It was gut-wrenching to watch when all she wanted to do was hold him, make it all better, love the pain away. But she couldn't. She just couldn't.

'I never said I didn't. I don't jump into bed with someone totally sober unless I feel something for them. I feel a lot for you. Perhaps too much.' The last three words were a concession. Something escaping from her bolted down heart that strained and bucked against the shackles under which she had secured it.

'How can you feel too much. I don't understand ?' This seemed to placate him a little. Gave him hope.

'I mean that I know what I'm about. If I fell deeply for someone else I could get lost. I think I could easily lose myself in you Jude and it scares me. Can you respect that ?'

'Of course I can.' No histrionics. No aggrieved male pride. No trying to assert his dominance at this point, or to throw wild accusations of her in an attempt to assuage the pain. True to form, he'd been totally different. Totally unscripted. Totally himself. Lauren couldn't help but believe she was starting to think the world of him. He was special. 'I'll speak to Star when she gets in. Ask if we can go home tomorrow.'

'Thank you.' She held his hands and smiled. 'You're lovely.'

'So I've been told.'

   Then silence returned and they both looked out of the window, pretending to watch the traffic, but really seeing nothing.

'Ayup mate. 'Ow's it going ? '

The cell door swung open and in walked the broad chested, bravado filled bluster and good cheer of Noah Aloysius Gimcrack. The last of the Whitby whaler's. So called because he always used to fall for the larger woman. Long before the days such a preference was known as chubby chasing. He just needed a bigger lass because there was an awful lot of him needed taking care of. Skinny vain birds just weren't up to the job. Nor were they ever much fun. Nor were they interested. The fuller figured woman kept him in check. As long as they had a personality to match their chips and chocolate habit then they generally kept him humble. Like his Debs. She definitely kept him humble.

He was smiling. A big friendly, problem engulfing smile. 'Looks like you landed yourself in a spot of bother.' He sat down next to Lee who instinctively threw his arms around his best friend and unselfconsciously started to cry. What a relief. Noah was such a huge fucking relief. 'Come on now fella. It's nowt we can't sort out. You're not on your own you know.'

The rest of afternoon had been awkward. Jude and Lauren had eventually returned to the flat to discover Star sitting in front of the TV working her way through Millie's DVDs. Mean Girls had followed Dirty Dancing which had been preceded by Moulin Rouge. It was a bit like being at home. She had immediately picked up on the fact that all had not gone according to plan. Lauren had made her excuses and taken herself into her room to read her book, take a nap and potter around on the internet. It was ever thus. The kind of routine she usually followed and particularly needed to today if she were not to have her world turned upside down by how she were feeling. Jude had sat with his best friend, finding conversation difficult when normally it just flowed. Randomly, effortlessly. He looked disconsolate. Star could feel his pain. It was awful.

'I think we should go home tomorrow Star.' He said after a long period of silence. He didn't look at her. Had no expression in his voice.

'But I thought..'

'Can we ?'

'Of course, if that's what you want.' She didn't know what to make of this. What the hell had happened between them ? Were these things normally this complicated ?

'It is.'

'You sure ?' This couldn't be right. Those two. They were so perfect. Utterly symmetrical. What was wrong ?

'I'm very sure.'

Answers might just have to wait.

That evening Jude and Lauren had barely been able to look at one another. The tension was difficult for Star and Millie to deal with. They tried their best to remain breezy but the atmosphere in the flat went beyond awkward. Moving through it was like running through glue.

Luckily Lauren had a date to keep. With her employer. It was hardly a prospect that filled her with much delight but a promises was a promise. With her head still full of the awkward delight and peculiarity of the day, she left the flat and stepped out into the night. The air was cold and cleansing. It was such a relief to be out of there. It was just a shame she had to subject herself to her employer's weirdness,

Lauren once again wondered what she was doing as she turned down Marygate. This frequently happened. Peculiar invitations would arrive out of the blue, she'd say yes to them before she'd had chance to think and then spend the time leading up to them feeling increasingly disorientated about the whole thing. This though was a newish boss. She needed to keep him on side, even if the employment was only part-time. Mr Lindacre had said he lived near the boarded up Bay Horse pub but Lauren was having trouble finding his address. A gang of cagoule wearing exchange students, possibly Spanish pushed past her on the pavement. One of the girls was giving her an evil sideways glance, so she stood her ground and made them walk round her. Small victories made life much more bearable. Just as she was looking up at the spire of St. Olave's church and wondering if she would bother after all, tell Mr Lindacre something had come up then retire to the Ackhorne for a drink and the paper, she heard a door click behind her.

'Ah Lauren.'

She turned with a start. 'Oh Mr Lindacre…hi.' Darn it. Her freedom dash thwarted.

'You found me.'

'Sure looks like it.'

'Excellent. Excellent. Well do step inside.' He held the door back and gestured for her to walk inside the little terraced house.

'Okay' This hadn't been a good idea. She really wasn't in the mood. If she hadn't of been so frickin desperate to get out of the flat she'd have texted her apologies. Just where exactly was he leading her ? For a second she thought of Mr Benn. The childhood cartoon where a little bowler hat wearing man entered a fancy dress shop, got kitted out in an outfit then disappeared into the time period from which it belonged. Perhaps inside she was going to become a Victorian lady, talking bashfully to a frock-coat wearing Mr Lindacre about the state of the Gladstone government. Actually, wouldn't such a conversation have been off limits for a lady at that point ? Maybe she'll just be sitting in the corner doing her needlepoint whilst Roger

Lindacre paces the drawing room reading improving verses aloud from scripture. Jesus frickin Christ on a pushbike. What a desperate thought that was.

For so many reasons she was glad to be a child of the late 20th century. That corsetry would have killed her. And have been totally unnecessary. She knew from bitter experience that more than a couple of hours in a skirt or a frock turned her mental. She always quite liked the idea of being one of those lounge suit wearing women from the 20s who smoked cigars, brilliantined their hair and got involved in horseplay. Not that she was particularly sure what horseplay actually involved, but she was sure there was nothing equine about it. Good job, animals didn't really like her.

God knows what people would have made of her strange androgynous self back then. A few centuries earlier she'd undoubtedly have been hanged for witchcraft. Maybe that's what Mr Lindacre had in mind ? Perhaps he was going to chuck her in the bath to see if she floated. Her mind was a strange place to inhabit at times. Where did all this stuff come from ? In the semi-real world she now found herself in, Mr Lindacre was leading her through to his dining room.

The house wasn't as she expected at all. The hallway had the original Victorian tiles on the floor, but the walls were tidy and painted a subtle cream. There were some interesting block canvas prints hung strategically. It didn't look as if it belonged to someone who lived in 1878. The dining room was similarly plain, functional and of modest taste. A small rectangular dining table was set with chairs at either end. It had a functional, slightly too perfect, almost unlived in feel. It was definitely the product of a male brain she thought. She could spot these things. There was little homely about it. All kind of assembled by numbers. A look decided upon, then completed with attention to detail, and ticks placed next to the serial numbers in sample catalogues. Maybe Roger was bordering on the autistic. It kind of fitted. There was a definite trainspotter tendency about antiquarian books. For Lauren, books were about the stories, or the information they contained, the insight into the human condition they could give. To a lot of the regulars at the bookshop they were about particular editions, or bindings and gradations in condition, or re-sell value. It was an odd way to view something so crucial to her life. Something as essential to her continued existence as food, clothes and shelter. Certainly far more essential than sex. Even if the sex she'd had earlier had been pretty damn hot. She could get used to that. No. Stop that right there.

'I'm so glad you could make it Lauren, I don't get the chance to entertain very often.' Roger Lindacre beamed. He looked genuinely pleased to see her. 'No, thanks for inviting me Mr Lindacre.' Well you had to return these kind of pleasantries didn't you ? If not you just looked difficult. She was difficult,

there was no need to draw attention to the fact. Particularly not with her employer.
'Please call me Roger.' He smiled, showing his teeth and allowing the skin in the corners of his eyes to fold. He held it for what to Lauren looked like a second or two too long. As if he'd learnt how to do it from a textbook but had missed the bit about releasing it before you started resembling a psychopath. One played by Jack Nicholson. It was mildly unsettling.
'Oh, ok Roger.' She stood there awkwardly and looked around the room. There didn't seem to be much in the way of clutter. Then looked at her host. He was still staring at her. ' Er..thanks.'
'Wine ?'
'Yes, wine. Wine would be good.' She nodded.
'Merlot ?'
'Pardon ?' Mer-low ? Was that some strange archaic form of acknowledgement she'd never had any reason to encounter ? What with having been born in 1974 and all that.
'Merlot ? The wine. The variety of grape. Would it be to your satisfaction?'
'Er sure, yeah. Mer-low. Sounds lovely.' Lauren knew nothing about wine and had no interest in rectifying this social omission. One of many seeing as she generally struggled with the word social. These kind of things didn't apply when you were her did they ? Leave that kind of carry-on to the regular folk. Were there not courses you could do of an evening in chilly parish halls where you sip wine with a load of self-important gimmers, being taught the mysteries of the grape ? Frickin weird. Occasionally Francis had attempted to educate her palate but with little real success. She still couldn't really tell them apart and didn't have any inclination to really try. On the rare occasions when she bought a bottle all that used to run through her mind was 'will it get me pissed ? Will I have change from a fiver ?' She knew where she was with lager. And vodka of course. Sometimes even in the same glass. When there was nothing on the telly.
'Well if you'd like to take a seat I will return shortly with an opened bottle.' He started to leave the room, before quickly double-backing on himself. 'Oh how remiss of me.'
'Sorry ?'
'I completely forgot to provide mood music. Are you a fan of the work of the Bee Gees ?'
'The Bee Gees ?' If she hadn't been so stunned she would have laughed. He'd just pronounced their name as if he were introducing her to some hip new underground New York noise merchants. Not a dangerously coiffured bunch of tight-trouser wearing freaks who hadn't had a hit since dinosaurs freely roamed around Harrogate. Actually, come to think of it, she was sure there were still plenty of prehistoric survivals trundling about that neck of the

woods.

'Yes, the Gibb brothers. Marvellously underrated talents I always felt. They had such a natural grasp of the song writing art. Don't you agree ?'

'Right. Yes. Saturday night fever and all that.'

'Oh there's so much more to their canon than their foray into disco.' As he said the word foray he made a showbiz hand gesture. Lauren wanted to pinch herself. Surely this was another of her seriously fucked-up dreams ?

'Well, if you say so Rog, you go putting on some Bee Gees. I'm sure it'll be fantastic.'

'Wonderful' He clapped his hands together and then made for a small expensive looking stereo which sat on a built in shelf in the corner. Pulling out a CD from a rack that appeared to contain all of five Cds. 'So just you sit down there Lauren, I'll get the wine and we'll let the Brothers Gibb do their thang !'

Did he really just say 'thang' ?

Millie and Star had shut themselves in the kitchen. They spoke in whispers ? Conspiratorially.

'What's happened ?' Millie asked.

'I've no idea. He's been like this all evening. Something went on but he's not telling.'

'Lauren was definitely off as well. Oh god, I'm going to die if I don't find out what's happened.'

'Whatever it is I don't think it went smoothly.'

'I thought they were ideal for each other.'

'Me too. Which just goes to show…'

'That you never can tell.'

'I'll try to find out from him. Could go out for something to eat actually. Can you recommend anywhere nice ?'

'There's a Loch Fyne place down the road. I went there with…'Millie hesitated a second. 'With Damian.'

'Seafood. He's partial so that's perfect. Should entice him out his misery. Seeing as it's our last night here and I'm paying.'

'Let me know what he says won't you ? My mind's going to be whirring until I get something definitive.'

' Will do. I'd better go tell his ladyship he's got a hot date.' She raised here eyebrows. 'Just not with who he'd like it to be with.'

Lauren was finishing off her bowl of pasta, meatballs and freshly grated parmesan. It had been surprisingly satisfying. The wine too wasn't bad. After the first glass, the incongruous Bee Gees compilation didn't seem to jar quite

so badly. The only thing that was really missing from this happy scenario was interesting company. The meal had been largely conducted in silence. She would be eating, only to look up and find Roger Lindacre staring at her, his fork held in his hand. By the third time of finding her employer in silent contemplation she felt compelled to say something.
'Er..is there something on my face ?'
'Pardon ?'
'It's just that you've been staring at me.'
'Oh I do apologise.'
'OK.' She rolled her eyes and put her bowl to one side. 'That was lovely thanks.'
'You too.'
'Eh ?'
'Lauren. I need to tell you.'
'Tell me what ? Can I have more wine ?' She'd reached for the bottle before Roger Lindacre had chance to respond. He stood up, and moved deliberately down the table to where she was sitting. Thinking he was about to collect her empty bowl she held it up for him with one hand, whilst taking a sip from the wine with another. She looked at him out of the side of her eyes as he paused and gazed at her intently.
'Lauren…I'
'What ?'
'I have an offer to make to you.'
She glugged her wine and put it down . 'If it's about more hours, I'm going to have to turn you down as I need the time to write you see. If I get drawn back into working full-time it's going to be…'
'Oh no, it's not about work. Can we leave business outside tonight ?' His voice had gone softer, his body was beginning to lean into hers.'
'Oh-kay…erm..do you mind if I just nip into your backyard to smoke a ciggy ?
She started to stand up, Mr Lindacre placed a hand firmly down on her shoulder. 'No, really this cannot wait any longer' He placed his other arm around her waist and leant in to kiss her. Realising just in time what was happening, Lauren turned her head away sharply and pushed him aside.
'Fucking hell no !'
I'm sorry.' He straightened up, held out his hands and looked hurt. She jumped to her feet and made herself big.
'What the fuck were you thinking ?'
'I'm sorry, I just…'
'Just nothing fella. Are you mad ?' This was ludicrous. Where exactly in her behaviour tonight had she shown him she was in the slightest bit interested ? The man was an antique freak with a passion for the Bee-Gees. That did not

hottie material make.

'No, I was merely..'

'Merely what ? Making a move.' This was deeply irritating. The evening had been alright up until now but the clueless sod had just gone and spoiled it. And probably made life difficult at work. 'That was what you were up to. Having a crack at your staff. Christ on a bike Rog, do you really think I was giving you the signs or something ?'

'Well I had thought…'

'Thought what ? That I was probably desperate enough to reciprocate. Fucking hell matey.' She shook her head and straightened herself up. 'I might be single and you might have some money but I 'aint interested fella.' She jabbed his chest. 'Do you really think I'd cheapen myself by getting off with someone just so they'd pay my frickin bills ? You really don't know me mate. I've got fucking standards.' Oh god. She'd gone on a swear-fest directed at her employer. It was hard to see how this could get much worse.

'Miss Seymour, I really don't think…' He sounded irritated now. This clearly wasn't the response he'd been expecting.

'Don't think what ? And it's Miss Seymour again now is it ? It might have escaped your notice Mr but I'm not a ten year old girl, I'm a 33 three year old frickin woman of sorts so for crying out loud call me fucking *Ms.*'

'Yes, of course I do apologise'

'I should hope so.' Her anger had started to abate a little. 'Frickin norah Rog man, what was going through your mind ?' She shook her head and looked at him confused. ' That's not the way you go about things either mate.'

'I'm sorry, I feel very stupid.'

She smiled at him. He just looked a bit silly and embarrassed. Poor fella. How must he be feeling ? How much courage must that have taken ? 'Look, I'm flattered, but I really do need a fag now, so if you don't mind I'll just nip outside. Why don't you put the kettle on and we can talk about it eh ?'

'Yes, yes of course.'

'Cool.' She darted outside past him.

Her hand was shaking as she clicked her lighter and moved the flame to the cigarette on her lips. Taking a long drag she looked up at the sky. Why did she keep getting herself into these situations ? Now it all seemed obvious of course. Why did she never see these things coming ? It never really crossed her mind that any man would particularly find her attractive, nor that she should be in any way cautious about judging their motives. If one showed an interest in her, or her in them, it meant nothing more than a tentative overture at friendship. Why did everything have to descend into these mannered sexual games everyone seemed to play ? It was bizarre. Like being the only sane person in an asylum that had split into two warring tribes who broke their shared enmity by shagging. She felt like she was standing on the sidelines pointing out the lunacy of everyone else whilst being told that she was mad not to play along.

Drawing on her cigarette she wondered how long it could be before she could realistically make a dash for it ? The urge to getaway was immense. It was an awful situation but she knew that if she did make a hasty getaway, then the situation at work would be intensely embarrassing if not unbearable. The job, hours and location of the shop really suited her. She didn't want to lose it. This meant she was going to have to either talk the whole thing out or gloss over it for the rest of the evening, acting as if nothing had ever happened. That way she could re-establish a working relationship with Roger and a pretence of the thing being forgotten maintained. She smiled to herself. Nothing had happened. She'd forget about it. She'd ask him how he got into books, what his favourite film was. That kind of thing. It was definitely for the best. Stubbing out the remains of her cigarette on the back wall of Roger's house she took a deep breath and went back inside.

Millie was alone. She stood at the window and watched the people passing, heading off for evenings out as town started to come alive for the night shift. Couples, groups of young people, occasional single stragglers breaking out into unlikely jogs to get where they needed to be in time. The flat itself was so quiet. The only noise was the anonymous street and traffic buzz, the sound of buses shifting gear that you got so used to living centrally. It became a kind of aural wallpaper. Inoffensive and ever present, only occasionally and unexpectedly jarring.

The noise was no comfort though. It was a non-intrusive nothing, a fizz that made little impression on the stillness of the room. Millie felt uneasy in stillness. She desired energy. She wanted buzzing, she needed conversation, and gossip and company. This wasn't her. Single. It was such a desperate word to her ears. Lauren found freedom in it, Millie only tragedy. But she had to persist with it. Keep it near her. See if there were any lessons contained within it for her, or if in its presence she could find something more of herself for a change. Maybe it would be a difficult bed-fellow, but it might just be the best partner she could ask for. She was still relatively youthful, she had a job she enjoyed, there were worse conditions in the world. In fact wasn't life now full of possibilities ? She sat back down on the sofa and resisted the urge to put on the TV. She wouldn't anaesthetise herself. Instead she'd force herself to experience the full-force of the solitude for a while. It would soon pass, but for now she perhaps had to learn to honour it, seek the stillness that lived somewhere beneath the perpetual whirlwind of her nature. It was there somewhere. Then the phone rang and broke her reverie.

Roger was waiting anxiously in the kitchen.
'Ms Seymour, Lauren I...'
'Look, you don't have to apologise.'
'No really, I must.'
'I'd rather you didn't.' No more. Please no more.
'But...'
'Let's just try and forget it ever happened shall we.'
'Forget it. Oh I'm not sure I can.' He was shaking his head furiously and looking rather alarmed. Oh god, he wasn't going to get difficult was he ? Maybe she'd be forced to look for something else.
'Please try Rog.'
'Right. Yes. More wine ?'
'No. Definitely no more wine. Tea would be good.'
'Yes, tea of course.' She noticed his hands were shaking.
'I'll go sit down.' She took herself back into the dining room and sat back down at the table. After a few minutes Roger returned with two white china cups and saucers.
'I've forgotten dessert. There's a double chocolate cheesecake in the fridge.'
'Well, I'm feeling a bit stuffed to be honest so if you don't mind I'll pass on that one.'
'No wonder you stay so skinny.'
'I think the Seymour genetic heritage plays its part. My dad's side are all tall and wirey. Mum's side are squat and fat though so you think it would even itself out.'
'Are you sure ? Do you eat alright. You mentioned something about your funny diet the other day.' He looked across the table at her meeting her eyes, but couldn't hold their gaze, the pain of remembering his earlier actions repelling him from her face. A face he thought was beautiful. And interesting. And quite unlike any woman he'd ever set eyes upon. There was something strangely other about it. As if she were an angel rather than a woman. 'Do tell me to shut up if I'm prying.'
'No, no, you're fine.' She drank some tea. 'I just eat a lot of crisps, drink a lot of tea and enjoy a Kit-Kat or two. It's not like it's all I eat. I do occasionally have a proper meal.' Lauren was trying to remember when this week, other than this evening, she had sat down to a proper meal. Did spaghetti on toast count ? Pizza Hut with shrimp that was it ! She'd even had salad, even if she had only eaten the croutons and the tomatoes. It was certainly a step in the right direction. That was yesterday. Other than that she was struggling. Not that it mattered. She always remembered to take a multivitamin. That way her hair would never start falling out.
'I try to maintain a healthy balanced diet. Food is such an important part of

an enjoyable life don't you find ?'

'Erm..I suppose so. I'm not really that much of a foodie to be honest. I enjoy a nice meal when someone else has cooked it for me, but I can't say I'm ever that bothered otherwise. I don't really do restaurants.' She looked as if she were considering something. 'Actually, don't you think it weird, like, all those strangers sitting around at tables eating ?' She shook her head in disbelief at the thought of it. Roger Lindacre looked at her as if she'd just landed from another planet.

'No, not really. It's enjoyable. Sociable. Good food is improved by good company.'

'Really ? I just feel dead trapped in a restaurant, which is why I avoid them if I can. Them and cinemas. I go occasionally but I don't very often make it to the end of the film. I have to escape.'

Roger chuckled.'You really are a solitary type aren't you.' He was relaxing again.

'I suppose so. I'm quite relaxed about it these days. It's just who I am. I'm happiest when I'm either watching something rubbish on the box, or with my head in a book, or writing of course.'

'Writing ? You write.'

Had she never told him ? 'Yes, when I'm not working at Ainsty I'm working on my novel. It's been a long held ambition to get one done. Just never got round to it.'

Roger's face lit up. 'Oh that's marvellous. That really is marvellous. I'm helping an emerging writer on her way.'

She returned his smile. Bless him. He was a gentle old cove wasn't he ? There was something of the Francis about him. Only slightly, but a definite something. His heart was in the right place. 'Yes, I suppose you are. Nice work fella.' She waved at him across the table. He smiled bashfully, then looked down at his feet.

Forever in electric dreams…

Town felt particularly full of casualties that evening. Not just the regular boozed up party girls and boys, but gangs of homeless men wandered, completely oblivious to anyone and everything. They were like a sorry decommissioned army. Something medieval, as if they'd slipped through a gash in time only to find themselves lost and redundant in the strange world in which they now found themselves. The stone walls and cobbled streets would have looked familiar though. There was continuity here. The ladder between the past and the present was still in place. At times it felt as if shadows from those earlier years had taken advantage of it, clambering into the present to play games.

Lauren was always anonymous. Despite her height and striking features she rarely figured in anyone's line of sight. It was as if she didn't exist at times. Which was just how she liked it. Invisible. You could move freely with less social encumbrance. It did her good to know that she was unknown. Life was emotionally messy at times. Being aware of the potential for situations to deliver heartache and upheaval minimised the hurt. She imagined what it must be like to be Millie. Forever surfing massive overwhelming waves of feeling from which she never shirked. The thought made her shudder. It wasn't that Lauren felt things any less intently, it was just that she was well practised in channelling it into controllable streams. Her personality had constructed massive flood defences that kept the relentless rain induced river of emotion from soaking her through. Then she heard her phone ring. It was the flat number. She'd better answer it.

'Hello'
'Lauren. It's me.' It was Millie. She was crying. Again.
'You alright sweetie-pie ?' Boys. It was always boys that made Millie cry. She couldn't live with them couldn't live…
'No, Lauren, look. Phone Francis.'
'Francis ? Why ? What's…'
'Just phone Francis.'
And with that the phone went dead. Lauren stood by the Parliament Street fountain clueless as to what was happening. But something wasn't right. She quickly rang the telephone to her former house. It was engaged. She waited then phoned again. It was still engaged. This time she left a message. 'Francis, it's me. Mills asked me to call. She was upset. Don't know what's happening but I'm worried. Give us a buzz mate.'

She closed her phone and waited for a second. This was no good. She needed to find out what was up. Something was definitely up. Something was wrong. She'd have to go round. She needed to go round.

Quickly, she turned around, headed through the empty stalls of Newgate Market, into Kings Square, and broke out into an uncomfortable jog as her feet hit Goodramgate. They had walked this route home for the best part of a decade and seemed to go into autopilot. They pulled her down back alleys, cutting across terraced streets until through the maze of two-up, two-down terraces she found her way to Diamond Street. The lights were on at her old house. She knocked on the door. There was no answer. She knocked again, this time louder. Then she remembered. She still had her key for the front door on her key ring. Francis had told her to keep it and just let herself in whenever she wanted. It was always her home and she was welcome whenever…where was it ? Where the fuck was it ? Until now she'd never had much call for the thing. But it was there. On her keyring. She stood before the door of her old life and breathed in. It was a struggle to get the key into the still stiff lock just as it always had been, Franny's ever-promised but never materialising can of WD40 was still absent. It turned with a familiar clumsy, clunking click. Pushing the door open she walked inside.

'Francis.' She shouted as she did so. No answer. Opening the door to the front room, she saw him. He was sat on the futon facing the wall, several buttons on his white shirt open, tears streaming down his face, his eyes blankly staring at the brickwork round the gas fire. He didn't even seem to notice her.

'What the fuck.' She flung down her bag and scurried across to sit with him. Placing her arms around her old housemate and tormentor, she urgently pulled him close. With feeling and intensity. 'What's wrong my love ?' She wiped a tear from his cheek. 'What's happened ? Where's Tony ?'
With the mention of that name he turned and looked at her.
'He's not well Lauren.' Tears started to pour again, as he unfolded a disintegrating tissue in his hand. Lauren intervened. She stood up, found a clean tissue in her pocket and handed it to him.
'Here, have this.' She sat back down. 'What's wrong with Tony ?'
'Yesterday, he went for a prostrate examination, all OK, no problems.'
'That's good isn't it ?' What was coming ?
'It is but, they found something else when they gave him his general check-up.'
'What ? What did they find ?'
'Pancreatic cancer Lauren. It's advanced I'm afraid. He's been feeling off for a while. But he didn't go to the doctor. Just took his painkillers, put it down to other things, denied there was anything wrong with him. He's very predictably male for a gay man.'
'But surely there's treatment cancer isn't a…' She hesitated. 'Death sentence.' Francis looked at her. 'Is it ?'
'In this case, I'm afraid so.' He looked so pale. So drawn. So utterly dejected. All the life had gone from him. He was an aching shadow of the man she loved so much.
'Oh my god.'
At the mention of the deity Francis snapped. 'You don't have a god Lauren. And mine is looking somewhat impotent.'
'I don't know what to say I…' There was the virgin statue. The Mexican one on top of the TV. Still looking sympathetic. Still looking as if she felt what you were going through. Still ultimately cold, meaningless and made of

plaster. A kitsch piece of tack iconography. The gay man and his colourful Catholic baubles. It was so cliché and so painful. She always hated that fucking statue. For its false hope. For what it said she should be, with its ceaseless passive sorrow and freaky looking Christ child. The misery it had caused so many people, the women it had ensnared into believing that all they could ever be were servants of some fucking father or son on a Big I Am trip. They didn't come much bigger than calling yourself a fucking Messiah now did they ? Well where was he now eh ? Where was that fat ugly baby ? What did he grow up to become ? Nothing more than another executed hothead. Another man on a mission to prove himself. Believing himself special. There was no hope in that kind of ancient posture or in his dumb compliant mother. Francis believed and Francis had been left bereft. There was to be no salvation for him from this. Lightning had struck, despite all those chanted rosaries, all those masses at which he'd exacerbated his dodgy knees by dropping to them every time it was expected. And what would the people in the pews be saying ? Even now she could hear some disapproving fucker in his congregation muttering 'ah well, he was homosexual wasn't he ? The lord doesn't repay his debts in pennies now does he ?' She wanted to pick up that statue and throw it through the window. Expunge everything it stood for from the room, from his life. She couldn't offer much in its place except her arms. And the knowledge that her love was real and that it bled for him. It was made of flesh and warmer to the touch than anything some cold church sanctioned piece of shit could ever offer.
'Nobody knows what to say. What can they say ? There's no words I want to hear. Apart from the ones that tell me this is all just a miserable dream.'
Francis howled with sorrow again.
'How long has he...'
'A few weeks probably. They'll treat him best they can. He has to stay in hospital.'
Lauren fell into stunned silence for a moment.
'I'm definitely going to give up smoking.'
Francis smiled. It looked incongruous but she was grateful for it. He could be reached. She so badly needed to reach him.
'About time too. But what else ?'
'What do you mean ?'
'What else are you going to do ?'
'I don't understand.'
'You frustrate me so much Seymour. I see someone in you who has so much potential, so much to give yet you're terrified of freeing it, or truly believing people could like you, or being brave enough to experience things.'
'What things ? I...'

'Love for instance.' He took her hands and placed them on her heart cupping his hands over them and not allowing her to wriggle them free. She looked down at her feet. To see that face so broken. So full of emotion. It was too intense. It threatened to completely overwhelm her. 'Because as hard as this is, I wouldn't swap it for never having experienced real love. For having been able to have known that special man lying in a hospital bed on Wigginton Road. I've been privileged. I've been blessed.'
'I know that but…'
'You do know it, but you don't feel it. You don't let yourself feel anything. People like Tony don't come along very often. We rarely meet someone who makes that much sense to us and when we do we should give them everything we have and expect everything in return. I only feel so empty now because I have felt so full of life and joy and beauty in his presence. We grieve because we feel things. That's why there's only two letters difference between love and loss. Does that make some sense ?'
She took hold of his hands, and tried hard to fight off the impending tears.
'It does.'
'So don't let people slip out of your fingers until you have to.'
'OK'
The silence returned.

    Lauren was running. The arrival of Francis's older sister at the house with an overnight bag had been the cue to leave. She would call again in the morning. Now she had other business. Her legs were going ten to the dozen, sweat was beginning to seep from her pores, her face was red, her hair flyaway and frizzy was working itself into an unflattering fuzz-ball. None of that mattered though. She just needed to get back to the flat, and when she did she found the place was in darkness. Where was everyone ? Looking in Millie's room, she saw a sleeping best friend fully-clothed and foetus like on top of her bed, Lauren charged in and shook her awake.
'Mills, where are they ?'
'Sorry, Lauren, who ?' She put a hand to her head and tried to focus.
'Jude and Star. Where are they ?'
'Oh, they're at that place down the road ?'
'What place ?'
'The fish place. The nice one.'
'Which one ?' Lauren couldn't think.
'In the old hardware store, loch thingy.'
'There ! Right, Ok. Seeya. Go back to sleep.' Lauren kissed her hand, placed it on Millie's cheek and saw her eyes close.

    She hurtled down the back stairs and onto the street, almost knocking over a semi-inebriated middle-aged man as she did so. It was all downhill and relatively easy, until she reached the big wide window of the restaurant. Catching a glimpse of her reflection she realised she looked terrible. There was a moment's hesitation. No, this had to be done. She looked through the door and saw them. Sitting at a table towards the back, Jude had his back to her, Star was talking animatedly about something. It looked very cosy. But she had to intrude. Flinging open the door one of the black-clad staff, a tall woman, her blonde hair tied back came to greet her.

'Can I help you…'

'Sorry, no..er..' She charged past her. The waitress stood momentarily lost as to what to do then quickly began to follow her. This was going to turn into a scene. She had been warned. These things could happen quite randomly.

'I'm afraid we're…' Be firm, decisive but remain unthreatening. Do not make the intruder panic. Try to keep the situation calm and under control.

People turned to look at the lanky vision of sweaty fury scything her way through the tables. Then Star noticed the slight shift in the atmosphere, that something was happening. She looked up from the last of her salmon fishcakes and saw a sweating, red-faced frenzy of a figure who roughly resembled her cousin.

'Lauren ?' Was that really her ? At the mention of her name, Jude turned sharply in his seat.

'Jude,' Lauren panted, trying to recover her breath. 'I need to ask you something.' She leaned over, placed her hands flat on her thighs and breathed deeply. Seeing as the woman seemed to know the seated couple, the waitress backed off a little.

'Er yeah.' He looked up at her, his face full of surprise, his eyes wide and expectant.

Lauren looked startled. Now what. She straightened up, looked distractedly around the room, her hands were shaking, no make that her whole body was shaking. She looked back at Jude and nearly melted. Took a deep breath, paused then gushed with a tremor in her voice, 'er…god…aw no..erm..Jude will you marry me ?'

'Marry…' Jude couldn't believe what he'd just heard. Had she really just asked him to marry her ? The woman who didn't do relationships ? Star dropped her knife and fork dramatically, her mouth flew open and she looked likely to pass out with shock at any moment.

'No..argh.' Lauren put her hands on her head and shook it wildly. 'Fuck it. Rewind a sec.'

You don't want to marry me ?' Jude's face sank ? Was she having some kind of a breakdown ? People didn't do this kind of thing did they ?

'Lauren are you alright ?' Star finally recovered herself. This was insane. What the hell was going on ? Ignoring her cousin, Lauren focused solely on Jude

Travers.

'No, I do. I'm meant to ask you some questions first.'
'Questions OK.' He shuffled in his seat a little. Whatever. This couldn't get any weirder. It was exciting and wasn't that precisely what they'd come away for ?
'Kids ? You don't want kids do you ?'
'God no, I'd be a crap dad.' What a thought. No. Definitely not.
'Cool right. Er.' She thought for a second . 'This whole sensitive pretty thing. It's not just a fashion statement is it ? You're not going to become a fat boring predictable bloke in a few years are you ?'
'I think I'd probably rather die Lauren. I've tried to be the real man believe me. It's just never been very convincing.' Lauren looked at Star who sought to reassure her.
'It's true cuz. He's always been like this. That's what he's about. He'll no more change than you'll get married in a big white frock.'
'Well in that case.' Lauren dropped to one knee, took his hand in her own, and looked the slightly shell-shocked pretty-boy in his huge beautiful doe-eyes and spoke. 'Will you marry me ?' She'd never meant anything so much in her life.

  A huge beaming smile covered his face. 'If you're serious and not at all loony and stuff.' Lauren shook her head, pushed out her lips and widened her eyes expectantly. 'Then I'd love to. I'd absolutely fucking love to.' He leaned down, put his hands either side of her cheeks, looked into her big brown eyes which were showing the first sign of tears, a mixture of elation and utter desolation at the news the evening had brought, and kissed her. It felt like the beginning of something. The first word in a new chapter.

  Star jumped to her feet and screamed in delight. 'Yay !', prompting everyone else in the restaurant to begin clapping. After the attention died down one of the staff brought over a bottle of champagne.
'It's on the house.' Star pulled out her chair, gestured for Lauren to sit down, and then excused herself.
'Don't go on my account.' Lauren said.
'No I've got to go see Millie. She told me to tell her any goss I found out, but she'll never be expecting this.' Star clapped her hands together and almost danced with delight. 'Hahaha…a wedding ! Jude's getting married.'

   Lauren and Jude sat at the table, swimming in the glory of each other's presence.
'That was a bit unexpected. I thought you didn't want a relationship.' Jude leaned in as he spoke. He couldn't take his eyes off her. And she was definitely his. You couldn't get any more certain than a proposal in a busy restaurant could you ? It was hard for him to fully articulate to himself

precisely how he was feeling. So instead, he just decided to ride it. To let the emotion and the romance carry him. To feel love. For that was what he felt. All the more real and glorious for coming completely out of the blue during a grey period in his life.

Stuff just happened. Good stuff, shit stuff. Whatever. It was all vital. It showed you still had a pulse. That you were capable of feeling.
'Things change. I was stupid. And you.' She leaned across the table and kissed him. 'Are absolutely frickin perfect.' So he was. In a way she could never expect anyone ever would be. Someone just like her.

He blushed. 'Thank you,' and hesitated a second. 'On the face of it this whole marriage thing is probably a bit ill-advised.'
'Are you saying you don't want to ?' She stuck out a sad bottom lip.
'No it's not that, I said on the face of it, it's ill-advised, but it just makes perfect sense. I don't know why but it does.'
Lauren smiled at him. 'You make perfect sense my love.' They kissed again. 'We both make sense.'

Another kiss. This time they both straightened up as another bottle arrived. It was a present from an elderly couple sitting nearby who had watched the proceedings with poorly-hidden, indulgent delight. The kind of indulgence that comes from fifty or so years of being together, of always remaining in love, of being a grey haired, happy counter to the tired burden of endless cynicism. In the strange young couple they saw sitting near them they recognised compatriots in the fight for beauty and trust and simplicity. For happiness in a world that told you it was right to never give completely, to not expect too much, to suspect the worse, to strip your life bare of romance and to expect to fail. The woman's big romantic gesture. It had blown them away and made them feel alive. A bottle of wine was the least they could do to show their appreciation.

Jude re-filled both of their glasses and then lifted his.
'Here's to making sense.'

They kissed again and lost themselves in the sense they seemed to be making.

Above a hospital bed a monitor made a crisp, clinical and totally sterile, silence piercing beep. A slender, silver haired man with refined features was gently sleeping below. Through reams of tubes and a maze of wires he was part of the mains. Plugged into the support system. Despite the artificial intrusions by which he was surrounded, tonight he was peaceful. Dreaming of his children, and the love that the decades had given him in countless different forms. Of sunny days. Winters by the fire. Laughter with his countless friends. Random hands shaken, money handed over, change given, pleasantries with strangers, admiring glances, the whole stinking, heaving, colourful, endlessly wonderful and inspiring web of humankind. That warm feeling of knowing that no matter what happened he never would be, or ever could be truly alone. That the strange dream through which he had struggled and transfigured for decades into something under which he could sign his name, was now leaving him. That a new reality, or lack of it was picking up the threads. Tying up loose ends in unseen ways which even those being bound with would remain perpetually unaware of. Even if occasionally they would briefly glimpse previously unseen notes in the margins of their lives. Lines in his handwriting.

His right hand tensed a little then loosened as something called him forwards. He followed. His sleep became dreamless. Then he drifted through a clear perfect blue sky, into a heaven of his own making, the mark of his embodied individuality, somewhere no-one else living or dead, could ever really know or experience, his imprint on the world beginning to slowly morph itself into stain. A deep permanent reminder that he had been here. It would be carried on the skin, of different intensities and sizes, of countless connected and random souls. As all around him everything was failing, and even the artifice of machinery, the far reaches of our science, could no longer hide anyone from the truth of what he was, what we all are. Fulfilment, in the midst of all this pain, this meaningless loss, was somehow being found. Deeply, his body made a huge involuntary sigh, his consciousness lost in the sense this all seemed to be making.

You can message, harangue, entertain and befriend the author @

www.myspace.com/martynclayton

You can do the same to the cover artist @

www.myspace.com/janjanowen